BURIED SECRETS

A NOVEL

ERIN LANTER

ISBN: 978-1-7357188-6-6

ISBN (ebook): 978-1-7357188-7-3

Also By Erin Lanter:

The Dark Hour

Saddle Hill Christmas Mysteries

Follow That Star
I'll Be Home For Christmas

Buried Secrets is a work of fiction. The location, characters, and businesses are either products of the author's imagination or used fictitiously. Any similarity to real people, living or dead, places, or businesses, is purely coincidental.

For the entire adoptive community—the adoptees looking for a place to belong and the parents who do their best to love their children well.

For Nora—you are loved in this world.

BURIED SECRETS

Prologue

THIRTY-TWO YEARS AGO

Startled, Sheila's eyes snapped open. Light filtered into the bedroom from beneath the door, and she could hear voices coming from downstairs. The glowing red numbers on the bedside clock told her it was three o'clock in the morning. She reached over to the left side of the bed to find that her husband, Thomas, wasn't there. The coolness of the sheets told her he'd been gone awhile.

The voices continued, and as they did Sheila's grogginess dissipated.

What's going on? Why would anybody be here at this hour?

Surely he's not having a meeting about a case, she thought, but as she continued to listen the hair on her arms prickled.

Throwing the covers aside, she slipped out of bed and walked quietly across the room. Opening the door a crack, she placed her ear against the opening. Holding her breath, her heart beat faster.

The voices echoing through the house were coming from the library.

"Did you really think you could get away with this?" growled a deep, angry voice.

"I'm not trying to get away with anything," Thomas replied.

Sheila opened the door wider.

Thomas spoke again. "Wait a minute. Think about what you're doing. You're not going to solve anything like this."

"You have no idea how I solve things. Do you think I got where I am by always playing by the rules?" Though muffled, Sheila recognized the voice.

It can't be, she assured herself. This must be a mistake.

Sheila grabbed her robe and rushed from the bedroom, her heart pounding wildly as the sound of breaking glass reverberated through the house. She willed her feet to move faster, and though she was desperate to help her husband resolve the situation that had woken her up, she was terrified of what she might be walking into.

"Stop! Don't do this!" she heard Thomas shout frantically. "Please, no!"

Silence.

Forcing herself to move through the paralyzing fear, she walked quickly through the living room, feet noiselessly padding on the plush carpet. Pausing when she reached the library door, a low groan escaped her lips when she saw her husband's limp body lying on the floor.

The light flickering from the fireplace cast an eerie glow throughout the room. From the corner, the twelve-foot Christmas tree still stood, cheerful twinkling lights contradicting the horror taking place in front of it.

A scream froze in her throat as she saw the gaping wound in her husband's chest and the poker from the fireplace lying beside his body. The crystal vase that had been a wedding gift three years earlier lay in pieces around him.

Kneeling in the shattered glass, she silently prayed he was still breathing. Adrenaline coursed through her so she didn't notice the deep gashes and the blood oozing from the bottoms of her feet.

Sheila raised her head and her eyes met those of her husband's killer. "What have you done? You killed him!" she shrieked.

Where had he been hiding? Or had he been there in plain view the whole time, watching her terror? Her mind raced. How could the man standing in front of her be a murderer?

"Sheila, darling, don't look so surprised. You must have known the kind of man I am." He was unremorseful and smug, not the person she thought she'd known. How could he be so calm after taking the life of another human being? How could he talk to her with such callousness after killing her husband?

"I never thought you were capable of *murder*!" she wailed, tears spilling down her cheeks.

Turning his back to her, he walked toward the fireplace and rested his forearm on the mantle. The dying fire cast a shadow across the face she'd once looked at with admiration.

"We were a mistake, Sheila, and I think you know that. We never should have gotten involved." His voice was quiet, barely audible over the crackling fire.

A chill raced up her spine. He was too calm. Only a sociopath would show this little emotion after killing someone. Fear knotted in her chest, almost choking her. Warning signals went off in her head, urging her to get away.

Rising on trembling legs, she ran toward the hall. Before she reached the library door, the killer was standing in front of her, a menacing smile on his face. Sheila's eyes darted around the room, looking for an escape.

There was none.

"What do you want?" she pleaded. "I'll do anything."

He chuckled softly, a cold, threatening sound, and reached out to stroke her cheek. "There's nothing you can do, I'm afraid. It really is a shame that things have to end this way, though. We did have some fun together."

In terror, Sheila watched as he stooped to retrieve the poker that had been lying next to her husband's body.

Before she could utter a sound, he raised the gloved hand that held the poker and brought it down hard against the side of her head. The sickening sound of iron shattering bone filled the room.

Sheila remained conscious long enough to see her murderer walk out the front door, resetting the alarm as he left.

As the darkness enveloped her, Sheila's last thought was of the baby she would never see again, and the man who'd made her an orphan.

1

I T WAS A gorgeous fall day. The kind that makes a person glad to be alive. Definitely not the kind you'd expect to find out your entire life had been a lie.

Late-afternoon sunshine angled through the small attic window, illuminating a dislodged floorboard. Alexandra Tucker couldn't breathe—and not because she'd spent the last two hours in a dusty attic.

She stared at the paper in her trembling hand, willing the words she was reading to change.

"Gram!" she called, her voice shaky.

"Be there in a minute, dear," her grandmother replied.

After what seemed like hours, Joan Shepherd's head bobbed up the ladder. "Sorry, I was hauling boxes to the curb. Who knew a person could accumulate so much junk?" Then, after studying her granddaughter for a moment, she asked, "Are you okay?"

Numbly, Alex shook her head. She wanted to speak, but the words wouldn't come.

A wooden crate screeched as Joan dragged it across the

floor, leaving a trail in the dust. "Sit down, dear. You don't look well."

Alex's legs wouldn't move. Feeling as though she was moving in slow motion, she extended her hand. "What is this?"

Joan took the paper, eyes widening as she read.

"What is that, Gram?" Alex demanded, pointing to the paper in her grandmother's hand.

Joan didn't respond.

"Gram!" Alex snapped. "What is that?"

"A birth certificate," Joan whispered.

"I can see that. Whose is it?"

Joan stared at the worn toes of her boots, still saying nothing.

"Whose birth certificate is that?" Alex asked again.

"Yours," Joan said, barely audible.

"I have a copy of my birth certificate," Alex contradicted. "It doesn't look anything like this." It crinkled in her hand as she grabbed the paper from her grandmother. "This says my last name is Stone. And Mom and Dad aren't listed as my parents."

"I know."

The room spun. Alex took a few careful steps forward and sat on the wooden crate. "This birth certificate was issued in Kentucky. I was born in South Carolina. Tell me what's going on."

"It's best that I don't," Joan said quietly.

Alex's face flushed hot. She held up the birth certificate. "This is mine?"

"Yes."

"Then it's best you do," Alex countered. "Why is my name listed as Alexandra Stone? And why are the parents listed as 'anonymous'?"

Joan took a step forward. "Your birth parents didn't want to be identified."

Alex glared at her grandmother. "My *what*?"

"Your birth parents," Joan repeated.

"I'm adopted? I'm adopted and nobody ever told me? How could they keep this from me? How could *you* keep this from me, Gram?" Alex's heart hammered in her chest; her hands grew clammy.

For the first time since she climbed into the attic, Joan's eyes met her granddaughter's. "Your parents thought it was best."

She might as well have shrugged as she said it.

"And what about you? Did you think it was best?" There were no words to communicate how betrayed she felt. Her whole life was a complete lie. The birthday parties, holidays, and family vacations—all based on lies.

"It wasn't my place to agree or disagree. You have every right to be angry," Joan said in a soothing voice. "The people you trusted most in the world kept some big secrets from you."

"I'm thirty-two years old, Gram, not a child that needs to be protected. I could have handled this. I *can* handle this," she added as she looked out the small window, squinting into the sunlight.

Worry flitted across Joan's face. "I'm not sure your parents would agree."

"And what's this?" Alex asked, nudging a dusty, leather-bound journal with her foot.

Joan bent over and picked it up. She flipped through the pages. "It looks like it's your mother's journal."

"It was hidden with the birth certificate. Is it about my adoption?"

Joan flipped to the first page and scanned it. "It would appear so, yes."

Alex rubbed her temples. "Why did it have to be such a secret that I was adopted? Didn't I have the right to know where I came from? And why was my birth certificate and Mom's written account of my adoption under the floorboard in your attic?" Questions swirled through Alex's head, but they were questions nobody was answering.

This time, Joan did shrug. "I didn't know it was up here until now. I assume your parents were afraid you'd find it if they kept it at their house."

Ironic, Alex thought.

"I haven't even been in the attic for years," Joan said, brushing a cobweb from the ceiling. "Your grandfather was always the one who took care of stuff up here. You remember how disorganized he always was. He probably didn't know it was here, either."

Narrowing her eyes, Alex said, "What aren't you telling me, Gram?"

Joan diverted her eyes and focused on something in the far corner of the attic. "Nothing, except this. You were given a wonderful home with a family that loved you very much. Out of respect for your parents, I think it's best you let it drop."

Alex rose on unsteady legs. "I can't do that, Gram. Not now." She tucked the journal under her arm, climbed down the ladder, and walked out the front door, still clutching the paper that had just turned her life upside down. As her feet moved swiftly down the sidewalk, she couldn't help but wonder what could have happened to make her entire family bury the truth and vow to never speak of her adoption again.

2

ALEX OPENED ONE eye and looked at the clock. She groaned. Six-thirty Friday morning, and she was supposed to be up and getting ready for work.

"Adopted," she said for what seemed like the millionth time in the last twelve hours.

What was she supposed to do now?

The information she had was minimal, but it would have to be enough. A last name and a location would get her started.

But did she want to get started?

She'd spent most of the night wondering that very thing. Questions came at her from every direction. Answers did not.

Should she accept this new truth about her life and move on with it, secure in the knowledge that she'd been raised by two people who'd loved her very much, or should she risk throwing her life into a tailspin to find out where she came from?

Who was she kidding? Her life was already in a tailspin.

The pain on her grandmother's face last night almost made her want to let the whole thing drop.

But she couldn't. She couldn't unlearn what she'd found out.

Quickly grabbing her cell phone from the nightstand, she turned it on and, ignoring a voicemail from Gram, scrolled through her contacts and selected her boss's number. There was no way she could go to work today. After leaving a message, she threw back the heavy down comforter and placed her feet on the hardwood floor. A chill went through her body. She crossed the small bedroom to the dresser and pulled out a pair of socks, then turned to the closet and grabbed her favorite jogging suit.

She had to clear her head. Talking to Gram would have to wait.

"Jack!" she called.

Within seconds, the ninety-pound Lab was in front of her wagging his tail. Jackson had been her constant companion since she rescued him from the shelter last year.

It was love at first sight.

As she bent to pet his shiny black head, his tail whipped from side to side. Just yesterday she'd had to clean up a vase of flowers that had been the victim of Jackson and his powerful tail.

Yesterday. It seemed like so long ago. Her whole life had changed in a moment and would never be the same.

Alex shook her head, determined not to entertain the questions forcing themselves into her mind. She looked down at Jackson, who now stood holding the leash in his mouth.

She smiled. "Okay, buddy, I get it." She attached the leash to Jackson's collar and slid her apartment key into the pocket of her running jacket.

Stepping out into the cool October air, Alex took a deep breath. Rain had fallen during the night, dampening the sea air she loved so dearly. Once summer ended, many of the people who frequented the beaches in Charleston returned to their normal lives. She couldn't help but feel sorry for them.

Taking one last deep breath, Alex began a light jog. As her shoes met the all-too-familiar path, she took in the scenery. The trees boasted cinnamon- and rust-colored leaves. Next month the trees would be bare, brown leaves covering the ground. But no matter the weather, this was a beautiful path and one of the few places Alex felt completely content.

She turned right and jogged through the gates of the cemetery. After running a few more yards, she slowed her pace to a walk and veered off the path to the left, Jackson following a few steps behind. She took several more steps and stopped. Grief washed over her as she looked down at the headstone. This was a place she'd visited too many times in the past year.

When the news came of her parents' death, she'd been numb. How could they have been on that plane? Her mother had accompanied her father on a business trip to San Diego on a chartered flight, and they weren't supposed to return home for several more days. Alex was heartbroken when she learned they'd changed their plans to surprise her on her birthday.

Tuesday would be the anniversary of their deaths.

Standing on the soggy patch of ground shared by her mom and dad, Alex had questions for them they'd never be able to answer.

"How could you not tell me?" she demanded as the tears streamed down her face. "Didn't I have a right to know? How will I ever know?"

She covered trembling lips with her fingertips, guilt nagging at her conscience for the resentment she felt for the two people who had raised her. People who couldn't defend themselves against the anger she threw at them now.

Jackson rubbed his head against her hand, as though he knew she needed comfort.

"Let's go home," she whispered. Expecting answers from a headstone wouldn't help her. Right now it seemed like nothing would.

Sadness settled in the pit of her stomach as she turned to leave. Would she ever be able to think of her mom and dad the same way again?

She mourned. This time because the parents she thought she'd known now seemed like strangers.

3

THE RINGING PHONE made Alex realize she was still standing under the water. She quickly turned off the faucet and grabbed the towel hanging just outside the shower. Wrapping it around her slender frame, she picked the phone up off the sink counter with still-damp hands and answered just before the call rolled to voicemail.

"Hey, Alex. It's Jeannie."

Despite her shivering, Alex smiled. "What's up?"

"I was going to ask you the same thing. We've missed you at work today."

Alex first met Jeannie Davidson when she was doing her postdoctoral work at the community mental health center Jeannie managed. After that, she never left.

"Yeah, sorry about that. I'm just not feeling like myself today." That's the understatement of a lifetime, Alex thought, using her free hand to squeeze the water from her mahogany hair into the sink.

"Everything okay?"

The concern in Jeannie's voice was welcome. She wasn't just a boss; she was a dear friend.

Noticing Alex's hesitation, Jeannie pressed. "Alex, it's me. What's going on?"

She could picture Jeannie's eyebrows furrowed over inquisitive hazel eyes.

Silence floated between them for several moments before Alex answered. "I'm adopted," she said quietly.

"I'm sorry," Jeannie said. "I don't think I heard you correctly. You're *what*?"

"Adopted," Alex repeated. Almost twenty hours later and she was still hoping it wasn't true.

"You're adopted and nobody ever told you?"

"Nope. Apparently Mom and Dad wanted it to be a big secret. Gram followed along. She still is." Alex remembered how odd her grandmother seemed when Alex asked her about the birth certificate. "Something weird is going on," she added.

Alex heard Jeannie blow a puff of air from her mouth. "So, what are you going to do?"

"I haven't decided," Alex confessed. "On the one hand, Mom and Dad really loved me and they were my family. I don't question that. On the other hand, who are my birth parents and why did they give me up for adoption? I might have a whole other family out there."

Jeannie didn't respond, a technique therapists use to keep their clients talking.

"It's just all so confusing," Alex continued. "Is it even worth looking into?"

"That's a decision you'll have to make," Jeannie said softly, a tone Alex recognized as her friend being in therapist mode. "What's your gut telling you to do?"

"My gut says I need to find out where I came from. We all have a need to know and be known. If nothing I've ever believed is even true, how can I possibly know myself or my family? And there's so much they don't know about me. Like who my birth parents are. The parents were listed as 'anonymous' on the birth certificate. Or maybe they did know. I have no idea." Alex took a deep breath. "Tell me what to do."

"You have to decide that on your own, but I'll help you however I can." Papers rustled, then Jeannie said, "Why don't we meet for dinner tonight. I can be your sounding board."

A smile tugged at the corner of Alex's mouth as she pictured Jeannie. She was most likely leaning forward on her desk as she spoke, ready to spring into action. Her unruly auburn hair had probably escaped from the clip that could never quite hold it back.

"The usual place?" Alex asked, strangely comforted by the monotony of eating dinner in a familiar place.

"Where else? What are your plans in the meantime?"

Alex chewed her lower lip. "Try to find answers, I guess. I'll do an internet search and see what turns up. After that, I don't know."

"That's a starting place but be prepared. You're not going to find any information of your adoption online," Jeannie warned. "Those records are probably sealed, and even if they aren't, they won't be posted on the internet for all the world to see."

"I know," Alex agreed.

"Maybe you should try a search for abducted children from the year you were born." Jeannie's voice sounded disturbingly matter-of-fact.

"Abducted? Why?" Alex shivered beneath her towel.

"Everybody has kept this a secret and your grandmother

is being tight-lipped and acting strangely. There has to be a reason. It's worth a try."

"I guess," Alex said, her stomach turning. It was too horrifying to even think about. "See you later."

Alex pushed the button on her phone to end the call, then closed her eyes and took a few deep, steadying breaths into her belly, just as she told her clients who struggled with anxiety to do.

Dressing in black yoga pants and a lavender hoodie, she made a quick lunch of salad, grilled cheese, and tomato soup.

Comfort food. Fast.

She carried the food to the coffee table and sat cross-legged on the floor. Jackson followed and plopped down next to her.

"I guess I'll rip the band-aid off," she muttered. Soon the laptop was open and Alex was using every search engine she could think of to find out about adoptions in Kentucky from the year of her birth.

As Jeannie had predicted, she didn't find anything. Most sites directed her to adoption agencies.

"I'm not trying to adopt, I want to find out about adoptions that have already happened," she complained to the computer.

The chance of finding out about the events surrounding her adoption seemed to be nil.

But she had a last name. Stone.

Fingers flying across the keyboard, she looked up "Stone" in Lexington, Kentucky. Nothing. But if she ever needed to buy stone in Kentucky, she now knew of a couple dozen companies that could help.

Discouraged, she closed the laptop. There was one place she could look. It would hurt, but it might hold some answers.

Alex twisted toward the end table next to the sofa and opened the drawer. She took a deep breath and grabbed the leather-bound journal she'd found in Gram's attic. She ran her fingers over the cover, feeling each crease and scratch. She opened it and stared at her mother's handwriting scrawled across the pages, yellowed by time.

Alex had placed it in the drawer last night when she got home, determined to not read it unless it became necessary. Under normal circumstances, she'd respect her mother's privacy and not read the words no one was ever meant to see, but these circumstances were anything but normal.

She scanned the pages, tears filling her eyes. The first entry was written on January second, thirty-two years ago.

Alex would have been just over two months old.

According to the entry, her parents had been in a hurry to pack. They'd gotten a call about a baby that needed a home quickly and were flying out first thing the next morning. The words were laced with excitement.

Mom was so happy, Alex thought. Because of me.

Later entries seemed anxious; splotches of ink on the pages indicated her mother had put the tip of the pen on the paper to write, then hesitated.

There was no indication in that entry that they'd ever met with the birth parents or even someone from an adoption agency.

"But that doesn't have to mean something shady was going on," Alex assured herself, but the nagging doubt in the back of her mind told her it did.

She replayed Gram's reaction over and over in her mind. Her grandmother was spooked, and it went far beyond honoring the wishes of Alex's parents.

Oh, Mom, Alex wondered. What did you and Dad get yourselves into?

4

"I SWEAR I didn't kill those people!" Benny Johnson shouted, shifting his rotund body in the wobbly aluminum chair.

The overhead light flickered, barely illuminating the dingy visitor's room at the prison. To Benny, it looked like an underground train station, only without the possibility of going anywhere.

John Carmichael shook his head. "Benny, you've been in jail for thirty-two years. They have solid evidence against you. Give it up."

"Listen. I done a lot of things in my life. You know that. Some I'm proud of, some I'm not. But I didn't whack those people! And if you think I did, why did you even bother to take my case in the first place? I'm here because people think I murdered someone in *your* firm. Or has that little factoid slipped your mind?" Benny's lip curled in a sneer.

John's face reddened. "I took your case because I believed in your innocence. Thomas and I weren't that close. I barely knew him, and let's face it, you needed a good lawyer. You'd been linked to loan sharks and your name was pretty well-known in the horse-racing circuit. You're not exactly a noble citizen."

Benny pointed a beefy finger at his lawyer. "And you expect me to believe that you decided to represent me out of the goodness of your heart? Don't pretend there was nothing in it for you."

Straightening in his chair, John replied, "You were being represented by a barely-second-rate public defender. You didn't stand a chance. And don't forget, the victims were personal friends of the governor at the time. If it wasn't for me, you'd be sitting on death row right now, waiting for them to stick a needle in you. Assuming they hadn't already done it." He leaned back in his chair and laced his fingers together on the table.

"They'd never have executed me. I did my homework. In the past forty years, only three people have been executed in the state of Kentucky, and two of them asked for it! Idiots…" Benny muttered and shook his head. "Anyway, I'm sure you've made some enemies because of me. Don't forget, I was convicted of killing one of your own."

The dim fluorescent light cast a shadow on Benny's round face while John Carmichael looked on in disgust. He stood quickly, legs of the chair screeching on the floor as he pushed it back. "I suggest you find yourself another lawyer. I won't waste my time on you and your pathetic requests for an appeal any longer." He took long strides toward the door, then turned his steel-gray eyes on Benny. "You were found guilty of murder and there is overwhelming evidence to that fact. Give it up, Benny, and while you're at it, you might as well get ready to meet your maker. Even though you won't get a lethal injection—thanks to me, by the way—somebody is bound to get sick of your mouth and take you out." With that, he pushed the buzzer to alert the guard that he was ready to leave.

"I bet you'd like that!" Benny shouted at John's back just as the door snapped shut behind him. With a mock salute, he said, "Adios, pal."

Minutes later Benny waited as the guard unlocked the door to his cell, wincing as it slammed shut behind him.

So this is it, he thought. This is how I'm going to spend the rest of my life.

"How'd it go with Carmichael?" Marty, Benny's cellmate asked.

"It's over," Benny said, plopping down on the sorry excuse for a bed.

"What are you going to do now? Can you afford another lawyer?" Marty asked.

"I couldn't afford that one," Benny said, hooking his thumb in the general direction of the parking lot. "I'd probably be better off with a public defender, anyway. Maybe some guy right out of law school that hasn't been following the case. Or a girl. Maybe she'll be cute." Benny smiled at the thought.

"I hope whoever you get next can get you off. Even if Carmichael doesn't believe you, I do."

"Too bad you can't be my lawyer, Marty. I could use somebody that believes in me. I don't think you'd look so hot in one of those skirts the girl lawyers wear on those TV shows, though."

Marty chuckled. "Sorry, pal. Lawyering ain't one of my gifts."

"No, grand larceny and assault are," Benny joked, then his tone grew serious. "I always hoped having someone from that firm representing me would help, but I think it might have shot me in the foot instead."

"Don't you think it's weird that he offered to represent you in the first place? Especially for free. Seems like it would've flushed that guy's career down the toilet," Marty observed.

Benny had spent the better part of three decades trying not to dwell on that very question. Deep down, he wondered if Carmichael had ever even tried to get him cleared of murdering those people. If he had, maybe Benny wouldn't still be looking down the barrel of a life sentence.

5

TAKING A DEEP breath as he exited the prison, John Carmichael was relieved he wouldn't have to deal with Benny Johnson any longer. He'd been a thorn in his side for decades. Maybe defending the man who'd been accused of murdering his colleague hadn't been such a great idea after all.

I've wasted more than thirty years of my career on that bum, John thought as he walked across the parking lot to his car. How could I have allowed myself to get tangled up with such a lowlife?

That's the nature of your job, a voice from somewhere in his head responded.

There's a reason I left my position as a public defender, he countered in his head. People just like Benny.

Initially John had taken pride in defending those who couldn't afford an expensive lawyer in a corner office.

Now he *was* the expensive lawyer in a corner office.

The day he was offered a position at the most prestigious law firm in town, he'd jumped at the chance. Most of the lawyers at the firm had a family connection to the partners, but when Terry Hughes, the senior partner, died suddenly of a heart attack on the racquetball court, there was an empty office.

Back then, it felt like he'd hit the jackpot.

When John made the decision to represent Benny, he was still relatively new to the firm and thought taking a high-profile case pro bono would earn him some extra press. It certainly had, and nearly ruined his reputation in the process. He quickly realized that if he didn't keep Benny out of the public eye, his career would be toast.

Upon arriving at his car, John ran a hand through his gray hair and lowered his athletic frame onto the plush leather seat. He never tired of driving around in luxury.

As he put the car in reverse, he caught a glimpse of his reflection in the rearview mirror. Usually, he saw a handsome man with sharp features who commanded attention. What he saw now was a man who desperately wanted to retire and live a quiet life. No more criminals, trials, and no more defending people he knew were guilty.

Enough was enough.

"Good riddance, Benny," he muttered as he drove away from the prison for what he hoped would be the last time. He'd announce his resignation first thing Monday morning with the understanding he would stay on until he finished his active caseload.

An hour and a half later, he paused before closing the door of his third-floor office. He turned toward his assistant, Julia Burke. "I'm not taking any calls the rest of the day."

"Yes, sir," Julia said, glancing at her watch.

Julia had been worried about him lately. John knew that. He'd been distancing himself from everyone in the office and spending more and more time either out of the office or asking not to be disturbed. Julia wasn't oblivious. She knew his meeting shouldn't have taken this long. He shrugged.

After shutting the door to his office, John leaned against it and breathed deeply. "Not much longer," he reminded himself.

Taking long strides to reach the other side of the room, he stopped at the floor-to-ceiling window to the right of his desk. He had a spectacular view of the fountains at Triangle Park. The leaves began to change a few weeks ago, and in a month or so skaters would be gliding across the ice rink below.

Reluctantly, he turned from the window. For years he'd relished the picturesque view and welcomed the acclaim he received as one of the top defense attorneys in the state. His reputation had been solid for most of his career, the only blip being when he'd first chosen to represent Benny Johnson. Eventually he'd been able to convince his colleagues and the media that getting Benny cleared would keep the police looking for the real killer.

Unfortunately, that never happened.

Even so, he was admired and never grew tired of it.

The past couple years had been taxing, though. Sure, his record was still impeccable, but he didn't have the same energy in the courtroom he'd had before, and the victories weren't as thrilling as they'd once been.

"John?"

He turned toward the door to see Susan Bentley, another partner at the firm. Just a few years older than he, she was the only other person who'd been there when Thomas was murdered. A workaholic who wanted to be taken seriously, she put in long hours at the office. She, like the rest of them, worked constantly and rarely took a vacation. It had been Susan who gave him the hardest time when he decided to take Benny's case.

"How'd it go with Benny?" Susan asked, her concern genuine.

He'd always admired Susan. She had a no-nonsense way about her, accented by a pantsuit and low-heeled shoes. Her shoulder-length gray hair was pulled into a bun. This was a woman who could strike fear into the witnesses testifying against her clients. Her dominating presence belied the fact that she stood only five feet three inches tall. In the courtroom, she was always larger than life.

"Was everyone right? Was I insane when I agreed to represent him?" John sighed and lowered himself into the high-backed leather chair behind his massive desk.

Susan half-smiled and shrugged one shoulder. "Maybe temporarily."

John smiled at her joke. Everyone wanted to plead a case of temporary insanity. Even him.

"I didn't think it would turn out this way. I really didn't. I thought we'd find the evidence we needed to have his sentence overturned. He's been screaming about his innocence for so long I actually believed it was true." He rubbed his eyes, exhaustion setting in.

"You wanted to believe the best about him," Susan said with a shrug. "There's nothing wrong with that. You're like a pit bull, which explains why you haven't been able to let go all these years. But John, the evidence against him was overwhelming. They found his fingerprints in the library where Thomas and Sheila were found. No one else's. The alarm system was set from the inside. The police responded when he broke into the house. They caught him red-handed. How does he explain that? That, on top of his rap sheet, made the case a slam dunk for the prosecutor."

He rubbed his face. "You're right," he sighed. "Who would guess a person could still be so naïve at my age?"

John glanced around his office. The degrees and awards hanging on the walls did little to comfort him.

He felt like an old fool.

Susan ignored his question. "What now?"

"We're done," John said, feeling every one of his sixty-three years. "He's finding another lawyer."

Susan cocked an eyebrow. "You've spent almost your entire career on that guy. You're sure you can just walk away?"

John nodded. "It's time. There's nothing more I can do, or want to do, for that matter." He began shuffling papers around on his desk. "Now, I really need to get back to work."

Susan nodded and turned to leave, then paused with a hand on the doorknob. Without turning back to face him, Susan said, "Thomas's murder was hard on all of us. We handled it in different ways. You did what you thought was best. Now maybe you can get some closure." With that, Susan pulled the door open and slipped out, allowing it to click shut behind her.

"Sure," he muttered. "Closure."

He pressed the intercom button. "Julia?"

"What can I do for you, Mr. Carmichael?" Her voice was tinny through the speaker.

"Please get the entire Benny Johnson file from archives."

"Sure thing," she responded, then was gone.

One more look through the evidence against Benny and he would call it quits.

Several minutes later, Julia entered his office carrying a thick stack of folders and set them on his desk. After more than thirty years, the records were voluminous.

"Thank you, Julia. That will be all."

John looked at the mountain of folders in front of him. Sighing, he looked at the clock.

Why even bother?

6

SIGHING HEAVILY, JOAN Shepherd settled into the oversized leather chair by the fireplace. Deep down, she'd always known the truth about Alex's adoption would come out, but after seeing the raw pain in her granddaughter's eyes, she regretted going along with the wishes of her daughter and son-in-law.

Joan knew loss. First, Frank died after having a stroke two years ago. That had been so devastating she thought she'd never recover. How could she just move on after fifty years of marriage? But the support of her daughter, Carla, son-in-law, Robert, and Alex had helped her begin again. She still felt empty, but others helped fill the void. Then, when Carla and Robert were killed in the plane crash last year, Joan nearly suffocated. First her husband, then her daughter. That was enough pain for a dozen lifetimes. She'd been able to pull herself together for Alex, but there were nights the loneliness almost crushed her.

Now that Alex knew the truth, Joan was terrified she would lose the last person she loved.

Joan always treasured the special bond she had with Alex. When Alex was a little girl, they'd giggled and shared secrets over cookies and milk. As Alex got older, she kept confiding in Joan about problems with school, work, and her parents. If possible, Carla and Robert's death brought them even closer. They'd clung to one another like a life preserver.

Now, the knowledge that she'd betrayed someone she loved so dearly made her feel like she'd committed treason against her own flesh and blood.

Except she isn't my flesh and blood, and now she knows it, Joan thought. There's nothing to keep her from taking off and making a new life for herself. One that doesn't include me.

Shaking her head, Joan realized it would be just like Alex to hop the first plane to Lexington to find out exactly what happened.

Covering her face with bony hands, Joan choked out a sob. Another followed and soon they were so close together she couldn't catch her breath.

Mustering every bit of strength she had, she straightened her back and made a vow. She had to protect her relationship with Alex. She would not, under any circumstance, lose anything—or anyone—else.

7

ALEX SLAMMED THE car door and darted across the parking lot. She was late and Jeannie, eternally punctual, would be getting peeved.

She scanned the crowded café, then spotted Jeannie at a table for two near a window. The setting sun glowed orange against the wild curls cascading around Jeannie's face. She wore a brown cardigan over a turquoise shirt. Under the table, Jeannie's ankle-length skirt in turquoise and brown tie-dye was pulled up slightly, revealing brown sandals and a hemp ankle bracelet. Alex wondered if Jeannie knew, or even cared, that it was late October.

As she weaved through the tables, she inhaled the aroma. Her stomach growled. She hadn't really eaten since lunch yesterday; her grilled cheese and tomato soup this afternoon went untouched.

Settling into the chair across from Jeannie, Alex began the apologies. "Sorry I'm late. I was reading Mom's journal and trying to find information about my adoption online but struck out. Big surprise."

Jeannie scowled at her plate. "I should know better than to eat curry. Now I have indigestion and I'm still hungry." She covered her mouth as a small belch escaped. "I got here early, so I went ahead and ordered. I had to skip lunch to cover someone else's client load." She winked at Alex, then noting Alex's attire asked, "Have you been doing yoga?"

"You know better than that, Jeannie. Lunge-and-hold isn't my thing." Alex dismissed her annoyance that Jeannie hadn't paid attention to anything she said. Though sometimes absent-minded, Jeannie was a wonderful friend. "I've been reading Mom's journal. What's got you so distracted?"

Jeannie shrugged. "Rough morning at the center. Having to take over your caseload today didn't help, either."

A stab of guilt worked its way through Alex's stomach.

"What did you learn? From the journal, I mean," Jeannie asked, shifting in obvious discomfort.

"Not much, really. According to Mom's journal, my birth parents were involved in some kind of tragedy, but it didn't say whether they were alive or dead. I guess that's why I was placed for adoption."

"Nothing else?"

"Just that some attorney contacted them, but she didn't mention his name or the name of his firm, just that he was from Kentucky. Apparently Dad met him at a convention. Why the attorney called them about adopting me, I have no idea."

Alex glanced in the direction of the cash register. The line to order was still ten people deep.

"If the adoption was legitimate, why all the secrecy?" Jeannie asked while she rubbed her upper abdomen.

Alex raised a shoulder and let it drop. "I've asked that

question again and again and can't seem to come up with a good reason. Maybe they were afraid if I found out I was adopted, I'd go off searching for my birth parents."

"A valid fear, I'd say, considering how quickly you've started looking for them," Jeannie observed.

Alex tilted her head and frowned. "Don't say that. I need to know the truth. I'm sure you can empathize with that."

"I suppose I can." Jeannie rummaged through her enormous purse for an antacid. "Did you run a search of abducted children?"

Shifting uncomfortably in her seat, Alex broke eye contact. "Uh, no, I haven't. There's no reason to. Mom and Dad would have never been involved with something so horrible."

"Maybe, maybe not," Jeannie challenged. "One thing that can't be overlooked is humanity's ability to do the unthinkable in desperate situations."

"Desperate? Come on, Jeannie. They were good, honest people," Alex corrected.

"Good, honest people who gave you a fake birth certificate." Jeannie finally stopped looking through her bag. "The nature of our job is to question everything and dig for the 'why' of things. That's why you're so determined to find out the truth of where you came from." She reached across the table and took Alex's hand. "Right now, I think you have reason enough to doubt them."

Alex inhaled sharply. She wasn't entirely happy with her parents at the moment, but she couldn't stand listening to Jeannie question their character. "I'm sure there's a perfectly good explanation," she defended.

"Sounds like cognitive dissonance to me," Jeannie said

with narrowed eyes, then released Alex's hand. "Now, are you taking care of yourself?"

Alex smiled, the first genuine one in twenty-four hours. Jeannie, always the boss, making sure her counselors were practicing self-care. "I'm okay. I didn't sleep well last night, as you can imagine, and haven't really eaten since lunch yesterday. I did go for a run this morning, and that helped clear my head."

"What about Steven? Is he still calling?" Jeannie asked, resuming her search for heartburn relief.

Alex rolled her eyes and settled against the back of the chair. "He is. For some reason he just can't let it go. We weren't even together very long. Last week he tried to give me a scarf. I hated to turn it down. It was really pretty."

"Are you worried?"

"No. He's a little intense and creepy, and everything always seems to be about him. After dealing with clients and their problems all day at work, the last thing I need from a boyfriend is for him to be so needy."

Jeannie nodded in understanding as she pulled a bottle of Tums from her purse. Shaking a couple into her hand, she asked, "So how are things going with Joan?" She popped the antacid into her mouth.

"Strained, as you can imagine, at least on my end. I haven't spoken to her since I found the birth certificate last night. She's left a few messages on my voicemail, but I don't have anything to say to her right now."

Eyebrows knitted together, Jeannie nodded. "I can understand that, but try to remember that Joan has been under a lot of emotional stress the last couple years. Perhaps she deserves a little grace."

"Maybe…"

"She does," Jeannie urged.

Alex sat in thoughtful silence for a moment, chewing her thumbnail. "I'll go over for breakfast tomorrow," she finally said. "Maybe she'll have more to tell me."

Like why Mom and Dad gave me a forged birth certificate, and how they knew how to get their hands on one in the first place.

8

ALEX OPENED HER front door and dropped her keys on the entryway table and exhaled. Dinner with Jeannie hadn't been as comforting as she'd hoped. Instead of being on her side, Alex got the distinct feeling that Jeannie was in Gram's corner.

Perhaps she deserves a little grace.

Maybe she does, Alex thought. But that doesn't excuse her keeping a lifetime of secrets about *my* life from me.

She sat on the sofa and leaned her head against the back and closed her eyes. Jeannie's words echoed in Alex's ears. Maybe she should check for abducted children after all. She didn't want to believe it could be true, but her grandmother's concern told her abduction was at least something to consider.

After a few deep breaths, Alex opened her laptop and waited while it hummed to life.

It's weird, she thought. I've never felt abducted.

She always figured abducted children knew something was off, that their caregivers gave some kind of indication that they'd stolen the child. She never would have considered it. Her parents loved her, and she loved them. She still did.

We were a typical happy family, she thought as she clicked on the search engine. Sure, there were times we drove each other crazy, and I felt like I didn't quite belong, but that's just being human.

She hadn't been the spitting image of either of them but looked similar enough to assume everything was as she believed it to be.

If she'd been abducted, the National Center for Missing and Exploited Children should have record of it. Once she had the database pulled up on the screen, she scanned the faces looking back at her. Nausea coiled around her stomach as she looked at columns of children who'd disappeared, never to be seen again. Faces of small children who'd been missing for months. Faces of people missing for decades that had undergone age progression to show what they might look like now. Alex's heart broke for the parents who spent their lives wondering what happened to their children and for the children who'd met a tragic end and whose bodies hadn't been found yet. Some of the parents probably died never knowing what happened to the baby they once held in their arms.

Tears stung the backs of her eyes. Quickly, she blinked them away.

Were her birth parents among those who went to sleep every night praying for the safe return of their child?

Rubbing her eyes, Alex glanced at the antique clock that had been her mother's. It was well past midnight. The web search yielded no information. No infants had been reported missing from Kentucky from her birth year. Grateful she hadn't found out she was a missing child, she was still disappointed. She still had no new information to tie her to her birth parents.

Except…

From the same end table that held her mother's journal, she retrieved the birth certificate she'd found yesterday. Without the names of the parents she'd never known, she'd put it inside and not looked at it again. It didn't seem like there was a reason to, but avoiding it wouldn't help, either.

She unfolded the paper and looked at it closely.

Name at birth: Alexandra Stone

Date of birth: October 29, 1990

Mother's name: Jane Doe

Father: Unlisted

"This is no help at all!" Alex growled, tossing the birth certificate to the floor. "Did I just appear out of thin air?"

Frustrated and exhausted, Alex decided to call it a night.

How could my parents have been involved in something like this? What *were* they involved in, anyway? she fumed.

Alex stood, noticing for the first time how stiff her legs had become. Placing her hands on her lower back, she arched backward to loosen her spine. Stifling a yawn, Alex looked wearily at her dog. Jackson was curled up on the dark red sofa, snoring softly. In this moment, she envied the simplicity of his life.

Walking quietly toward her bedroom at the end of the short hallway, she flipped off the light and climbed into bed without bothering to change her clothes.

All she wanted was sleep. Deep, peaceful sleep.

But after the past thirty hours, Alex wondered if she'd ever be at peace again.

9

"HEY, TONY! I finally dropped that weasel from your brother's office," Benny Johnson called across the prison yard.

"Oh yeah?" Tony Caldwell replied as he made his way across the basketball court, dodging a ball that came flying toward his head.

The day was sunny and warm, and several of the inmates of the Kentucky State Penitentiary were in the middle of a pick-up game. Unpredictable Kentucky weather could be beautiful one day, with frost on the ground and snow in the forecast the next. This could be the last warm day until spring, so the inmates were making the most of it.

"Yeah. That guy never believed me when I told him I didn't off those people. I don't know why he hung around so long in the first place. Did that brother of yours ever say why?" Benny asked, picking his teeth with a mangled toothpick.

"Simon never discusses cases with me. Professional ethics and whatnot."

"Then he must have stayed for my electric personality," Benny remarked, flicking the toothpick to the ground.

Tony grunted. "Must have."

If he had a dollar for every time another inmate asked him for advice about the legal system, he'd have been able to buy his way out of prison long ago. That was the burden of having a defense attorney for an older brother.

"What good is it to have a lawyer for a brother if you don't learn nothing?" Benny asked.

The truth was, Tony and Simon couldn't have been more different. In fact, sometimes Tony wondered how they were even related at all. Given Tony's current predicament, it wasn't like he'd been walking the straight and narrow. While Simon was graduating from law school at the top of his class, Tony had been pushing drugs. In some ways, he was proud of himself for lasting eight years in that line of work before his arrest at age twenty-six. Unfortunately, it all came crashing down when he was caught selling drugs to high school students during a sting operation.

Tony shrugged. "Beats me. Seems like I struck out in that department. I did learn not to get caught selling drugs, though."

When he was first arrested, he thought he would hit the jackpot and Simon would get one of the lawyers in his fancy firm to represent him. Instead, Simon told Tony he needed to face the consequences of what he did. The irony that Simon made his living defending people who'd been arrested for doing the same kinds of things he did gnawed at him. His own brother wouldn't even throw him a bone. Instead, the district attorney, determined to make an example of him, came at him full force during the trial. Now twenty-eight, Tony was two years into serving a ten-year sentence and still had three years to go until he'd be eligible for parole.

"How does a guy like you end up in a place like this, anyway?" Benny chided. "Seems like your family's got it out for you."

"Whaddya mean by that?" Benny had read his mind, but it still irked him that someone like Benny Johnson would say it out loud.

"Isn't it obvious? They think you're a piece of trash, no better than the stuff that's clogging up landfills. Why else would you be sitting in here?"

"Shut up, Benny," Tony warned. "You don't know what you're talking about."

Tony hated Benny and his ability to find and push every button he could. Everyone hated Benny. Still, he hated himself more for letting that piece of scum get to him.

"Oh, come on! Get serious for a minute. Your brother is a defense lawyer. He represents filth like us every day, then goes home to his nice, big house that people like us pay for, but he wouldn't even help his own brother. And don't even get me started on your dad—"

"I said shut up!" Tony yelled, the muscles in his forearm rippling as he clenched his hand into a fist. "Don't you dare bring my dad into this." His dark eyes were fixed on Benny's.

Ignoring the threat, Benny taunted, "Your dad's a cop, for crying out loud. He could have gotten the charges dropped, or at least reduced. He wasn't even willing to do that. What kind of family do you come from, that won't look out for its own? What about your mom? Did she turn her back on you, too?"

The basketball game had come to a halt. The inmates moved closer. Most of them would be happy to see Benny put in his place. A voice from the crowd yelled at Tony to do something about it.

Benny outweighed Tony by sixty pounds, but Tony had lean muscle and rage on his side. He stuck a finger in Benny's face. "You are *never* to bring up my mom again, do you understand?" he growled through clenched teeth. His only urge at the moment was to beat Benny to a bloody pulp. Instead, he spun and stalked to the other side of the yard and unleashed his anger on the punching bag near the fence until his knuckles bled.

"Whatsa matter with you, Benny?" a voice called from the direction of the basketball game. "He coulda killed you."

Without answering, Benny settled onto a concrete bench and squinted against the sun. The guards would be making them go inside in a few minutes, and he wanted to soak up the last bit of fresh air. Inside, it smelled like mildew.

His hope of getting out of prison had gone out the door with Carmichael. Now he could act however he wanted. If his own attorney wouldn't believe him, nobody else would, either.

"What was all that about?" Marty asked, sitting on the bench next to Benny. "Are you trying to make sure nobody else takes your case? Word gets out about how we act in here, and that guy's brother works with Carmichael. I hear he's a big deal."

"What's it matter now? I've been in jail over thirty years. We all know my chances of getting out are slim. If they were going to let me out, they already would have. Most people convicted of murder don't have to stay in this long. Why me? They've got it out for me. Maybe it's time for me to face that and make the most of it." Benny began working his teeth with a grimy thumbnail.

Marty raised his eyebrows. "And that involves getting your brains beat out? I've heard about Tony's temper. He tries to hide it, but he looks like he's about to unravel. If you keep it up, the only way you'll be getting out of here is in a body bag."

"He's soft," Benny mumbled. "Only in two years and he's already falling apart. Anyway, why don't you mind your own business? Huh, Marty?"

Benny was sick of people telling him what to do. The guards told him when to go to bed, when to get up, when he could eat, even when he could take a shower. Benny just couldn't accept that. It ate him up that his lawyer was the one that told him when he could make an appeal and what he could talk about to other inmates. Those should be decisions he made.

"A man in his fifties should have the freedom to do what he wants," he'd said many times, though it seemed that nobody listened. "I hate being treated like a child who needs a babysitter."

He was sick of it all.

"Come on, Benny," Marty consoled. "I'm probably the only person around here that actually likes you. Don't ask why. Maybe you remind me of somebody. But don't you think that means you should be a little nicer to me?"

Benny lifted his shoulders and let them drop. He picked fights with everybody and always made sure he had the last word. He took for granted that anyone might be willing to stick by him. Instead, he alienated everyone. He knew that.

"Sorry," Benny muttered. "I've kinda been on edge since my meeting with Carmichael yesterday. I've always believed that someday I'd get outta here. Now I just feel like a caged animal."

Marty chuckled. "Look around, Benny. We got rapists, murderers, child molesters. We *are* caged animals."

"Maybe you think you're an animal, and maybe you think the rest of these guys are animals, but I ain't no animal. I didn't do nothing," Benny protested, then began laughing.

"It's not funny, ya know. In my opinion, we're no better than a stray dog on the street. We belong here."

"Sure it's funny. I'm so proud of being innocent even though I'm stuck in here with the rest of you. I'm the biggest sucker of all. Wasting away in this hole when I should be out there walking the streets with decent folks." He jabbed himself on the chest with his thumb. "*I* don't deserve this."

Benny would keep them going around in circles, blaming everyone else for being parasites to society while he was wrongfully accused.

Always the victim.

Benny Johnson was a class act at playing the victim.

The guards signaled that it was time to go inside. Marty helped Benny hoist himself off the low concrete bench.

Tony Caldwell was already standing at the door, waiting to go inside. His hands were no longer balled into fists, but his knuckles were bleeding and the muscles in his jaw rippled as he clenched his teeth.

Benny was lucky this time. The hatred on Tony's face communicated that he wouldn't get that lucky again.

In fact, to anyone paying attention, it looked like Benny's luck had just run out.

10

ALEX WALKED UP the sidewalk in front of her grandmother's house Saturday morning, her stomach in knots.

Pausing on the porch, Alex let the childhood memories sweep over her. She'd spent so much time here as a child. Even though many years had passed, the deep, sea foam green of the wooden siding was still as vibrant as she remembered. The white shutters and door sparkled in the sunlight.

To her left, the porch swing gently rocked back and forth with the breeze. Alex had spent many hours on that swing with Gram and Papa as they read stories together and drank lemonade. She'd always loved this place.

The large red maple tree in the center of the yard had been where she and Gram had their picnics. Gram always made her special oatmeal-raisin cookies for dessert.

Now it all felt like a lie. All the good times, the happy memories. Gone.

She turned her back on the yard and nostalgia and tapped lightly on the front door as she pushed it open. "Gram?"

"I'm in the kitchen. Come on in, sweetie," Joan called.

"Hi, Gram," Alex said, her eyes never leaving the floor.

Joan walked toward her granddaughter and lifted Alex's chin with her thumb and index finger, forcing Alex's eyes to meet hers.

The blue eyes that had been so vibrant just two days ago now looked dull. The energetic woman Alex had always known looked every day of her seventy-five years. Standing there in her jeans and rumpled gray sweater, Joan looked weak and vulnerable. In that instant, she realized she wasn't the only one affected by this. Her grandmother was paying the price for burying the past.

"How are you holding up, dear?"

"I'm okay, Gram. The shock is starting to wear off. How are you? You look tired." Alex hated to see this woman suffer any more than she had the past two years, but this hurt could have been avoided.

"I haven't been sleeping well."

Guilt tried to work its way into Alex's mind, but she squelched it. She was here for answers. "Why didn't anybody ever tell me I was adopted?"

Joan sighed. "Your parents thought it was best. Why don't you take our coffee into the dining room? I'll bring the cake and we'll chat."

Alex obediently carried a try containing coffee, a bowl of sugar, and a small pitcher of cream into the dining room. The gold and sage color scheme and the sunflower arrangement in the middle of the dining room table were meant to bring joy, but this morning the cheerful colors couldn't overpower the cloud of distrust hanging over the house.

Joan set the tray of coffee cake on the table. Tension built as the two ate in silence. Finally, Joan spoke. "You have every right to be angry, Alex. I don't deny that. The people you trusted most in the world kept a huge secret from you. I'm sorry your parents never told you, and I'm sorry I never told you." Her chin-length gray hair slid forward as she looked into her coffee cup.

"I'm not a child that needs to be protected anymore. I can handle whatever you have to tell me," she said, taking a sip of coffee, her eyes never leaving her grandmother.

Joan leaned back in her chair and crossed her arms over the midsection, as if trying to protect herself from Alex's mounting anger. "When your mother found out she couldn't have children, she was devastated. She became severely depressed and there were days she hardly got out of bed. Some people are born to be mothers. She was one of them. It had always been her dream to have a big family and knowing it would never happen was really hard for her." Joan paused and took a sip of coffee. "They began looking into adoption, but things kept falling through. It seemed the birth mother always changed her mind at the last minute. Each time it didn't work out, your mother became even more discouraged. Then, one day, somebody called your mom and dad. They said there was a baby girl that needed a home quickly. Your mom and dad didn't even ask questions, they just said they would take her. You. The whole process took less than two weeks." Joan diverted her gaze from Alex and looked out the window. "When they brought you home, they told me I must never tell you that you were adopted. She was finally happy, so I didn't press the issue."

"But why did it have to be a secret?"

"I told you, I don't know. After the first few months, they

began to relax and really enjoy being parents. There was such a change in your mom. I hadn't seen her that content in years."

Alex cut a forkful of coffee cake. "What about the birth certificate I found? The only thing listed is my name. The mother was listed as 'Jane Doe' and the father isn't listed at all. How did they pull that off? All I know is that my last name was Stone, and I was born in Lexington, Kentucky."

"I told you I didn't know it was there. That's the truth."

"Where did they get a forged birth certificate?" Alex pressed. It seemed like Gram knew shockingly little for someone who should have known what was going on back then. She took the bite of coffee cake from her fork.

Joan extended both hands, palms up. "I have no idea. But I've been doing some thinking. Why don't we just forget all about this? We still have each other, and things can just go back to the way they were."

Alex stopped chewing. "Things will never be the way they were, Gram," she said over the mouthful. "I can't just forget. My whole life is different now."

Joan looked down at her hands. Tense silence floated between them until Alex broke it. "Gram, I'm going to Kentucky."

Joan's head snapped up. "That's a bit impulsive, don't you think?"

"Probably, yes. But I need to know."

"Can't you just leave it alone?" Joan pleaded. "Your parents loved you and I love you. Why do you think you need more than that?"

"I need the truth, Gram, and frankly, I don't think you're giving it to me. I understand why you don't want me to go, and I know you think it's unnecessary, but to me it isn't an option.

You know I've never been satisfied with half-truths, and right now, I don't even have that much."

The cheerful chirping of the bird sitting on the windowsill was a sharp contradiction to the discomfort in the room.

Alex was sure she wasn't the only one wishing her parents were here to take the brunt of the questions.

"I can only imagine how terribly difficult this has been for you," Joan said, her voice softening. "But Alex, are you sure you want to do this? Even after what I've told you? Your mom and dad were scared of something. Doesn't that tell you all you need to know? It could be dangerous."

"They were probably scared because they had an illegally forged birth certificate," Alex snapped. "The point is, we don't know what happened. So something terrible happened. Big deal. It could have been a car accident or a house fire. Mom was prone to overreacting; we both know that."

Joan nodded her agreement.

"You could come with me," Alex suggested. "That way you'll know I'm safe. You said you were sorry you never told me, but you can help me now."

Joan shook her head tightly. "I wish I could help you, but your parents didn't want you to find out. I have to respect their wishes."

"Fine," Alex growled. "I'll do it myself."

"Please don't be mad," Joan said gently. "I have to do what I think is best for you."

Unexpected tears sprang to Alex's eyes. "I know. I'm sorry. Please understand that I have to do this. For me. I have to find out where I came from." The determined thrust of Alex's jaw communicated the discussion was over. She wouldn't be dissuaded.

"I understand," Joan acquiesced. "When are you leaving?"

Alex sat up straight. "Today. As soon as I pack."

Joan slumped deeper in the chair. "I see."

Alex rose and circled the table. She gave Gram a quick hug and a kiss, then turned toward the front door.

"Alex? Please be careful." Joan's anguished eyes pleaded with her granddaughter.

"I will," Alex replied as she opened the front door and stepped outside.

I don't know what Gram is so worried about, she thought as she walked to her car. Chances are I won't be in any more danger than I would be if I stayed home.

11

H E STARED AT Alex's apartment with cold, vacant eyes as he inhaled deeply from his cigarette.

She was leaving him. He knew she was.

Even though she said she was there for him, she was leaving. How could she betray him this way?

Slowly exhaling, he considered what he ought to do about it. He'd trusted her, told her his deepest secrets, and trusted she would be there when he needed her.

Everyone in his life had abandoned him. He thought this time was different—that Alex was different. Her leaving confirmed that she was the same as everyone else.

She would have to be punished.

No one got away with abandoning him. Throughout his life, he'd already let too many people get away with causing him pain.

No more.

This time he'd have to make an example of her. Then no one would ever dare try to leave him again.

He sat straight up as he watched her come down the stairs

of her apartment building. She was carrying a small suitcase and rolling a larger one behind her. A big, black dog was at her heels.

He didn't know she had a dog. Something else she'd kept hidden from him. What else was she hiding?

She struggled to keep the suitcase from tipping as she carefully wheeled it down each step. It looked heavy.

Where does she think she's going? he seethed. Looks like she's planning to be gone for a while.

Even under the strain of the suitcase, her movements were graceful, like a gazelle in the savanna. She walked with confidence, a woman secure in who she was.

There's something different about her today, though, he thought. What is it? The ease with which she carried herself was still there, but the smile that was ever-present in her green eyes was missing.

She's moving like she's worried. Like she's being hunted.

He smiled. Does she know there's a reason to be worried? Can she sense the danger she's in, like the prey that realizes the lion is just moments away from attack?

He'd always thought animals had a sixth sense and knew they were being hunted. Do humans feel the same way? he wondered.

Alex pulled a cell phone from her pocket and tapped the screen, then brought it up to her ear. He leaned forward, straining to hear what she was saying.

"Jeannie, I won't be at work at all next week... I'm going to Kentucky... I've got some sick time and vacation I'll use... Sorry for the short notice... Yes, I know I owe you one... I promise I'll be careful. Bye." She slid the phone back into her pocket and loaded the suitcase into the trunk of the car. The dog happily jumped into the backseat.

A moment later, she backed the car out of the parking spot and pulled out onto the street. She was on her way—to Kentucky, apparently. He followed, a safe distance behind her.

The corners of his mouth lifted in a satisfied smile as he imagined the fear in her eyes when, like the prey of a lion, she knew her time was up.

12

JOHN CARMICHAEL SAT in his favorite leather club chair watching the flames dance in the fireplace. Though the day started warm, the temperature had dropped significantly in the evening hours. The setting sun cast an amber glow through the window on the opposite wall. Other than that faint bit of light, the room was lit only by the fire. Scotch in hand, John rested his head on the back of the chair and closed his eyes.

He loved this evening ritual. For years it had been reserved only for weeknights, but recently he'd started drinking on the weekends, too. The scotch initially served to dull the regret he felt when he'd gotten an obviously guilty client acquitted. Early in his career, it bothered him to know he was being paid to make sure guilty people were released to walk the streets. As the money rolled in, though, he'd learned to squelch his conscience. Now it bothered him that getting guilty people off no longer bothered him. As a result, the scotch was more of a fixture that John cared to admit. It was no longer reserved for the evenings when he got home from the office, and he frequently found himself pouring a glass at all hours of the day, even occasionally at his desk while he was at work.

Now that he was alone and away from the office and the expectations of the firm, he wondered how he'd allowed his life to get to this point. As a child, he never would have believed he would be wealthy and powerful. Always the kid who stammered, he'd been on the receiving end of endless cruel jokes by his classmates. His mother was a nice lady, but she always went from one job to the next trying to make ends meet. He'd only met his father a couple times and opted not to attend his funeral when he died twenty years ago.

John's father had been a successful surgeon who had no time for a child; his mother was a pretty, young nursing assistant who had aspirations of one day becoming a nurse practitioner. The unplanned pregnancy ended those dreams.

Because his mother and father had never been married, their split left his mother virtually penniless. His father always found a way to avoid paying child support, his mother often holding two or three jobs at a time in order to pay the bills. She'd died of heart failure when she was only forty-five years old, just after John graduated from college.

Sometime during his high school years, he'd found his voice and was able to stand up to the ridicule his classmates subjected him to. He remembered the first time he stood up to those harsh words. A classmate, the son of a wealthy businessman, had been mocking his labored speech and drawing attention to John's worn shoes and ill-fitting clothes his mother had bought at a thrift store.

The final straw had been when his classmate said, "If your father ever cared about you or your mom, maybe you wouldn't look like you went shopping in a dumpster. Your mom wasn't good enough for him, and you were probably such a disappointment that he couldn't stand to look at you."

He'd shouted back, "That's enough! If you ever talk about my mom again, you will regret it for the rest of your miserable life!"

Even to his own ears his voice sounded like someone else's. His voice was clear and strong, and there was no trace of the shy boy who'd been bullied most of his life. It was then that John knew he could take care of himself.

He remembered his mother's excitement when he got his acceptance letter from the University of Kentucky. He'd been accepted to other schools, but attending the local university allowed him to attend classes and hold a job without incurring extra living expenses. Finally, he'd been able to take some of the burden off his mom.

For forty years he regretted that she hadn't lived long enough to enjoy it.

In college, he decided to become a lawyer. He'd relished the thought of prosecuting wealthy defendants who thought they were above the law. It was as if he would finally be able to get his revenge on every entitled kid who'd ever wronged him.

Now, sitting in the den of his large home in the most exclusive part of town, the irony of how his life turned out brought a chuckle from his throat. He wasn't prosecuting criminals, he was defending them. Somewhere along the way he'd turned his back on his reason for going into law in the first place.

He'd become the very person he despised.

The money and power had seduced him, and he willingly turned away from his own moral compass.

He held the scotch to his lips and tilted his head back,

draining the last bit of liquid. Raising his lean body from his chair, he walked to the bar and refilled his glass. He'd been living on the edge so long he now had the sense he was about to lose his footing and topple off.

John lifted the decanter and splashed more scotch into the glass. Just as he was about to take a drink, the phone rang.

He stared at it, hesitant to answer. It was a burner phone and almost never rang.

Exhaling, he slowly walked over to the corner table and picked up the phone. Suddenly glad he'd had a couple drinks to calm his nerves, he pushed the button to connect the call. The voice he heard on the other end of the line was one he recognized all too well. He'd heard it many times in the past but was grateful they hadn't been in contact in a long time.

Briefly explaining the reason for the sudden communication, the caller uttered words that chilled John to his very core.

His past wouldn't stay buried much longer.

13

J OAN SHEPHERD POURED a cup of tea and looked at
the clock. It was seven-thirty, and Alex still had two more
hours of driving before she reached Lexington.

If Jackson behaved.

Her granddaughter loved that dog, but he could be ornery
when he was excited.

Knowing she wouldn't be able to relax until she knew Alex
had arrived safe and sound, she'd done her best to stay busy
around the house. She'd puttered around in the garden, pulling
weeds and digging up dead plants, then cleaned the house from
top to bottom.

The hard work had drained her as much physically as
worrying about Alex and what she'd be digging up drained
her emotionally.

Taking a sip of tea, she leaned against the counter and took
a deep breath. Only the light above the sink was on, bathing
the kitchen in muted warmth. Once upon a time, this room
had been the center of so many happy times. The whole family

would gather in there on holidays and special occasions, each person performing their assigned duties.

Joan and Frank bought the house as a fixer-upper shortly after they were married and spent many years putting their personal touch on it. Now in her mid-seventies, almost all Joan's happy memories were here.

Until Frank died two years ago, she felt content in this house and couldn't imagine ever leaving. Now she felt lonely. Acknowledging that she didn't need a house this size for just her, she'd considered selling, but couldn't bring herself to part with all the memories it held. She felt as though she'd be betraying Frank if she did.

Although, betrayal does seem to be my specialty these days, she thought wryly.

Shaking the thought from her head, she chewed the tip of her thumbnail. She'd put off what needed to be done long enough.

Reaching for the phone, she prepared herself to make the phone call she was sure would make Alex never want to speak to her again.

14

*T*HE PLANE HIT *turbulence and rocked back and forth. Alex looked at her mother, seated to her left, then to her father, seated to her right. They both stared straight ahead, faces devoid of expression. As the ride became rougher, Alex fastened her seatbelt and dug her fingers into the armrests. The plane went into a free-fall as the pilot struggled to regain control.*

Her heart pounded wildly; her body went numb.

Overcome by fear, she screamed. Her parents didn't look at her or try to comfort her. She turned her head to the right and looked out the window on the other side of her father. The plane was descending quickly toward the earth at a forty-five-degree angle. The seatbelt dug into her abdomen as the descent forced her forward.

Why aren't you scared? she wanted to scream at them. The plane is going to crash!

Suddenly, Alex was struck by the realization that her mom and dad didn't know what was happening. They were in limbo, somewhere between life and death, taking the final plunge into the afterlife.

Alex continued to scream as the plane plummeted toward the earth, then nothing. It was dark and cold.

She couldn't move.

Alex sat up and rubbed her eyes. A bead of sweat dripped down her spine. Palms damp, she wiped her shaking hands on her pajama pants and crossed the room to turn up the heat. Drenched in sweat, the cool hotel air chilled her.

She'd had nightmares about her parents' plane crash before, but this was the worst one yet. It was also the first time she'd dreamed she was on the plane with them. Her stomach rolled as she remembered how scared she was in the dream. The terror her parents would have felt must have been awful.

Alex fought the urge to throw up.

I guess I should have expected this, Alex thought. The first anniversary of their death is in two days.

She shook her head, trying to force the sadness from her mind. Sometimes, especially since her parents died, she was able to use the therapeutic techniques she'd learned from her academic training and clinical experience to talk herself out of a mild depression or panic. Other times it didn't work. This was one of those times.

But there wasn't time to mope. She had work to do and needed to get ready for the day.

After driving nine hours, she'd made it to the hotel just after nine o'clock last night. She'd quickly brushed her teeth, changed into pajamas, and fallen into bed, exhausted.

Jack was still snoring softly on the floor next to her, completely unaware that his human had been on the verge of a nervous breakdown only moments earlier.

Desperately wanting to feel close to her parents again, Alex opened her suitcase and took out a small box that was filled with old letters and photos of her parents. Now, more than ever, she needed to remind herself of the mother and father she'd always known.

She read each word and looked at each photo, carefully placing them back in the box. Reliving the happy moments was a journey she needed to take. The anger and hurt she'd carried since finding her birth certificate dulled the memories of the happy times she'd shared with them. She closed her eyes and remembered her mother's smile, a smile that brought joy to everyone around her. Even as she aged and the fine lines around her eyes and mouth deepened, the smile remained bright.

Her father's strong arms had picked her up time after time when she was learning to ride a bicycle. She remembered the box of chocolates waiting on her bed when she got home from school each Valentine's Day. Alex always had a special relationship with her parents, and she was angry because she'd let herself forget how much they loved her.

And how much she loved them.

Tucking the box back in her suitcase, Alex stood and exhaled. The drab color scheme of the hotel room certainly didn't have the same welcoming feeling her apartment had. She didn't feel welcomed at all. In fact, the only color in the whole place was the outdated floral bedspread. Why do these places always insist on ugly bedspreads? she wondered as she retrieved her clothes from the suitcase.

After a quick shower, Alex flipped on the local news just as the meteorologist promised the day would be sunny and brisk. Looking out the window, she wondered how any of these people kept their job.

It was raining.

She dressed in a green, fitted, long-sleeve shirt, jeans, and a chocolate-brown, calf-length sweater coat. This was her favorite cold-weather outfit. The green shirt enhanced her bright green eyes and the brown sweater coat was only a shade or two lighter than her mahogany hair.

Once she completed a quick application of blush and mascara, she fed Jackson. "Have a good day and don't get into trouble," she warned him, gently stroking his head. "I'll try not to be gone too long." Jackson leaned into her when she scratched his ears.

Before leaving, she switched the TV to Animal Planet and kissed the top of his furry head. She hadn't been very good company for him the last few days and felt guilty for leaving him. Maybe she'd try to find a dog park later if the weather cleared up.

After stopping at a nearby bakery for breakfast, she headed to the downtown branch of the Lexington Public Library. Since it was Sunday, the street parking was mostly empty.

"Thank God for GPS," she muttered as she pulled into one of the parking spaces right off the main street.

Born with a terrible sense of direction, she'd spent countless hours driving around town and stopping at gas stations for directions.

When she walked into the library, she was greeted by the scent of books, each one picking up a different smell every time a new person checked it out. She loved the library. It was filled with knowledge and good entertainment. To her, it also represented freedom. Thousands of books offering thousands of different opinions were at the tips of her fingers and she loved it.

After a quick stop at the information desk, she was directed to the Kentucky Room on the third floor. She settled into a rather uncomfortable chair and began looking at newspaper articles starting with the date of her birth. Three hours of reading yielded a headache and two interesting things: the University of Kentucky's football team must have been absolutely dreadful that year, and there and been a violent double murder.

She leaned against the back of the chair, rubbed her eyes, and stretched her neck from side to side, then returned her focus to the article covering the murder of a husband and wife in their home. An affluent couple who'd been personal friends of the governor at the time, they'd been involved in many charitable organizations. Thomas was a successful criminal defense attorney and his wife, Sheila, had been born into old Lexington money, making a career out of sitting on boards for various non-profit organizations.

A model couple, Alex thought.

The happy couple celebrated the addition of a baby girl on October 29, 1990. The newspaper reported the infant had been under the care of a family member the night of the murders and wasn't present at the home. Based on the tone of the article, Alex suspected there was doubt about that, but one of Thomas's own colleagues confirmed this fact and contacted the family member, arranging for the baby's care until permanent guardianship could be established.

Scanning the article a third time, Alex felt with certainty that things didn't go the way it was reported, and that she was the daughter of the two victims, Thomas and Sheila Stone.

15

ALEX GRASPED THE edge of the table. The room spun.

Thomas and Sheila Stone had been murdered in their home on New Year's Eve thirty-two years ago. Stone. Thirty-two years ago.

The timeline fit.

According to the article, they'd been murdered on New Year's Eve and the first entry in her mother's journal was dated January second. Only two days had passed between the murder and the phone call to her mom and dad about a baby that need to be adopted quickly.

And Stone. Their last name had been Stone. So what if her birth parents' names hadn't actually been listed on her birth certificate? Hers was, and it was Stone. On top of that, their baby had the exact same birthday Alex did.

She didn't believe in coincidences.

Taking a few deep breaths to regain her equilibrium, Alex closed her eyes, trying to talk herself down from her psychological high dive.

In through her nose, out through her mouth, just like she told her clients. She repeated the breaths until she began to feel more grounded.

Hands no longer trembling, she opened her eyes. The shrill ringing of her cell phone erased the calm she'd begun to feel.

Groaning inwardly, she pressed the button to connect the call. "Hello, Steven."

"I'm worried about you, Alex." Since the breakup, he had a way of sounding creepy every time he said her name.

Not again, she thought. "Thank you, but there's no reason to worry about me. I'm fine." Grimacing at her clipped tone, she scolded herself for answering the phone in the first place.

"Just because you don't want me anymore doesn't mean I don't still care about you," he said quietly.

Rolling her eyes toward the ceiling, she snapped, "What exactly do you need? I'm in the middle of a project and really need to get back to it."

I'm such a jerk, Alex thought. But Steven was clingy and couldn't seem to take a hint. They broke up three months ago, and he still found an excuse to keep calling. Did I leave my iPod in your car? Last night I watched the movie we saw on our first date... do you remember how much we laughed? Have you gotten your oil changed lately?

There was always something.

"I know where you are, Alex. You need to be careful."

Her head jerked back. "Excuse me?"

"I know where you are and what you're doing."

This *has* to be a joke! Alex's mind screamed. Surely a camera crew is going to pop out and tell me I'm on *Candid Camera* or *Punk'd* or one of the other shows that used to be so popular.

How did I ever get mixed up with such a head case? she

wondered. As a mental health professional, I should be able to tell the difference between the normal guys and the ones that want to set your house on fire. If it wasn't so creepy, she'd laugh.

Keeping her voice as steady as possible, she said, "Steven, I appreciate your concern for my well-being, but I have to be honest. All the attention you've given me since we broke up is starting to make me uncomfortable. I realize you've had a hard time accepting that we're no longer in a relationship, but that in no way gives you the right to keep tabs on me. I don't need you to take care of me."

Movement in her peripheral caught Alex's eye. An angry-looking librarian was coming straight toward her. She slouched in the chair, trying to make herself invisible.

The woman stopped just a few feet from her and pointed to a sign on the wall above Alex's computer.

CELL PHONES PROHIBITED.

"Ma'am, I'm going to have to ask you to turn your phone off."

Why do librarians always have to sound so brusque? she wondered.

Still reeling from what she'd discovered in the newspaper and trying to reason with an obsessed ex-boyfriend, she was also being scolded like a child by a very large woman who clearly took it upon herself to make sure the library existed in complete silence.

"Hold on, Steven." Alex covered the phone and turned to face the woman who was now tapping her foot on the carpet that was designed in multiple shades of brown. "I need to take this call. Will you please make sure no one else uses this computer while I'm gone? There are some very important articles I need to print." With that, Alex rose from the chair and quickly trotted down the stairs and out the front door. She was met with a light breeze and sunshine glistening on the wet pavement.

Maybe the meteorologist should get to keep his job, after all.

She raised the phone to her ear. "Okay. As I was saying—"

"It's not like that. Look, I—"

"No, Steven, you look. We're done. We have been for three months. I don't know how else to say it so you'll understand." So much for her personal rule of treating everyone with respect, she berated herself.

"Your grandmother called," he said, his voice barely audible.

"What did you say?"

"Your grandmother called. She's worried about you."

Alex felt as though she'd been slapped. "Gram called… you."

"Yes."

"What did she tell you?" She'd been betrayed. Again.

"She told me you recently found out some information about your past that you were having a hard time dealing with. She said you left town to try to find out what happened. She also said you weren't really speaking to her, and maybe I would have better luck. I told her that I've never had any luck with you, but she insisted. If there really is a reason for her to be worried, I wanted to make sure you're okay. You know, hear it for myself." He sounded so concerned and genuine.

Alex hated that.

Gram knew her relationship with Steven was over and that his continued attention made her uneasy. Why on earth did she call him, of all people? Why not Jeannie?

"I suppose she wanted to share her concern with someone who loves you," he said as though reading her mind. "I mean loved."

She pinched the bridge of her nose. For someone who was supposed to help people through tough times, she certainly didn't hesitate to pummel Steven for calling her during a tough time she was having.

"I'm sorry. I've been under a lot of stress the last few days. It was wrong of me to snap at you the way I did. I really do appreciate your concern. Even though we're not together anymore, it's nice to know somebody still cares."

A beat passed before Steven answered. "No apology necessary. Your spunk is one of the things I love most about you. And I do care, Alex. I always have. Maybe I always will…"

Alex shifted from one leg to the other as the damp air saturated her warmth. "I have to go now, Steven. I'm okay, though. Promise. Bye."

"Goodbye, Alex."

She heard a click and then a dial tone. A shiver raced up her spine that had nothing to do with the chilly fall air. There was something odd about the way he said "goodbye." As she turned to go back into the library, Alex wondered if he'd finally accepted the end of their relationship.

If he hadn't, just how far would he go to get her back?

16

PACING AROUND THE living room, Joan was completely oblivious to the sun shining or the birds chirping in the oak tree outside the window. The last couple days were taking a toll on her. She couldn't eat or sleep, and she was sure she'd lost weight. All she could think about was how she was about to lose Alex.

In desperation, she'd called Steven last night. Her relationship with Alex was already strained, and she was afraid anything she said might damage it even more. Telling Steven about Alex's adoption was risky; Alex herself had only known about it a few days.

The truth was it really wasn't any of Steven's business. Joan knew that. Alex had made it perfectly clear during the past few months that Steven wasn't part of her life anymore.

But he seems like such a nice young man, Joan had reasoned, and he cares so much about her. Maybe she'll give him another chance once he offers her a shoulder to cry on.

She looked at the clock above the fireplace. Ten minutes

past noon. Her stomach growled, but she was too anxious to eat. Perhaps a cup of tea would soothe her.

As she walked past the small table in the corner of the living room, she looked at the pictures it held. Pictures of happy times, before she knew what it was like to experience such devastating loss. She and Frank on a boat during one of their many trips to Maine; Carla and Robert gazing lovingly at their infant daughter; the whole family gathered around a beaming Alex when she completed her doctorate.

Frank had died six months after that photo was taken.

Now a secret had been unearthed and threatened to rip all those memories apart, leaving only the question of what might have been.

Clasping her hands together to stop the shaking, she walked quickly to the kitchen. Again, she brewed a cup of tea. Over the past few days, she'd downed more tea than the entire royal family.

As she poured the steaming water over the tea bag, the phone rang. Startled, she splashed the scalding liquid onto the back of her hand.

"Hello?" she answered, trying to sound cheery just in case it was Alex calling.

"It's taken care of," the husky voice on the other end of the call said.

Joan exhaled. "How'd it go?"

"I called. It's taken care of. That's all you need to know."

"What do you mean 'that's all I need to know'? I told you what was going on like you asked and now you're not going to tell me anything else?"

"I upheld my end of the deal. Now it's time for you to uphold yours. Find a way to get us back together."

Adrenaline shot through Joan. He sounded so agitated, angry even. Beads of sweat dotted her upper lip. "What do you want?" she choked.

"What I've always wanted," he said. "And you're going to make sure I get it."

"You know I can only do so much," Joan tried to reason. "I mean, Alex is her own person. A stubborn one at that. Certainly you must realize I can't *make* her do anything." She blinked. What exactly did he expect her to do?

Steven snorted. "You're a bright lady. You'll figure something out."

The phone clicked in her ear, and for the first time Joan saw Steven for what he really was. Alex had been right about him after all.

"Oh, Alex," she whispered. "I'm so sorry. What have I done?"

17

STEVEN DORSET DISCONNECTED the call and tossed the phone beside him on the tattered sofa. Jaws clenched, he glared at the framed picture on his lap. Alex was stretched out on a blanket, reading a book. He'd taken the picture at a park when he saw her there one Saturday afternoon in June. She had no idea he'd taken a picture, or that he was even there that day. She was like an addiction, and sometimes he just had to see her.

On that particular day, he'd followed her to the park. For hours he sat in his car and watched. She'd packed a picnic lunch for herself and read most of the afternoon.

She'd been an angel.

But that was then. He gripped the frame so tightly the wood dug into his skin. She wasn't an angel anymore. Now she was the woman who broke his heart.

He stood and paced around the tiny living room, still clutching the photo. He needed her. He had to get her back. She was his only reason for living.

But she doesn't want you, a voice from somewhere in his mind taunted.

"Yes! Yes, she does!" he shouted.

No, she doesn't. Can't you take a hint?

"She does. She needs me just like I need her."

She doesn't need you. She never did. Let her go.

"I will never let her go!" he screamed and threw the picture frame to the floor with such force that glass shards scattered over the threadbare carpet.

Sobbing, Steven knelt in the broken pieces. "I'm so sorry, my love." He pressed the marred picture to his chest, rocking back and forth. "I'm so sorry," he whimpered again and again.

Finally, he held the picture to his face, gave it a kiss, and said, "I will get you back, Alexandra Tucker. No matter what I have to do, I'll get you back."

18

MUFFLED VOICES SEEPED into John Carmichael's consciousness. He realized his hand was still on the handle of the coffee pot. Monday morning, and he was paying for self-medicating all weekend. His head was pounding, his thinking fuzzy. He was losing control.

The decision to retire was confirmed after the phone call on his burner phone Saturday night. He'd spent the rest of the weekend downing scotch after scotch to calm his nerves. Unfortunately, his nerves were still frazzled and now he had a hangover.

"Good morning, Mr. Carmichael." Julia's cheerful greeting was like a hammer beating against a sheet of metal.

"Good morning, Julia," he replied. "You're here early."

"My car is in the shop. I had to catch a ride with a friend," she explained, then narrowed her eyes. "Are you okay? You don't look well."

He nodded. "I'm fine."

"Are you sure? You look a little pale," she insisted.

John wanted to answer that of course he looked pale. He'd been working a minimum of sixty-hour weeks for the last thirty-five years, often coming in on weekends when others were enjoying the great outdoors. Instead, he said, "Yes. It's probably just one of those twenty-four-hour bugs or something. I'm sure it will be gone as quickly as it came."

"Okay. Let me know if you need anything." Julia turned to leave, then pivoted to face him. Eying him curiously, she said, "Perhaps you should see a doctor. You seem to be catching a lot of these bugs lately."

As he watched her walk away, he was certain she'd caught on to his increased drinking. She certainly wasn't stupid, and she would know whatever was wrong with him wasn't a twenty-four-hour bug.

John usually considered himself lucky to have an assistant like Julia Burke. He was a hard man to work for, but she rose to the challenge and never complained. He could count on one hand the number of times in the past two years she didn't have something ready for him when he needed it. One of the most competent people in the office, he'd always thought it a shame she hadn't gotten the education to match her intellect.

He watched the cream swirl in his coffee as he stirred.

The secret he'd kept all these years, the carefully constructed persona, was about to unravel. The phone call Saturday evening assured him of that. He'd been too careless, too confident. He was sure nobody knew his secret now, but they would. There were times he'd practically dared people to dig into his background, sure they'd come up empty. He was arrogant and thought he was invincible.

No more.

His worst nightmare was about to happen, and there was nothing he could do to stop it.

He could only try to outrun it.

A vice clamped around John's chest. He couldn't breathe.

Head spinning, he felt trapped. At his age it just wasn't worth it anymore. The best years of his life were gone. If he was lucky, he'd have another twenty.

Over the years, he'd built a large savings account that was more than enough to last that long. He'd have to scale back on his lifestyle, but he could do it. He had to get as far away from the law as possible.

After a few deep breaths, John walked methodically back to his office. One foot in front of the other, he reminded himself. He didn't make eye contact with Julia as he passed her desk but could feel her eyes on his back.

He shut the door and walked to his chair. A few minutes to compose himself, and he'd announce his decision.

Twenty minutes later, after summoning the entire staff, John stood in front of his coworkers in the large conference room at the back of the office suite. Shifting from one leg to the other, he cleared his throat.

His colleagues shared suspicious glances with one another.

Just get it over with, he commanded himself.

Inhaling deeply, he looked at each person in the room. He could only imagine what was going through their minds. Some of these people had known him for more than a decade and had never seen him so rattled.

"I know you are all very busy, so I'll make this quick," he began. "As you all know, I've spent the better part of my career representing Benny Johnson, the man convicted of murdering Thomas and Sheila Stone." Immediately, he wondered why he felt the need to explain who Benny Johnson was. Of course they knew who he was.

The room remained silent except for the ticking clock in the back of the room. He went on. "Many of you know why

I represented him, and most of you didn't agree." His eyes shifted to Susan Bentley, who was now looking at the floor. "As of this past Friday, I am no longer representing him. He has been a parasite to my career for too many years, and I'm relieved to no longer have any further dealing with that man. Upon thinking more about the direction my career has taken, I have decided that it's time I retire."

Susan's head snapped up. Eyes wide, she sputtered, "John, you can't be serious."

Susan and John had been working together for three and a half decades, both sharing an unquenchable desire for prominence and prestige. He'd known that out of everyone, she would be the most shocked.

Quickly scanning the reactions of everyone else in the room, John's eyes met Julia's. Her face was pale, eyes rimmed with unshed tears. He frowned. Those tears weren't out of concern for him or because she'd miss working with him. She was worried about what would happen to her. He'd already braced himself for that conversation, but it would have to wait. It would be up to his replacement to decide if he or she wanted to keep Julia or hire someone new for her position. He would put in a good word for her, but that was all he could do.

"I realize this announcement comes as quite a shock to you all, and that many of you will have questions for me. However, I do have some work to get done and don't wish to be disturbed at this time."

Walking briskly from the conference room, he felt dozens of eyes on his back. Taking a relieved breath, he strode to his office, not noticing the woman who'd entered the conference room as he left.

It was almost over…

19

THE EMPLOYEES OF Hughes, Stone, and Bentley sat quietly a few moments before murmuring to one another. As the talking grew louder, the visitor slipped out of the room and followed the path John had taken.

"Excuse me. Sir?"

John stopped in his tracks and slowly turned to face the person following him. "May I help you?" The words seemed helpful, but his tone didn't invite further questions.

"My name is Alexandra Tucker. I was wondering if I could speak to someone regarding a man who used to work here." The tremor in her voice betrayed her anxiety.

"I'm sorry," John said, already turning away. "I can't help you. Please excuse me." He marched to his office and closed the door with a decisive click.

Behind her, Alex heard someone approaching. She turned to see a woman whose eyes were red-rimmed, as though she'd been crying.

"I'm Julia Burke, Mr. Carmichael's assistant." She extended her hand toward Alex. "May I help you with something?"

"I hope so. I was trying to ask that man a question, but he said he couldn't help me. I assume that's Mr. Carmichael?"

"Yes." Julia sniffled and dabbed her eyes with a tissue. "I'm sorry. This is a difficult morning for the firm. He's just announced his retirement. It's quite unexpected."

"I'm sorry. I'll try not to take much of your time. I came to find out about a man who worked here many years ago. Thomas Stone. I was wondering if anybody might know something about him."

Julia cleared her throat. "Actually, yes. Mr. Carmichael worked with Mr. Stone. So did Ms. Bentley. They're the only two still around from those days."

Alex's hope soared. Maybe it wasn't such a long shot after all.

"Clearly this isn't a good time for Mr. Carmichael, but I wonder if Ms. Bentley would be willing to speak with me for a few minutes."

"I can check," Julia offered. "Please have a seat in the reception area." She waved her hand toward the front of the office.

On the other side of the door, Alex found a small grouping of leather chairs. She sat in one and picked up a copy of *Kentucky Living* magazine. She soon realized that trying to focus on the picturesque horse farms was useless and dropped the magazine back on the table. She was perched on the edge of her chair, drumming her fingers anxiously on the table when Julia appeared.

"Ms. Bentley has a very busy day today, but she would be happy to give you fifteen minutes," Julia said in a professional tone, obviously regaining her composure.

"Thank you," Alex said with a quick nod, then followed Julia past several desks in the main area of the office suite. Alex assumed they belonged to assistants and other administrative staff. Most of the office doors were closed. They turned left down a well-lit corridor and paused at the only door on the left.

Julia tapped lightly on the door and gently pushed it open. "Ms. Bentley, Alexandra Tucker is here to see you."

"Please, have her come in."

Julia moved aside to allow Alex to enter the office. When Alex turned to thank Julia, the woman was already gone.

Behind the desk, Ms. Bentley rose to greet her. Alex figured she must be in her early sixties. She also noted the woman's small frame seemed lost behind the enormous L-shaped desk.

"I assume you're Ms. Tucker."

"Yes, and please call me Alex, Ms. Bentley."

"Susan. Please, have a seat." She waved toward a high-backed leather chair opposite her desk before sitting back down in her own.

"Thank you." Lowering herself into the seat, Alex had the incongruous thought that Jeannie, a longtime vegan, would have a fit if she saw all the leather in this office. "I assume you're the Bentley named in the firm?"

"Actually, that was my father," Susan corrected. "This was his office. I haven't changed it since I moved in here. It might sound crazy but keeping things the way they were helps me get inside his head—to think the way he did. He was an extremely talented attorney."

Alex nodded. That would explain the masculine decor. Between the walnut desk, tan walls, and maroon leather chairs, there was hardly a touch of femininity anywhere in the room. If not for the small orchid on the far corner of the desk near the window, the office would be basically colorless. Other than the framed degrees from college and law school, the walls were empty.

It was the exact opposite of Alex's own office, where it was decorated in calming, muted colors with nature-themed artwork hanging on the walls.

"So," Susan began. "Julia tells me you have some questions about Thomas Stone."

"I do," Alex confirmed.

"How did you know Thomas?" The older woman's voice softened when she said his name. "I can't imagine you're old enough to have known him well."

"I didn't know him at all, actually," Alex confessed, then took a breath and forged on. "I found out I was adopted a few days ago."

Susan's expression relaxed. Her face was almost filled with compassion. "I imagine that was quite a shock."

Alex nodded. "It was. My adoptive parents never told me. They passed away last year and can't answer my questions. I found my original birth certificate and my adoptive mother's journal a few days ago. They both indicate I was born in Lexington."

"And what does that have to do with Thomas?" Again, her voice lilted at the mention of his name.

"According to my birth certificate, my last name was Stone, but my birth parents aren't listed. After I arrived in town, I went to the library and looked up old newspaper articles beginning with my birth date. My mom's journal indicated something terrible had happened to my birth parents, so when I found the article about Thomas and Sheila Stone, I knew there was no way it could be a coincidence. The more I read, the more convinced I was that they were my birth parents. They had a daughter my age."

"Yes, they did. From what I know, she was taken across the country to live with some distant relatives. Actually, one of our own attorneys was involved in the placement."

"That's what the newspaper said, but I suspect it's wrong," Alex countered.

She was met with silence.

"Their daughter and I share the same birthday, and I have the same last name as the murder victims."

Susan's eyes narrowed. "There is some resemblance, I suppose. But I assume you also must have looked like your adoptive parents. Otherwise, you might have suspected something sooner."

"Yes," Alex agreed. "I looked like my mother. Except my eyes. I could never figure out where I got my eyes."

Alex's shoulders slouched. *Did I make a terrible mistake in coming here?* she wondered. *Is this the danger Gram tried to warn me about? Disappointment and discouragement?*

Susan shrugged slightly. "I'll try to find out what I can about the placement of Thomas and Sheila's baby, but please understand that because of legal issues, the information I gather will be limited. It will be mostly the recollections of people involved in the placement. Many of them have since passed away, though. Please try not to get your hopes up."

Too late, Alex thought, looking down at her hands. "I'll try."

"I truly hope you find what you're looking for." Susan's voice was tender, as though she meant what she'd just said.

"Thank you," Alex said, standing. She'd taken enough of Susan Bentley's time. "I'm sure you can empathize with how difficult these last few days have been for me. My grandmother, the only other person who knows about the adoption, refuses to help me. She thinks I could be in danger."

"Let's hope she isn't having some kind of premonition," Susan said, her voice taking on a chilly tone. "Leave your phone number and I'll call you if I find anything."

Alex scribbled her name and phone number on a piece of paper and handed it to Susan. "Again, thank you so much for your time."

"Would you mind pulling the door closed on your way out?"

"Of course," Alex said, then pulled the door closed and leaned against it. Eyes closed, she whispered, "She seems nice enough."

Her eyes sprang open when a voice from nearby said, "Don't let her fool you. The woman is a barracuda."

20

ALEX TURNED TO see a man leaning with his shoulder against the wall, arms crossed over his chest, legs crossed at the ankles. He uncrossed them and took several steps forward, extending his right hand. "Simon Caldwell."

Alex returned the handshake, noting the calluses on his hand. He was wearing navy blue suit pants, a crisp white shirt, and a tie in a pattern of various shades of blue. He stood about five inches taller than she, with a lean build. His tanned skin and sun-bleached hair told her he was a man who enjoyed the outdoors.

"Alexandra Tucker," she offered.

"I assume you're not a client. I guess you know Susan?"

"Um, no on both accounts. I just met Susan about twenty minutes ago. I wanted to ask her about somebody that used to work here," Alex volunteered.

"Oh yeah? Who are you looking for?"

She waved her hand, dismissing his interest. "A man named Thomas Stone. He was here while you were probably still in diapers, so I doubt you can help me."

Simon cocked an eyebrow over his deep blue eyes. An amused smile tugged at the corner of his mouth. "I've been potty trained for quite some time now. Try me."

"Okay. Do you know anything about Thomas Stone?"

Simon shrugged. "I've heard of him." He glanced at his watch. "I just had a lunch meeting get canceled, so my afternoon just opened up. Care to join me for lunch?"

Alex's stomach picked that moment to growl loudly. She cringed at its timing.

"I'll take that as a yes." Simon smiled brilliantly at her and led the way back toward the front desk.

"Aida," Simon said to the secretary, "I'm heading out for lunch."

"Yes, Mr. Caldwell," the small, seventy-ish woman replied.

"I think my car is one level down," Alex said as they opened the door from the stairwell to the parking garage.

Jerking his head in the opposite direction, Simon said, "I'll drop you there after lunch. My car is this way."

When they approached a ten-year-old Honda, he unlocked it and opened the passenger door. "Ms. Tucker," he said in his best chauffeur voice.

"This is your car?" Alex said with a chuckle.

The corners of his mouth drooped into a frown. "What's wrong with my car?"

"Oh, uh, nothing," she stammered, giving herself a mental slap. "It's just that I guess I expected something different."

"It suits me perfectly." If Alex didn't know any better—which of course she didn't—she'd think she offended him.

"I'm sorry. I didn't mean to laugh. In fact, my car looks just like this," she offered.

His killer smile returned. "Oh, yeah? So you're more practical than you look, too, I guess."

Alex returned his smile. "I guess so."

She slid into the car and her eyes fixed on a bone on the floorboard. "You have a dog."

Simon nodded as he backed the car out of its parking spot. "Murray. Golden retriever and hiking buddy extraordinaire." He guided the car into traffic. "What about you? Any pets?"

She nodded. "A black Lab. Jackson. I rescued him last year."

"How old is he?" Simon asked, weaving between cars on the busy road.

"Just over two. He's still in the puppy stage and will play fetch until he drops." She settled back into the seat, relaxing into Simon's company.

"Murray's seven, but he still gives the pups a run for their money when he chases them." He paused and pulled into a parking lot. The sign on the front of the building said "Josie's."

When they walked through the door, they were greeted by the sound of chatter and utensils clanking on dishes. Judging from the crowd, Alex decided this place must be a favorite spot for the lunch crowd.

The hostess seated them immediately, saying, "Nice to see you again, Mr. Caldwell."

As they settled into a booth, Alex picked up her menu.

In her line of work, she'd learned to read people quickly. Simon was obviously confident and self-assured, but he was also quick to open the door for her and didn't mind driving a car that was probably far beneath his financial means. He seemed like an influential man but genuinely interested in others. The combination intrigued her.

Simon closed his menu and placed it on the edge of the

table. His eyes met hers. "So, tell me about yourself. I know your name and that you have a dog. What else?"

"You first," she suggested. If she was going to ask this man to help her find out about her past, she needed to know if she could trust him.

He tilted his head back and chuckled, revealing a row of perfectly white teeth. Against his tanned skin, they practically glowed. "What do you want to know? I'm an open book." He extended his hands, palms up, in front of himself.

"Well, first—"

"Are you ready to order, Mr. Caldwell?" asked the waitress who seemed to have arrived out of nowhere.

"Yes, Marie." He turned his attention to Alex. "Ready?"

Alex nodded. "I'll have the grilled pimento cheese sandwich, please. With sweet potato fries if you have them."

"And I'll have the spicy burger with pasta salad. And can we get some sweet tea?"

"Right away." Marie winked before turning and walking in the direction of the kitchen.

"Everyone seems to know you here," Alex observed.

Simon nodded. "I come here a lot. I like the food and it feels so relaxed. With my job, I'll take any opportunity I can get to unwind." Locking eyes with Alex, he said, "Now, where were we?"

"I was about to ask you about yourself."

"Ah, yes. Ask away." He leaned back and crossed his arms loosely across his chest, more relaxed than defensive.

He seemed so charming, and she felt foolish for having her guard up. A quick reminder to herself that many a serial killer and con man have won over their victims with an easy smile and some flattery helped her feel less absurd.

"Are you a trustworthy guy?" she finally said, hoping it didn't come out as harsh as it felt.

"I don't really know how to answer that," he acknowledged. "Obviously I like to think so, but the final determination is yours."

Alex shrugged. "You seem to be. Unfortunately, my line of work doesn't allow me to take many people at face value. I'm always looking for what's behind a person's actions. Occupational hazard, I suppose."

Simon smiled again. "My mother taught me to be respectful of women. If I didn't open the door for her or any other female in the vicinity, she'd give me a tongue lashing and a thump on the head as soon as we got home."

The corners of Alex's mouth twitched. "I think I'd like your mother. Tell me about the rest of your family."

Before he could answer, the waitress returned with their lunch. Marie repeated each order as she slid the plates in front of them. "Can I get you anything else?"

"No thanks, Marie." When the waitress was gone, he turned his attention to Alex's plate. "Pimento cheese, huh?"

She nodded. "Tastes like home." Alex picked up a sweet potato fry and took a bite. "You were telling me about your family."

"Well, my mother is part of the reason I know about Thomas and Sheila Stone."

Alex's heart rate kicked up. "Did she know them?"

Simon took a bite of his burger and chewed slowly, as if giving himself time to think about his answer. "The Stones were a well-known and very connected couple, but no, she didn't exactly *know* them." His phone rang. He checked the caller ID and placed the phone on the table next to his plate. "They didn't socialize in the same circles, but she got to know *of* them very well. Their murders made her famous."

21

SUSAN BENTLEY PROPPED her elbows on her desk and lowered her head into her hands. Her eyes stung. A trip down memory lane wasn't exactly what she had in mind first thing this morning. Ever since that young woman left, she'd been unable to focus on much of anything.

The sun shining outside her office window was lost on her. Too many things were out of her control, and she hated it.

First John's resignation, then some stranger popped into her office to dredge up old memories that were better left alone.

What a way to start the week.

Susan leaned her head against the back of her chair and closed her eyes, remembering how things had been all those years ago.

Her chest ached. There was a time she believed her career was all she needed. Desperately wanting to be accepted as a woman in a firm dominated by men, she'd made it her life's mission to be viewed as one of the boys. She'd realized too late that the price she paid was far too high.

She and Thomas had been close, but nobody knew how

close. Both were young and ambitious, often working late, long past the time everyone else had gone home. Their friendship developed over pots of coffee that kept them going late into the night. It wasn't long until the friendship took a romantic turn. Soon, Susan began talking about a future together, but Thomas had made it painfully clear that he had no intention of leaving his wife. Despite that, they'd continued their relationship until his murder. Even though she knew she should, she just couldn't bring herself to break it off. Somewhere deep inside—the naïve part, she guessed—she'd assumed they'd always be together.

That was why, after Thomas was murdered and John agreed to defend Benny Johnson, Susan objected so vehemently. She might not be able to openly grieve her loss, but she could fight like the devil to make sure the man who'd taken Thomas from her paid for his crime.

To this day, Thomas was the only man she'd ever loved.

Opening her eyes, Susan blinked away the tears that had gathered behind her eyelids. As planned, she'd gained the status she'd coveted. She was a successful and sought-after defense attorney, but she'd sacrificed too much to make it happen.

Glancing at the pictures of her sister's family on her desk, she had to face the realization that she had no family of her own. Working a minimum of twelve-hour days the bulk of her career didn't allow it. She couldn't even have a pet. When she left the office, she returned to an empty house and was greeted by silence.

And now this.

Seeing Alexandra Tucker nearly took her breath away. As soon as she laid eyes on Alex, she knew she was looking at the face of Thomas Stone's daughter. They had the same graceful gait, the same tall, lean body. She even had his mahogany-colored hair and startling green eyes. Though Sheila was a beauty in her own right, hers was the kind that would fade as she got older. Not so with Thomas. He had classic features that would only get better with time. He would have still looked handsome and distinguished at age ninety.

Susan wrapped her arms around her midsection. She would never know what Thomas would have looked like. While she was fighting and losing the battle against getting older, Thomas had never gotten that chance.

And John tried to get his killer off the hook, she fumed. I should be saying "good riddance" to him.

Rising from her desk, Susan placed her hands on top of it to steady herself. She had to talk to John.

She would never have imagined he would even consider hanging up the career he thrived on. He'd even mentioned on several occasions that he'd go to his grave helping accused criminals walk. The statement made Susan's skin crawl. He'd always been in it for the money. The rest of them just couldn't bear to think about an innocent person sitting in jail.

As she strode across the expansive office suite that held the Law Offices of Hughes, Stone, and Bentley for more than fifty years, she admitted to herself that she really shouldn't be surprised by John's decision. His behavior had been erratic lately, and though she had no proof, she suspected he'd been drinking more.

Whatever happened to make John decide to call it quits must have been big.

Heels clicking on the wooden floor, she inhaled deeply. The clamor of the busy office sounded as though she was hearing it for the first time. Phones ringing, faxes coming in, voices promising that at Hughes, Stone, and Bentley the caller would, indeed, find the help they were looking for.

Forty years ago, these sounds had filled her with excitement. Now they served as a reminder of what she'd given up.

And for what? she asked herself as she approached John's office door. The things that seemed so important back then were the very things that took from her everything that had been important.

22

"JOAN, ARE YOU okay?" The concerned voice broke through her fog.

"I'm fine," Joan lied. She was far from it and wasn't sure if she'd ever be fine again.

She hadn't heard from her granddaughter since Alex phoned to tell her she'd arrived safely in Lexington. Now that she'd meddled and told Steven, Joan was sure Alex would never want to see or speak to her again.

Not that she blamed her. She could hardly stand to look at herself these days.

"Are you sure?" Francine urged.

Only two years older than Joan, Francine was the motherly type. She wore thick cardigans and was always worried that others would catch a cold. While Joan stayed active by gardening and going for walks, Francine preferred to crochet and work on her needlepoint. Despite their differences, though, Joan was genuinely fond of Francine.

"Really, Francine, I'm fine," she repeated, then turned her attention back to the meeting.

After Frank died, Joan was in a daze. She was numb, and it took months to regain feeling. Then, as the numbness gave way to pain, Joan needed a distraction. She'd started volunteering at the local hospital. Soon, she was on the committee to come up with ideas as to how the volunteers could better serve the patients and their families.

Somehow managing to show enough interest to avoid further questions, Joan darted to her car as soon as the meeting had adjourned. As she was unlocking the door, Francine caught her arm.

"Joan, tell me the truth. I know you said you're fine, but you're lying. I can tell when something isn't right. What's troubling you?" Francine insisted, worry filling her eyes.

Joan turned toward Francine, her gaze settling on the rows of cars in the parking lot. Cars belonging to people waiting to hear how a friend or family member was doing after an accident or sudden illness. Cars waiting to bring home a happy family after the birth of a new baby. Tears would be shed in those cars.

Tears of joy and tears of grief.

Joan knew both all too well.

"… if you need me."

She furrowed her brow at her friend. She hadn't been listening.

"Why don't we go get some coffee, dear?" Francine suggested, showing the patience that had earned her the nickname "Saint Francine" among her friends.

The company sounded good. Joan had been alone with her thoughts for days, and the idea of being able to unburden herself lifted her spirits.

"A cup of coffee would be nice." Since genuine smiles had been hard to come by the last few days, Joan forced one.

How much should I share? she wondered. I've already made a mistake in telling Steven. Alex would be furious if she knew I told someone else, too.

Ten minutes later, Joan and Francine were seated in the hospital cafeteria, drinking their coffee from large paper cups. At a corner table, without mentioning the adoption, Joan told Francine about Alex being angry with her and her consuming worry that Alex would never forgive her for what she'd done.

Francine listened as Joan went on about her fear of losing the last person she truly loved, but as Joan spoke, she could tell Francine knew she was leaving out something big.

23

H E WATCHED FROM behind a pillar in the parking garage as Alex got out of the old Honda. A man in navy blue suit pants and a white shirt held the car door open for her. The way he bowed as she stepped out and her laughter at whatever he'd said made him even angrier.

He cracked his knuckles. His face felt hot.

Alex smiled up at the man as he kept his hand on the small of her back as he walked her to her own car. Their handshake seemed to linger, then he said something to Alex, causing her to blush and look down at her shoes. With his thumb and index finger, the man lifted her chin, forcing her eyes to meet his. She nodded and he saw her mouth form the word "yes."

"She's agreeing to see him again," he growled through clenched teeth.

His body tensed.

How could she do this to me? Doesn't she know what I'm capable of? After everything she's learned about me, does she really not know?

He knew this feeling. He'd only felt it once or twice before.

The blackouts after this kind of episode lasted for days, and he'd never regained the full memory of what happened during that time.

He shivered.

Last time, he woke up covered in dirt. He smelled of alcohol and cigarettes—both of which he usually tried to avoid—and there was dried blood on his hands and shoes. He didn't know what he'd done, but he knew one thing now: Alex and the man she was with were in a great deal of danger.

"I'm sorry," he whispered. "You shouldn't have left me. Now you both have to pay."

24

ALEX'S CELL PHONE rang as she slid under her steering wheel. She breathed a sigh of relief when she saw the number on the screen. "I'm so glad you called!"

"It's nice to be wanted," Jeannie said. "How's the detecting? Find anything yet?"

"I think so," Alex said with a nod even though Jeannie couldn't see her. "When I got here, I went to the library to search newspaper archives. I found an article about a double murder two months after I was born. A lawyer and his wife were found stabbed and bludgeoned to death in the library of their home. It happened in an upscale neighborhood and it shocked the whole town."

"Sounds promising," Jeannie encouraged. "I mean, not for the victims, God rest them."

"It does. Especially since the victims' last name was Stone." Jeannie whistled.

"I know. I did a bit more digging at the library, then this morning I went to the law firm where the husband worked.

You know, just to see if there was anyone still there from those days."

"You did what?"

"I said I went to—"

"I heard what you said," Jeannie interrupted. "I guess I just didn't expect that, but maybe I should have. Still doing things on impulse, I see."

Alex felt her eyebrows furrow into a frown. "Apparently. I did get a chance to talk to a woman who worked there with Thomas Stone."

"And how did that go?"

The parking garage darkened as a cloud passed over the sun. "She seemed nice enough," Alex offered. "She said she could see some resemblance between me and Thomas. She said she would ask around to see if anybody who worked the case remembered what happened to their baby. She said some distant relatives on the other side of the country adopted her."

"You keep saying 'she said.' Do you not believe her?" Jeannie questioned, clearly doing some detective work of her own.

Alex chewed her lower lip while she considered Jeannie's question. "I'm not sure. There was something about her that bothered me."

"How so?"

"She looked like she was seeing a ghost." Alex's hands suddenly felt clammy, and she had the urge to get out of the parking garage. At first, Alex thought she felt awkward with Susan because she was discussing something so personal with a total stranger. Now she had the feeling that it was personal to *Susan*.

"Did you talk to anybody else?"

A few beats passed. How should she approach the topic of the handsome lawyer who'd taken her out to lunch?

"Hello?"

"I ended up having lunch with one of the other attorneys at the firm. He said he might be able to help me, and I was starving, so I agreed."

Silence floated through the phone, then finally Jeannie asked, "Was he cute?"

Alex rolled her eyes. "He's okay, I guess. Anyway, he wanted to know how I knew Susan, the attorney I talked to. He'd heard of the Stones and said he might be able to help."

"And did he?"

Putting her palm to her forehead, Alex sighed. "Not yet. We were having lunch and I asked him about his family. He said that murder case made his mother famous."

Jeannie gasped. "He has a personal connection to the murders of the people who might have been your birth parents? How did his mother become famous from that?"

"I wish I knew. His phone rang before he could tell me anything else. There was some kind of emergency and he had to leave lunch right away. He seemed upset and didn't speak the whole way back to drop me off at my car." He'd certainly turned on the charm when he dropped me off, though, Alex remembered, heat creeping up her neck.

"That's too bad," Jeannie consoled. "Hopefully you'll have another chance to talk to him."

Alex cleared her throat and drummed the tip of her finger on the steering wheel. "Actually, I'm having dinner with him tonight, so hopefully I'll get more from him then."

Jeannie's chair squeaked, and Alex could almost see her leaning forward, not wanting to miss a thing.

"That was quick," she observed.

Trying to keep her voice nonchalant, Alex said, "He probably felt bad about having to cut lunch short. Anyway, I need to find out what he knows about the murders. He might be the only one that can help me find out if they were my biological parents."

The two friends were quiet for a minute, both lost deep in their own thoughts. "So, what's next, besides dinner?" Jeannie finally voiced.

"I have no idea. I want to go to the police station with my suspicions, but I don't have anything to give them except a birth certificate with no names and one that was forged in another state. They probably get enough crazy tips without me going in there with the harebrained idea that I'm the daughter of two murder victims from thirty-two years ago."

"Makes sense. Have dinner with—"

"Simon."

"Have dinner with Simon tonight. Find out what he knows. Then, if you think you have enough information to take to the police, go tomorrow. This isn't a situation to be impulsive," Jeannie warned.

Alex exhaled. Impulsivity—her fatal flaw.

That does sound reasonable, Alex reminded herself. I'll even have a few hours to spend with Jack before dinner. Poor guy has been so neglected the past few days.

"I know you're there to work," Jeannie continued, "but try to relax and have a little fun, too. You need to find balance."

She wanted to hug her friend. "I will, Jeannie. Thanks for being there."

"Always. Let me know if you need anything. And please, take care of yourself," Jeannie admonished.

"I will," Alex said through a smile. "Bye." Alex tapped the screen to disconnect the call and took a deep breath. Both curious and frightened about what she might learn about Thomas and Sheila Stone tonight, she let her mind wander to the worst possible scenarios.

Another shadow passed over the parking garage as she backed out of her space. A shiver raced down her spine. As she pulled out onto the street, she wondered why it felt like everyone was telling her to be careful.

And why the parking garage suddenly made her feel so uneasy.

25

ONY CALDWELL'S EYE twitched as he looked across the table at his visitor. Aside from a brief "hello," he hadn't spoken.

"This is a fine welcome," Simon said, annoyed. "I took time out of a very busy day—and left the company of a very charming woman—to come see you. At your request. Now you won't even speak to me." Simon was usually patient with Tony, but after being called away in a hurry for a so-called "emergency," his patience was wearing thin. Especially since the emergency appeared to be that his little brother was peeved.

"Maybe I had time to think about some things and don't feel much like talking anymore." Tony's jaw muscles bunched as he chewed a wad of gum.

"Look, I know we don't have much in common, but I'm your brother and I care about you. You can talk to me." Despite the fact that Simon had always been a bookworm and Tony was always out with friends—mostly getting into trouble—Simon had a soft spot for him.

"Benny Johnson. That's what's going on." Tony's fists clenched; his knuckles went white.

"Again? What's his beef with you, anyway?"

"I think you know," Tony said, crossing his arms over his chest and leaning back in his chair. It was a move he'd been making since he was a kid whenever he got mad at someone. "Dad arrested him, and since Benny can't take it out on him that he's been sitting in jail most of his adult life, he tortures me for it."

"He's a real piece of work and has a big mouth. What did he do this time?" Simon asked, rolling his eyes.

Tony's eyes had a hard glint in them. He turned them to meet Simon's. "Running his mouth, as usual. But he said some interesting stuff that got me thinking."

Simon could only imagine what kind of ideas Benny put in Tony's head. He came across dumb as a post, but the truth was that Benny was a master of manipulation. Tony had always been a follower and was easily influenced by a stronger personality. Putting the two of them together was trouble.

"What did he say, Tony?" Simon urged, trying to soften his tone. Even as kids, dragging anything out of Tony that he wasn't ready to talk about was next to impossible. When he wanted to shut down, he did.

Tony broke eye contact and dropped his eyes to the beat-up old table in the visitor's room. Finally, he spoke. "Oh, you know. Just wondering why I'm still sitting in jail when my brother is a big-shot defense attorney, and my father is a cop. That got me wondering the same thing."

Simon took a deep breath. They'd been through this before. "First, Dad wasn't a cop anymore when you were arrested. Second, you know neither Dad nor I could get involved because it would have been a conflict of interest. We've gone around and around about this. You're doing time because you broke the law and got caught. You know that. Dad and I don't owe you anything. We didn't force you to sell drugs. Please don't start this again." He'd accepted Tony's bitterness about his place in the family a long time ago, but the longer Tony sat in prison, the more it consumed him. He was turning himself into the victim. What would eight more years of this do to him?

"But you defend people like me, Simon," Tony whined.

He sounded desperate. Simon wanted to help his little brother, but he knew it was the last thing he should do. Tony started getting in trouble as a kid, and Simon had always tried to talk some sense into him. When the trouble escalated, Simon stopped interfering. Tony needed to learn a lesson and grow up. Unfortunately, he'd held a grudge ever since.

"What brought this up again, Tony?" Simon asked gently. "You're even more agitated than usual. Did this just happen today?"

Tony shook his head tightly. "Saturday. In the yard."

"And you've been letting it fester for two days? No wonder you're so angry." Simon lowered his voice. "You know they have counselors available to help when things in here get to be too much to handle. Why don't you try talking with one?" he suggested.

Tony shook his head and gripped the edge of the table. "It's not that," he said quietly. "Look at you, dressed in your per-fectly tailored suit. Now look at me," he complained, waving his hand the length of his torso at the prison-issued orange jumpsuit. "I hate it here. I'm not a bad guy, I just made some bad decisions. I'm cooperating with the rules here, keeping my nose clean. Where has it gotten me? Nowhere. I let the other guys steamroll me so I can get paroled sooner, but it's not helping. I have a reputation in here as a wimp, and I'm tired of it. Just get me out of here. Please, Simon," he begged.

Simon sighed. "What happened, Tony? You're really playing the victim card here. This has to be about more than Benny Johnson running his mouth and reminding you that Dad and I could have pulled some strings for you."

Eyes filling with tears, Tony sniffed and said, "He brought up Mom."

"Oh…"

For the past year and a half, it had been eating at Tony that he'd missed her funeral. Tony never wanted to talk about it, even with his own family. Even though Tony never voiced it, he couldn't stop punishing himself for disappointing her. He held her up as a saint and thought of himself as nothing more than a scoundrel who wasn't worthy to breathe the same air she did. Simon and his dad suspected that on some level, Tony even blamed himself for her death.

"I want to get out of here and do something she would have been proud of. Every day is nothing but a reminder that I'm a failure, that I'm no better than the people I'm locked up with. She'll never get the chance to see what I could have done with my life."

It tore at Simon to see his brother like this, but the pain in Tony's face was a relief. He'd always worried that prison would harden Tony. Now he knew he didn't need to lose sleep over it. A person's heart, their character, didn't change.

"You will get that chance, Tony," Simon encouraged. "I promise. You're doing all the right things. I wish I could help you get out of here, but I can't. Just know that I will do anything I can to help you get through this. Dad, too. When you get out, we'll help you get back on your feet."

"I know," Tony muttered, then quickly changed the subject. "So, tell me about this girl I dragged you away from." He leaned forward and interlaced his fingers on the table. The mischievous twinkle in his eyes told Simon his brother was coming around.

Simon felt his body relax. "Well, her name is Alex. I bumped into her at the office today."

Tony raised an eyebrow. "She's not a criminal, is she? Because that would be a conflict of interest."

Simon let Tony's shot at him slide by. "No, she's not a criminal. She was asking questions about somebody that used to work at the office. We were having lunch when I got the 'emergency' call," he said, hooking his index and middle fingers in the air.

"Sorry 'bout that," Tony said sheepishly.

Simon shook his head. "It's done. Don't worry about it."

The brothers nodded together in understanding. Everything would be okay between them.

"Anyway," Simon continued, "she's a real knockout. And smart. She kept me on my toes."

"Good. You need somebody that'll call you on your bull," Tony teased. "All that knight-in-shining-armor stuff you used to pull made me sick. I hope she hated it."

"I get the feeling she doesn't need a dragon slayer. She did agree to have dinner with me tonight, though. She's coming over and I'm going to grill some ribs. This might be the last warm day we have, and I can't miss the opportunity to impress her with my skills as grill master."

Tony snorted. "Show off." A few years ago, before he went

to prison, Tony gave Simon an apron for his birthday that had the words "Grill Master" emblazoned across the front.

"Dad will be there," Simon added.

"You're already introducing her to the family? Don't you think it's kind of soon to show her how messed up we are? I don't want you to scare off possibly the only woman in the world who isn't impressed by you." Tony had fallen into the old banter that characterized their childhood.

Simon missed the simpler times, when all they had to worry about was getting along well enough to agree on an ice cream flavor at the supermarket.

"I think she'd want to meet him." Simon paused, then said, "She wants to know about Thomas and Sheila Stone."

Tony leaned back in his chair and whistled. "That could be trouble."

Simon nodded.

The banter was over. They both knew the kind of trouble that could be coming.

26

JOHN WATCHED THE door, wondering when this would all be over. He took a sip of scotch, his second since he arrived at the bar. At four-fifteen, most of the seats were unoccupied, making it the perfect spot to be if you didn't want to be seen. He chose a corner booth, mostly hidden by the shadows but with a clear view of the door.

When his associate entered, John waved him over.

"You look terrible," Clarence said as he scrutinized John.

John knew he was right. Last week he looked strong and confident, years younger than his age. Now he looked haggard and worn. The slight wrinkles around his eyes and on his forehead had deepened and his skin was ashen. Even he couldn't believe he was the same person that could strike fear into any prosecutor he came up against during a court trial. The John Carmichael sitting in the corner booth of this shadowy bar didn't bear any resemblance to that John Carmichael.

"Thanks," John said. "I guess I won't be making the cover of *GQ* like you." If he were in better spirits, or had a few more drinks in him, he would have chuckled. The man sitting across from him was rail-thin with sunken cheeks and hollow eyes. John didn't know his exact age, but figured Clarence was probably pushing at least seventy based on his appearance. Either that or he'd lived a hard and fast life. John guessed that even in his younger days, Clarence hadn't turned many heads.

"Ouch. No need to be so grumpy." Clarence paused, took a pack of cigarettes from his breast pocket and looked around the empty bar before speaking again. "So, what's this all about? I thought we agreed never to meet in public."

They'd decided years ago it would be too dangerous for them to be seen together. John's demeanor and carelessness now evidently concerned Clarence.

"It's all about to unravel." John's tone was flat, thanks to the scotch.

"Everything's been running fine for years. What changed?" Clarence asked with an edge to his voice as he absently spun the pack of cigarettes on the table.

A chill raced up John's spine. "I got a call Saturday night. Apparently somebody is snooping around and trying to find out what happened thirty-two years ago. If that information gets leaked, I'm finished."

Clarence's fingers flexed around the pack and jammed it back in his pocket. Clarence usually lit up when he was angry, but the smoking ban for public spaces kept him from doing that now. He wouldn't risk bringing attention to himself for breaking the law for something so trivial. Especially in the company of John. So now, John would take the brunt of Clarence's anger.

"So, what are you going to do?" Clarence demanded.

"I don't know, but I'll have to think of something quick. It won't be long before someone finds out Thomas and I weren't just coworkers. I guess I always knew it was bound to come out sooner or later…" Despite the two drinks, John was on edge. His life was falling apart.

"Whatever you do, it better be enough to make sure you're not exposed. This is happening because you left loose ends last time. It's time to finish. You can't let anyone know you had a reason to want Thomas dead. If anyone finds out the reason, I'll finish you myself," Clarence warned.

John knew better than to cross him. Clarence's frame might be small, but John knew firsthand that Clarence was ruthless and didn't care about a person's social status—a lesson he didn't need to learn a second time.

John had always been careful not to get his own hands dirty. He played the part of the upstanding citizen while being the puppet master from far away. It was a position he relished, getting high on the power it gave him to have so much control over the lives of others, some of whom he'd never met.

Now that power was slipping through his fingers. He felt like a wild animal cornered by a predator.

He looked at Clarence. In a way, he was just that.

Sitting in front of the man who wouldn't hesitate to send him into oblivion, the only thing on his mind was survival.

At any cost.

27

A LEX RANG THE doorbell and waited. She wasn't
sure what she expected the home of a successful young
attorney to look like, but a single-level house with
lawn ornaments wasn't it.

At least he doesn't have a garden gnome, she thought,
amused.

She covered her mouth as a yawn escaped. She'd only been
in Lexington forty hours. With everything that had been going
on, time was relative. Evenings ran into mornings with sleep
occasionally interrupting the flow of time.

The door opened, but instead of seeing a tall, handsome
man in his thirties, she looked down into the face of a man in
his sixties sitting in a wheelchair.

That would explain the lawn ornaments, Alex realized.

"Oh, I'm sorry," Alex began. "I think I have the
wrong house."

Alex started to turn away when the man spoke. "You must
be Alex. I'm Sam Caldwell, Simon's father."

She extended her hand. "I'm so sorry. Simon didn't mention you'd be joining us."

Sam's hand enclosed hers. She was surprised how big it was. At first she didn't notice, but now realized he was a big man, probably even taller than Simon and with broader shoulders. Though the years had taken a toll on Sam's face, she could certainly see a resemblance between the father and son. Sam Caldwell was a very handsome man.

It looks like Simon came by it honestly, Alex thought.

"Please, come in," Sam said. The ease with which he turned his wheelchair indicated he'd been in it for quite some time.

The front door opened into a small living room, occupied by a matching sofa and armchair. The decor suggested a woman's touch, but there was a certain coldness that indicated it had been missing for a while. She stopped to observe a black and white framed photo hanging on the wall over a small table adjacent to the armchair. It was of a young couple, probably in their mid-twenties, smiling into the camera on their wedding day.

She turned to Sam. "This must be you and your wife."

Sam wheeled closer to her. "Yes. It seems like that was taken so long ago." Sam's voice held a wistful tone. Sadness clouded his aging face. He shook his head quickly as if to clear his thoughts. "Follow me. Simon is in the backyard."

Alex followed him from the living room to a small kitchen. Though there wasn't a lot of space, it was bright and airy. The appliances appeared to be relatively new and in excellent condition, and the white cabinets practically glistened as the evening sun streamed through the kitchen window. Everything was arranged so Sam would have easy access from his wheelchair.

"Your home is lovely," Alex commented.

"Thank you. I'm all thumbs when it comes to cooking. Betty—my wife—was an extraordinary cook. She passed away last year, so now I exist almost entirely on frozen meals and takeout. I never thought I would be living like a bachelor again at this stage of life, but Simon comes over at least once a week to make sure I have a decent meal."

"I'm so sorry."

"Don't be. He knows his way around a kitchen better than I do."

"Oh, no. I mean, I'm sorry for…"

Sam winked at her, communicating he knew what she meant. "You're going to be fun."

Alex decided she liked Simon's father.

As they moved toward the kitchen door that led to the deck, Alex couldn't help but smile when she saw Simon. He wore a floppy white chef's hat and a red apron with the words "Grill Master" across the front. In his right hand he held tongs covered in barbecue sauce and in his left hand he held a glass of water. A goofy grin spread across his face when he saw her.

She decided she liked Simon, too.

Walking toward him, she noticed Sam stayed inside and closed the kitchen door.

"So. You're a 'Grill Master,' huh?" she asked as she stepped out onto the deck.

"Yes, ma'am. One of the best. You'll see." Simon smiled proudly.

"Then I guess this is a bad time to tell you I don't eat meat?"

Simon's smile crumbled as he looked at the meat sizzling on the grill, seeming to wish it into an eggplant. Alex watched his eyes as he thought back to their lunch. Grilled pimento cheese sandwich. No meat.

"Are you serious?" Simon asked, looking for all the world like a little boy who'd just been cut from the baseball team.

Alex laughed. "Nope. It looks delicious."

Simon breathed a sigh of relief and pointed the tongs at her. "You scared me. Don't do that again."

She chuckled again. "Sorry, I couldn't resist." She paused, then said, "You didn't mention your father would be here."

Simon's face dropped again. It seemed like she had a special talent for making him frown. "Sorry I didn't tell you before. I was afraid you'd back out, and I really think you should talk to him."

Alex shrugged. "It's fine. I was just surprised."

"Since my mom died last year, he's been pretty lonely. His neighbor, Mrs. Cline, keeps him company some, but I try to have dinner with him at least once a week. It usually falls on Monday. This time I asked if I could invite someone."

"Did you tell him what I want?" She wasn't sure how comfortable she'd be discussing everything in front of him. On the other hand, if the case really did make Simon's mother famous—whatever that meant—Sam might be able to add any details Simon didn't know. After all, Simon had only been a toddler when the murders took place.

"*I* don't even know what you want. Not really. I told him you were asking about the Stones. He could help you a lot more than I could."

"You said the case made your mom famous, but nothing else. How did she get famous from a murder?"

"We'll discuss it over dinner. Can you hand me that plate?" he asked, pointing to a large oval platter.

Alex picked up the plate and handed it to Simon. While he piled the ribs on it, she tried to squelch her annoyance.

She was at the mercy of his willingness to talk. She needed to know what he knew. She couldn't let herself do anything to jeopardize getting that information, even if she thought he was being unfair by not even discussing it until his father was around. Instead, she bit the inside of her bottom lip until it hurt.

"Is there anything else I can do?" Alex asked, hoping her frustration didn't come out in her voice.

"Don't be mad. You'll see why I'm making you wait in a few minutes. Would you please help Dad get the dishes out of the cabinet?" His tone was calm and even. He seemed perfectly in control.

Alex, in contrast, felt about three inches tall. Simon was being a mature adult, and she felt like a child, ready to throw a tantrum just because she wasn't getting her way. Her parents always told her she was stubborn and impulsive. Looks like they were right, she thought.

With a sigh, she did what Simon asked and went into the kitchen.

Seeing the look on her face, Sam wore an amused smile. "He's a pretty cool customer. It takes a lot to upset him, and he enjoys watching people squirm. Probably a little too much. He always has a reason for what he does, and it's usually a pretty good one. It's easy to be frustrated with him when he seems so calm, but give him the benefit of the doubt."

Sam had her pegged. Either he was extremely observant, or he'd been in her shoes a time or two himself.

She was surprised to see several bowls and plates already filled with food sitting on the kitchen counter. It smelled delicious and she was hungry.

"Can you help me carry these outside?" Sam requested. "We'll be eating on the deck."

"Of course," she agreed. She grabbed as many of the side dishes as she could carry and made her way outside, then returned for a small stack of dinner plates. The sun was starting to go down and there was a slight chill in the air as a gentle breeze blew.

Fall had always been her favorite time of year.

The plate of ribs was already in the center of the table. As Alex arranged the baked potatoes, green beans, and corn on the cob around it, Sam came out of the house with a plate of rolls balanced on his knees.

Saliva filled her mouth in anticipation.

Simon ducked into the house and returned shortly, carrying a pitcher of iced tea, a bucket of ice, and three glasses tucked into the pockets of his apron.

After they settled around the table, Alex heaped generous amounts of food onto her plate. She looked up and met the eyes of her dinner companions, both of whom were watching her with amusement.

"What?" she said over a bite of potato. "You had an emergency to take care of at lunch and made me leave before I was done. Remember?"

Simon nodded with a chuckle. "I remember."

He hadn't even given her time to get a to-go box.

"So, tell me about yourself, Alex." Sam's request reminded her that Simon didn't know much about her either. He didn't even know why she was interested in the Stone murder case. This would be a bombshell.

"Well, I'm a psychologist," she began. "I work mostly with clients who have severe and persistent mental illness, such as schizophrenia and bipolar disorder. Occasionally I get people who have been court-ordered to get help for substance abuse or anger-management problems. That's tough, because if the court tells them they need help, they haven't necessarily admitted they need it and it's hard to make progress. But when I get to work with somebody who society has given up on build a new life... that's so rewarding. I collaborate with the client's psychiatrist, and we work to get the client the correct medication and dosage. When they regain lucidity, it's like meeting them for the first time. Then we work on skills to help them function in their new lives, such as problem solving, communication, and emotional management."

"Sounds interesting. There has to be a story about how you got into that," Sam pressed, sounding genuinely interested.

In her experience, not everyone wanted to hear about her work. Most people are uncomfortable with mental illness and just want to forget it exists.

"It just seemed like the natural career for me, I guess. From the time I was a child, my friends would come to me with their problems. Somewhere along the way, I realized everyone needs a safe place to go. Everyone needs at least one person they can trust who will give them a different perspective on what they're going through. I enjoy being that person." Alex knew how she sounded when she started talking about work. Sometimes she was self-conscious, but not today.

Simon had been listening intently as she spoke. He even looked like he cared. Alex's respect for him grew.

"And where are you from?" Sam asked.

"I grew up in Charleston, South Carolina," she replied, reminding herself that if she wanted something from them, she had to be willing to give a little of herself as well.

"Are you close to your mom and dad?" Simon queried.

Alex's eyes suddenly burned. She cleared her throat. "Yes. We were very close." She dropped her gaze to her untouched food. "They both passed away last year. Tomorrow is the one-year anniversary of their deaths." She looked up from her plate and into two pairs of concerned blue eyes.

"I'm sorry," Sam soothed.

Though heartfelt, Alex was tired of the "I'm sorries" she typically got when people found out she'd recently lost her parents. This was different, though. These men had been grieving a loss the same time she had.

Simon spoke up. "Tell us more about what brings you to Lexington. I told Dad you were interested in the Stone murder case but couldn't tell him more than that since I don't know either."

"It's odd that you would travel all this way to learn about a case you've had no prior knowledge of." Sam narrowed his eyes and studied her. "What exactly is your interest in the case?"

She had the distinct impression her motives were being vetted before they would give her any information. That piqued her curiosity even more.

Deciding a direct approach was best, Alex plunged forward. "I found out on Thursday I was adopted. My parents never told me. I'm here to find answers."

The two men stilled, then exchanged a quick glance. "What does that have to do with the Stones?" Simon asked.

As Alex went through the details of finding her birth certificate and her mother's journal, plus the suspicious lack of paperwork, her small audience hung on her every word.

"The only information my grandmother would give me was that I was adopted thirty-two years ago at two months old. I came here to find my birth parents. After reading about the murders of Thomas and Sheila Stone in the newspaper archives, I think I've found them. It can't be a coincidence that my last name on my original birth certificate was Stone. Plus, there's the birthdate to consider."

Sam and Simon diverted their eyes.

They know something, Alex thought. I know they do.

"This is why I thought you needed to meet Dad," Simon pointed out.

"Why?"

Sam looked directly into her eyes and said, "Because I was the arresting officer for that case."

28

"YOU WERE WHAT?" Alex blurted. The words flew out of her mouth before she could stop them or think of something better to say.

"Like I said," Simon reminded her, "you needed to talk to my dad."

Alex turned to Simon. "You told me the case made your mother famous but never mentioned anything like this!"

Sam leaned back in his wheelchair and rested his elbows on the armrests. "Why don't I tell you how our family is involved in all this?"

Even though he was a little on the gruff side and posed every question like he was conducting an interrogation, Alex appreciated Sam's kind spirit and his openness toward her.

"As I said before, I was the arresting officer in the Stone murder case. Thirty-two, almost thirty-three, years ago, on December thirty-first, police responded to a triggered alarm at the Stone residence. When the police showed up, they found a husband and wife dead in the library of their home. He'd been stabbed in the chest with a poker from the fireplace, she'd been bludgeoned on the head with the same poker. Since the killer didn't bring his own, more efficient weapon, that told us the killer probably didn't enter the house with the intent to commit murder, that it was probably just a burglary gone wrong. We lifted the prints of a man named Benny Johnson from a jewelry box in the master bedroom and the safe in the library. We arrested him for breaking and entering and murder. He confessed to breaking and entering but denied any involvement in the murder. He still denies it."

Alex read most of the information she'd just been told in the newspaper archives but hearing it herself from someone who'd been involved made the story come alive. It was horrifying, and she could picture it just as Sam described.

She glanced at Simon out of the corner of her eye. He, too, was hanging on every word his father said.

Sam continued. "Soon there were a half-dozen police cars and an ambulance with their lights whirling parked in front of the house. I was in the second car to arrive at the scene. Even though I was young, the chief thought I showed promise and punted the case to me. As soon as I saw the victims, I knew it would be a high-profile case. Thomas Stone was a rising star in the criminal defense world and had strong political ties. He had a knack for making even the most seasoned law enforcement professionals look like fools. Unfortunately, I played that part a time or two myself when called to witness against one of his clients," Sam confessed. "I can't say I cared for the man. He always seemed to be a power-hungry egomaniac. Altogether an unpleasant package, in my opinion."

Despite the fact that the murder took place more than three decades ago, Sam recalled the details like they'd happened yesterday.

"Anyway," he continued, "when we started digging, we found that Benny Johnson was a small-time goon who roughed people up to get them to pay off their debts. He worked for a loan shark he swears he never met and we were never able to track down. When a forensic accountant looked at the Stones' accounts, he found that Mr. Stone was quite a gambler, and not a very good one at that. He was in debt up to his eyeballs and was working his way through his wife's trust fund. His whole life—the fancy car, big house, expensive suits—were all a front. That made Benny look even more guilty, like he went to collect on a debt and went a little too far."

"So you arrested Benny Johnson," Alex stated, her chin resting on her fist.

Sam nodded. "I did." He shifted in his wheelchair. "He was the strongest lead we had. All the evidence seemed to point to him, so the judge issued an arrest warrant and we picked him up. He was found guilty on two counts of first-degree murder and received back-to-back life sentences. He's been a resident of the state penitentiary ever since."

Alex pursed her lips. "But how does your wife fit into this? Simon said the case made her famous."

"Betty was a journalist, and a darn good one at that," Sam offered. "The newspaper gave her the exclusive on the story. Journalists from all over came to cover the case, but no one could turn a story like Betty. She even won a Sigma Delta Chi Award for her coverage of the story." Sam leaned forward with a sly grin and a twinkle in his eye. "I fed her inside information. She never revealed her source, though."

Something clicked. "Her name was Elizabeth Caldwell." Alex read her coverage of the case at the library and had been impressed by her ability to tell a story.

"She was Elizabeth to everyone else. To me, she was Betty."

"But what about the baby?" Alex pressed. "That's what I really want to know."

Sam picked at a thumbnail. "There was no baby in the house when police searched the home. The following day, when some officers were talking to Mr. Stone's colleagues, a couple of them corroborated that she was staying with relatives out of town. Apparently, Thomas and Sheila had thrown a big New Year's Eve bash that night and didn't want a baby to be in the way."

"Were the relatives ever located?" The out-of-town-relative scenario didn't ring true in the newspaper, and it didn't ring true now.

"We were given the contact information for them. After speaking with them and the other attorneys in Mr. Stone's firm, one of them volunteered to handle the adoption so the relatives would be granted immediate guardianship of the child. From what I know, that's the way it happened." Sam was still picking at his thumbnail.

Alex narrowed her eyes. He was awfully concerned about that thumbnail. Concerned enough to avoid eye contact the whole time he talked about the baby.

She cocked her eyebrow and took a shot. "But you don't really believe that's what happened."

Sam looked up but still didn't make eye contact. A wry smile tugged at his lips as he shifted his gaze to watch a cardinal that was occupying the lone oak tree in the backyard. "You're very perceptive, aren't you?" He shook his head slowly. "It wasn't my job to decide guilt or innocence, right or wrong, truth versus lies. My job was to follow orders and uphold the law to the best of my ability. I didn't have the luxury of pursuing an unsanctioned investigation."

When he finally looked at Alex, she was certain. He didn't have to use his words to say he had doubts, his face told her he did.

But if the official account of what happened wasn't true, she wondered, what really happened to the baby?

29

JULIA BURKE OPENED the door of her small apartment and tossed her keys onto the table just inside. It had been a horrible day, and all she wanted to do was put her feet up and watch something mindless on television.

She'd been just as shocked as everyone else when John announced his upcoming retirement. Sure, he hadn't been himself lately and she was getting concerned about the increase in his drinking, but the news that he wouldn't be around much longer had blindsided her.

Some mornings he came into the office with alcohol still on his breath from either an early morning drink or a bender the night before. Either way, she'd known for a while that something wasn't right. Still, the thought of his impending retirement made her sick to her stomach.

Walking down the tiny hall that led into the living room, Julia shook her head at the mess. A pizza box lay open on the coffee table with two shriveled pieces of deluxe meat pizza inside. Beer bottles littered the floor, and Mikey was sprawled out on the couch.

She rolled her eyes. I guess I'm going to be watching something mindless on the sofa instead of the TV, she thought.

He was wearing the same dirty sweatpants he'd been wearing the night before and when she left for work that morning.

My knight in shining armor.

She thought back to the last conversation she'd had with her mother. Julia had big plans for her life. She was going to make something of herself, but her mother, Edna, had only laughed. "You're not meant to have that kind of life, Jules," she'd taunted. "The job, the money, the decent man. It's all too good for you."

With her head held high, Julia had snapped back at her, "Maybe it's too good for you, Edna, but it's not too good for me. I'm not going to be stuck living the kind of life you have. I'm better than that."

That was two and a half years ago, and they hadn't spoken since.

From even her earliest memories, Julia had always called her mother "Edna." Never "Mom."

Now looking around the filthy apartment with the deadbeat lying on the sofa with all the motivation of a jellyfish, she was disgusted to realize that she was, in fact, living her mother's life. The only difference was that she had a better job. But now that job was in jeopardy.

Mikey finally noticed Julia. "Hey. You're home late."

"Hey. You haven't moved since I left this morning."

"Sure, I have," he contradicted. "I got up to get the pizza from the delivery guy. I got up to get more beer. I got up to take a leak a few times. See? I moved."

She snorted. "Well, aren't you the picture of productivity?"

Mikey could have a nasty temper and she usually tried to

watch her step around him. This time she didn't care. Let him get mad. Maybe it would light a fire under him to stop lying there like something that washed up from the sea.

"Why are you in such a bad mood? I didn't do nothing," he defended, then turned his attention back to the TV.

No kidding, Julia thought.

Her father had been a bum who walked out on them when she was four. All of her mother's subsequent boyfriends had been bums. In her family the woman always supported the man, and she'd been determined to break the cycle. She'd vowed that when she finally met someone, he'd take care of her. Now fate was laughing at her.

In the beginning, she'd been able to overlook Mikey's flaws and supported him as he tried to make a career out of his music. Lately, though, his lack of drive and his dependence on her to pay his bills was getting old. He hadn't even picked up his guitar in weeks. There had been a time when his free spirit intrigued her, awaking something in her she'd always wished she had. He'd made her feel alive and she envied his ability to follow his passion, despite the instability.

Now she felt used and broke, and the instability in her life terrified her.

"John Carmichael is retiring," she said, her gut clenching in fear and uncertainty as she said the words.

"Who's he again?" Mikey asked, half listening to Julia, half listening to the game.

"He's my boss, you idiot."

"Don't call me an idiot just 'cause I don't know all those fancy people you work with," Mikey pouted.

When she'd gotten the job at Hughes, Stone, and Bentley, Mikey had been excited. All he could see were the dollar signs and a get-out-of-jail-free card if he ever landed on the wrong side of the law. The more time that passed, though, the more her job strained their relationship. He thought she was getting uppity, and she was beginning to see him for the loser she'd always known he was.

They'd even called off their engagement, and most of the time Julia wondered why they were still together at all.

"John Carmichael, the senior partner at the law firm where I work, is retiring. I am his personal assistant. I have been for two years. Remember?" She spoke slowly, as though she was addressing a child.

"Oh, yeah. He's the guy that's loaded. Sure wish I had that kind of money." Mikey shook his head in self-pity.

"Imagine how much pizza and beer you could buy with it," Julia said sarcastically, then added, "His retirement could mean big trouble for me."

Mikey sat up and clicked off the TV. "Whaddya mean?"

Wishing the concern in his eyes was for her, she knew that what Mikey was really afraid of was that her trouble would turn into his trouble. He was afraid of losing his meal ticket.

"I'm his personal assistant. He hired me specifically to work for him. When he retires, it's not guaranteed that I'll keep my job. If his replacement decides he doesn't like me or has someone else in mind for the job, I'm toast."

Mikey stood up and paced. Julia figured that was the most he'd moved all day.

"You mean they could just, like, fire you?"

"Yep. Just like that." Julia snapped her fingers.

"What are you gonna do?" he whined.

"I don't know, Mikey," she snapped. "I didn't get a chance

to talk to him today. In the meantime, you could look for a job and do something useful with yourself."

Mikey sat back on the sofa, staring at the black TV screen. Apparently the football game had lost its appeal. The prospect of having to work for what he had tended to sour his mood.

Julia crossed the room in front of him and walked into the bedroom, closing the door behind her. Sitting on the edge of the bed, she buried her face in her hands. She was dangerously close to losing everything. Her relationship with Mikey was a sham and might as well be over, and now she had no guarantee that she'd have a job in a few weeks.

It hadn't been easy to get a job at the most prestigious law firm in town, and she'd been more surprised than anyone when John hired her.

Now it was all slipping away. Everything she'd worked so hard for could be gone in a matter of weeks. Her life would look even more like her mother's.

Julia gritted her teeth. No way. I can't let that happen, she resolved.

She still had one card she could play. One she'd tucked away for years and hoped she'd never have to use.

30

"WHAT DO YOU think?" Simon asked as he dried a serving dish and placed it on the counter.

"I'm not sure," Sam replied. He'd been unusually quiet since Alex left thirty minutes ago.

The sound of running water and dishes clanking were the only sounds filling the silence between the two men. As he cleared the table and washed the dishes, Simon thought of the information he'd just learned. Alex hadn't revealed much about herself at lunch, always deflecting the questions and inquiring more about him.

Now he knew why. This must be really hard on her.

The look on her face when she'd talked about her parents reminded him of how he felt when his own mother died, but at least he'd still had his dad. To lose both parents at once, only to find out later that someone else had been her biological parents... he just couldn't imagine how she was getting through this alone.

A smile tugged at his mouth. Alex was vulnerable and strong, and Simon knew he didn't stand a chance.

Simon respected her tenacity, but at the same time he wanted to protect her from the heartbreak she'd be facing when she finally learned the truth. She would either find out she'd been orphaned twice or be sent back to square one, and he'd already learned enough about her to know she wouldn't stop until she found the truth.

"Could be," Sam said.

He'd been so quiet, Simon almost forgot he was there. Looking at his father now, he realized he'd seen that look on his father's face countless times. While Simon was growing up, each time Sam was working a case and became certain the only possible answer couldn't be possible, he would sit quietly, thick brows furrowed, unconsciously rubbing his chin.

"Are you on to something, Pop?"

Sam shrugged. "I don't know. Maybe."

Simon waved his hand in a tell-me-more gesture.

"You know I've always had lingering doubts about this case. It's the kind that will haunt a cop long into retirement. Too many loose ends, too many unanswered questions. The jury might have been convinced Benny Johnson was guilty without a reasonable doubt, but I'm not. Never have been." Sam shook his head. "The biggest case of my career, and I can't stop thinking we got it all wrong."

Dropping the dish towel on the counter, Simon turned to face his dad. "What kind of loose ends are you talking about?"

"Well, the baby, for one. What really happened to her? I never even saw her. It was reported that she was staying with relatives at the time of the murder and that they obtained legal guardianship without ever having to come to Lexington. We all thought it was a good idea that she never had to stay in the foster system. It all ended so smoothly. I was still naïve back then, but now I wonder if it went too smoothly."

Simon's pulse quickened. "You don't think the baby was really with relatives? Do you think whoever murdered the Stones also kidnapped the baby?" Simon tensed at the thought of Alex being kidnapped as an infant.

Shaking his head, Sam said, "I just don't know. An attorney from the victim's practice supposedly contacted the relatives. Because it was such a high-profile case, the chief worked with the attorney and relatives. I never even spoke to them."

"Why didn't you contact them anyway? It's not like you to bow out of something so important," Simon pointed out.

"I was given strict orders," Sam admitted. "The chief told me he'd already spoken with the family and there was no need to put them through any unnecessary questioning. He said he wanted to make it as easy on them as possible. We were all instructed not to contact them." Sam's shoulders sagged as though the weight of a decision from decades ago was suddenly too much to bear.

"Didn't that sound weird to you?" Simon insisted.

"It does now, but it didn't at the time. You remember Greg Long. He was great with families, very empathetic. He dealt with the families of the victims on many occasions. Especially if it was a particularly disturbing case. That was his style. We didn't question it." Sam rubbed the creases on his forehead.

Simon remembered Chief Long well. Everyone thought highly of him, and his decisions were rarely questioned. The fact that Sam was even considering the possibility that his former boss had been involved in anything unethical spoke volumes. "And now you think he might have been up to something? A cover-up, maybe?"

Sam thought about it for a moment, then admitted, "I wish I knew. Under normal circumstances I would say 'absolutely not.' Now I'm not so sure. It was a unique case. Everything was handled more delicately than a regular case would have been. Thomas and Sheila Stone were personal friends of the governor. Thomas had his sights set on a political office. If I wasn't wondering about the baby, I'd assume everything was done according to protocol. I can't even believe I'm letting myself entertain the thought that Greg might have been involved in anything fishy."

Simon sat down at the table across from his father. "What now?" It was in Sam's blood to find out what really happened. Now that he was retired, there was no badge to hold him back anymore.

Sam splayed his hands in front of him. "What can I do? Greg died three years ago from Parkinson's Disease. Without having him to talk to, I don't even know where I'd begin."

"You can always talk to the district attorney from those days," Simon suggested. "I think I heard Clark Matthews retired about ten years ago and is living somewhere in Montana."

"I doubt he'd know anything about this," Sam challenged.

"Wouldn't he? If Chief Long took care of the family aspect, wouldn't he have told Matthews about it?"

"I guess he would have, yeah." Relief flooded Sam's words. "Thanks, kid."

Simon reached over and gave his father's shoulder a squeeze. Maybe he was more concerned that Chief Long was doing shady business than I realized, Simon thought. Changing the subject, he asked, "So, what did you think of Alex?"

"She's tough. I like her. You know I've got no time for weak women. I like knowing a woman can take care of herself and won't be depending on me for everything." Then Sam added, "Your mother was tough."

Simon smiled. "I know she was, Dad." He squirmed in his chair. He felt awkward and ridiculous, like he was in seventh grade again.

"Be careful not to get too attached, though, son," Sam advised. "You don't know where she stands. Besides, she has enough on her plate right now and might not be interested in swooning over your charm."

Leaning forward, Simon said, "I hear you. I don't think it's just me, though. I think she likes me. I'm going to ask her out again. This time, you're not invited."

"Oh, sure. Go out on the town and leave the old geezer at home with a TV dinner."

"I'll bring you a doggie bag." Simon winked at his father.

Sam's tone became serious. "No dates, Simon. Not yet. What she needs from you is support, not wining and dining. Especially if her hunch turns out to be right. She's vulnerable. Don't take advantage of that."

"I know, Dad," Simon agreed. "Strictly business. For now. I like her, though. I really do."

Sitting in his father's kitchen on that beautiful fall evening, Simon had no idea how close he and Alex were about to become.

Or how much she was going to need him.

31

STILL HUNGRY AFTER yet another missed meal, Alex stopped at a local deli for a sandwich and decaf coffee to go. Mind still reeling from her dinner with Simon and Sam, she was too distracted to enjoy the food. Her favorite sandwich, turkey and Swiss on rye, was flavorless and dry. She took a gulp of coffee to wash it down.

When Simon told her he might know something about Thomas and Sheila Stone, she never would have guessed how deeply his family was involved. His mother was a journalist who covered the story, his father the arresting officer. The convicted murderer, a man named Benny Johnson, had been sitting in prison all these years while Sam had doubts about whether or not he was really guilty.

Talk about holding someone's fate in your hands and being completely unable to change it, Alex thought.

And the baby. What happened to the baby? Alex wondered. Sam wasn't sure about it either, and she was more certain than before that she was on the right track. The records might say one thing, she told herself, but the look on Sam's face told her he believes something else.

Crumpling the sandwich wrapper into a wad, she tossed it across the room into the trash can beside the desk. Jackson sat patiently beside her with his head resting on her lap, content that his best friend was finally back. She stroked his silky fur as she thought about what her next move should be.

Of course she wanted to know where she came from and was glad to have some leads, but everything was happening too fast. In the span of four days, she'd learned she was adopted, determined that her biological parents very well might have been murdered, and had dinner with the retired detective who worked the case.

Maybe jumping into this so fast wasn't such a good idea after all, Alex acknowledged. Again, her impulsivity had gotten the better of her.

She was eager to learn the truth, but what if she hit a wall? That was a possibility she wasn't ready to face. She also wondered if she'd be able to handle the truth once she found out what it was. The past few days had already taken an emotional toll on her. A step back could do her a world of good.

"What do you think, buddy? How about we find a nice park tomorrow morning so you can run around?" Alex asked as she scratched Jackson's ears.

He responded by putting his front paws in her lap and licking her face.

Spirit lifted, she continued, "I do need to take care of a few things tonight, though. We'll get started on our day of fun bright and early tomorrow morning."

Jackson responded with a satisfied sigh.

Nudging Jackson off her lap, she stood and crossed the

small bedroom and grabbed her laptop. She wondered how many emails she'd missed the past few days. After logging into her email account, she quickly glanced down the left-hand column at the senders. Several emails promised great deals and free shipping if she acted quickly. Others were from coworkers expressing concern for her and asking if there was anything they could do.

I guess the secret's out, Alex mused.

She also had an email from Gram, Jeannie, and Steven. She read Gram's email first. In it, Gram said she didn't want to call because she knew Alex was busy, but wanted to know how things were going. *I'm sorry for everything. Let me know how you're doing. No rush.* That kind of thing.

Jeannie's email was the same. She knew Alex would call when she could. She also wrote that J.A. had missed his appointment that day.

J.A. was Jeffery Anderson, a client she suspected was becoming fixated on her. He'd been diagnosed with paranoid schizophrenia in his early twenties but had been doing much better the past several months. According to Jeannie, Alex was the only counselor who'd been able to make any progress with him. Initially, Alex was flattered and felt a great sense of accomplishment. Lately, though, his growing attachment to her made her uneasy. Alex couldn't help but wonder if it was a coincidence that the first appointment he'd ever missed was on the one day she was out of town.

But how could he know? At least I'm in a totally different state and don't have to worry about him until I get back. There won't be a need to look over my shoulder and wonder if I'll see him. She shuddered at the memory of seeing him places he had no reason to be.

Alex thought, maybe I should have told Jeannie my suspicions about him. She sighed. She'd worry about that when she got home. There was enough on her plate right now.

Last, she opened the email from Steven. After the phone call yesterday, she couldn't imagine what else he had to say. Expecting the same kind of thing she'd been hearing the past few months, Alex quickly scanned the email. There were no pleas for her to give him another chance. He didn't tell her he knew they were meant to be together or that he dreamed of her last night. Instead, he said "goodbye" and told her to enjoy the rest of her life. *One day,* he wrote, *you'll be sorry you refused me.*

What a weird way to say goodbye, Alex thought, but maybe he's finally accepting that it's over.

She wanted to be relieved, but everything she knew about Steven told her it would take a lot more than a simple "goodbye" for him to really move on.

32

SUSAN HAD BEEN on edge since Alexandra Tucker came in to see her yesterday. She'd spent years grieving Thomas's death, but somehow managed to put it behind her. She'd never been able to grieve openly because no one knew about their relationship. To everyone else, they'd been coworkers. Nothing more.

Any time someone was suspicious about how hard she took his death, she explained it away by telling them she and Thomas started working at the firm around the same time and were the same age. She'd told them it just makes you think a little more about how short life really is.

Most of the time they nodded in agreement.

Instead of being viewed as a grieving lover, she'd managed to convince them she was merely thinking about her own mortality. One coworker even suggested therapy.

She'd been able to lay low most of yesterday and so far this morning, but couldn't hide in her office forever. Her caseload was light, and she had a hard time staying as busy as she'd like. For the past twenty-four hours, though, her mind had been drifting to the past too much to be productive at much of anything.

Tired of being cooped up in the drab office that was just as her father had liked it, Susan went to the break room for a second cup of coffee. It was unusually quiet around the office today, the silence broken only by her heels clicking on the floor as she walked to the break room.

As she passed John's office, she noticed his door was shut. Again.

What's going on with him? Susan wondered.

Julia sat at her desk working quietly. She seemed to purposefully avoid eye contact as Susan passed.

Simon's door was open, but he wasn't in his office. The rest of the staff were either staring blankly at their computer screens or speaking quietly into the phone.

If I didn't know any better, Susan thought as she entered the break room, I might think everyone has figured out what I've been hiding. Of course that was ridiculous. No one had a clue.

In reality, the whispered conversations were more likely about John and his abrupt retirement, she assured herself as she poured coffee into her mug.

Movement in her peripheral caught Susan's attention. She turned slightly to see Simon bent over, looking in the refrigerator for something that obviously wasn't there.

"Lose something?" Susan asked, trying to keep her tone light.

Simon looked up and flashed a smile at her. "Oh, hi, Susan."

"Did somebody steal your lunch?" she joked.

Simon laughed. "No. Just searching for unclaimed goods."

He paused then added, "I haven't seen much of you the past couple days. Caseload picking up?"

Of course he knew her workload was light. Everybody knew. "I've been very busy," she replied, nodding in agreement. Vague, but true. He didn't have to know what she was busy doing.

She'd been impressed with Simon the first time they met, and in a way, she envied him. He had several years of experience in the courtroom, but he hadn't yet been jaded by the realization that the human capacity to hurt one another was virtually limitless. She also guessed he had yet to lose a night's sleep because he knew the client he was defending was guilty. Eventually, even the most seasoned defense attorneys felt at least a passing feeling of regret over their choice of profession.

Except John Carmichael, Susan realized.

"I heard you met Alexandra Tucker yesterday."

Susan cringed. This was exactly what she wanted to avoid. "Yes, I did," she answered, noncommittal.

"It would be pretty wild if this turned out to be true," he said as he began to rummage through the cabinets.

"Very," she agreed. "But you know, I really don't think anything will come of it. It's pretty far-fetched if you ask me."

"Oh, I don't know about that. She seems to have a pretty good reason for thinking what she does," Simon said, pulling a box of Wheat Thins from the cabinet. He checked the expiration date and put them back.

"Oh, yeah?" Susan asked, trying to sound disinterested.

"Yeah. She said you offered to ask around for information about the case. That's very nice of you."

Susan shook off the paranoia that was creeping in. "I did. I honestly don't think it will go anywhere, though. The case was closed a long time ago. Most people have probably forgotten about it. Many who worked on it died years ago."

"I'm not so sure it's been forgotten," Simon countered. "It was a huge case. It still makes the news occasionally when Benny insists on a retrial."

Susan shook her head tightly. "Benny Johnson is as guilty as they come. A judge would have to be out of his mind to let him out." As soon as she spoke the words, she wished she could pluck them out of Simon's brain. The look on his face communicated clearly to Susan that he knew what she meant by that.

"Do you think John represented him knowing without a doubt that he was guilty of killing a coworker? John's a go-getter, but that's quite a statement."

Susan bit her tongue and clicked the handle of her coffee mug with her thumbnail. Her silence answered his question.

"You do think that. You've known John a long time, way longer than I have. Why would he do that? I mean, he's taken some cases where everyone knew the client was unquestionably guilty, but why that particular case?" A frown creased Simon's forehead.

It was too late to backpedal, so Susan shrugged. "John has always said he truly believes Benny is innocent of that particular crime. Breaking and entering, sure. Being a lousy human being, sure. But not murder. For thirty-two years he's been adamant that he doesn't believe Benny killed Thomas and Sheila. To say I've had doubts about that is an understatement, but it's not my place to pass judgment. We've all taken cases where we know our clients are guilty, even if it's only a gut feeling. This one just hit a little closer to home. I've tried to stay objective about the whole thing, but I don't think I'd ever be able to represent someone that had been charged with killing my colleague. I can tell you one thing. Not everyone here took his decision to represent Benny well. He made a lot of enemies because of it. They're long gone, though. I'm the only one left from those days."

Susan did the best she could to put the attention on John. This conversation would lead Simon to raise questions about *him* instead of her. She'd do whatever she had to in order to encourage that.

But what if he started having questions about her? A chill raced down her spine. That was a different story. There were things she couldn't let Simon—or anybody else—find out about her.

Ever.

33

TUESDAY STARTED OUT beautifully. A gentle breeze sent leaves swirling to the ground. By late morning, though, it had become cold and rainy. Even then, the leaves shone like glass when the sun came back out that afternoon.

If possible, Alex thought, I think Jackson is smiling at me. Of course it's possible, she corrected herself. The connection she felt with her dog was incredible.

She threw the ball as far as she could and watched as Jackson ran after it. From the way he ran in circles, Alex could tell he was just as restless as she.

After an early massage, she spent the rest of the morning at the dog park. Anything to keep her mind off the anniversary of her parents' death.

And her birthday.

She wondered if she'd ever be able to enjoy her birthday again.

Arm sore from hours of throwing the ball, she whistled for Jack and the two of them walked toward the car. A quick lunch and a drive around town, then she'd have to get back to business.

A bit of research on Lexington revealed that it was known as the Horse Capital of the World, with more than a hundred and fifty horse farms in Lexington alone, and approximately three hundred more in the surrounding area. As much as she loved Charleston, she had to admit the horse farms added something most places just didn't have. Here she could experience a taste of city life with a certain quaintness that whispered Southern charm. She'd also learned she could make a reservation to tour one of the many farms but determined it would have to wait. Maybe as a celebration of finally getting to the bottom of where she came from.

Maybe Simon would go with me, she thought, immediately squelching the thought. She shouldn't even entertain the thought that anything would ever happen between them. Whatever relationship they'd ever have would be born out of the necessity of finding out about her birth parents. When she was done here, she'd return home. That would be the end.

Back at the hotel, Alex slid her key card into the hotel room door and removed a note taped to the door. Once in her room, she dropped it next to her laptop and turned her phone on. She'd turned it off first thing that morning, determined to have an uninterrupted day of fun, without anyone checking on her to see how she was doing. The concern was nice, but right now she just wanted to be left alone.

Several voice mail messages were waiting. Gram wanted to know how her day was going and needed to hear the sound of her voice. Jeannie wanted to know how dinner with Simon went and was busting to hear what she'd discovered.

I'm glad my life is providing interest for somebody, Alex thought wryly.

There were also a couple messages from Simon, who was curious about how she was this morning, it being the one-year mark since her parents died and given the bombshell he and his father had dropped on her the night before. He'd left another message a couple hours later, concerned that she was overwhelmed. He said he knew a great Italian place that would knock her socks off.

Alex smiled as she listened to the message. His voice was soothing in the midst of her chaos. Besides, Italian food was her favorite.

After a quick shower, she'd pick up where she left off. The information Sam Caldwell gave her last night was, in her mind, more than enough to take to the police. She'd make a list of all the things that point to her being the Stones' daughter, then call Simon back to ask him if she'd missed anything.

Before that, though, I need to call Gram, Alex thought. She'd sounded so tired and hesitant in the message, as if she was afraid of saying the wrong thing but also afraid of saying nothing at all.

She pushed aside the pang of guilt, reminding herself that she didn't have anything to feel guilty about. I'm just trying to find out where I came from. She—along with my mom and dad—lied to me my entire life. If it wasn't for them, I wouldn't have any questions to begin with. Gram is also the one who called Steven and told him about the adoption... and where I am. She knows how I feel about him. She had no right to interfere in my personal life.

Jeannie's words from Friday night echoed in her mind. *Perhaps she deserves a little grace.*

It was unfair to push all the blame on Gram. She knew that. Right now, though, and on this particular day, she couldn't bring herself to be angry with her parents.

Fifteen minutes later, after a brief but tense conversation with her grandmother, Alex looked at the paper she'd started making notes on.

She'd go to the police. But first, she wanted to talk to Benny Johnson. With no idea how she'd get in to see him, she knew in her gut that if anyone could tell her what happened that night, it would be him.

34

"WHAT DO YOU mean you won't represent me?" Benny thundered. "I've been held here thirty-two years for a crime I didn't even commit!"

"I understand that, Mr. Johnson," Richard Wade said, struggling to keep his tone even. "I just don't know what you want from me. You've had top-notch representation for those same thirty-two years and have still been unable to get your conviction overturned. I'll be honest. I'm good at my job, but I'm not half as good as John Carmichael. If he couldn't get you out of here, what makes you think I can?"

Richard Wade was in his late thirties and had been a public defender for several years before taking a job at a small firm. With thinning hair, round wire-rimmed glasses, and a slight paunch in his midsection, he always looked slightly disheveled and wasn't exactly the picture of poise in the courtroom. Even so, he did have a knack for discrediting witnesses for the prosecution. That success, and his lower fees than many other defense attorneys, guaranteed a steady stream of clients.

Because of pressure from his father, he'd first worked as

an accountant in his family's accounting firm, but decided he wanted more excitement than tax preparation and audits could offer. That was when he made the decision to go to law school.

His father never forgave him.

"Carmichael wasn't trying to get me out of here," Benny snarled. "He said he was, but I don't think he was trying at all. That's what I want you for: to pick up where he let me down."

Richard was incredulous. "You can't really believe that! You think he tried to keep you in here? That's ridiculous," he said, shaking his head.

"All I know is I didn't kill those people and I shouldn't be in here with common criminals," Benny argued.

The corner of Richard's eye twitched, a sure sign that he was frustrated. "You know that to the rest of society, you *are* a common criminal? Besides, you're acting awfully entitled for someone who needs another person—me, apparently—to help you look good." He'd heard about Benny Johnson, and from what he could tell so far, it was all true. The man's temper tantrums could rival any toddler's. He'd also heard taking this case would be career suicide, and he believed it.

Then what am I even doing here? he wondered.

The evidence was stacked against Benny, and even the best criminal defense lawyer in the state hadn't been able to keep him out of prison.

"I *am* entitled!" Benny shouted. "I'm entitled to a good defense. I was wrongly accused. Someone needs to make it right."

Richard could see that thirty-two years behind bars only served to make Benny think he was a legal expert.

"And exactly how do you intend to pay anyone that takes your case? You're not secretly wealthy, are you? Although, you'd have to be able to afford someone like John Carmichael." Even Richard didn't couldn't have afforded Carmichael's rates, and he made a good living.

"You'll work for free, of course, just like Carmichael did." Benny's statement was matter-of-fact, as though what he'd said was the most reasonable thing in the world.

Richard laughed, a harsh sound that communicated he wasn't too happy with the idea. "You can't be serious. Work for free? No way. I've got bills to pay. And I have a hard time believing anyone, especially someone like John Carmichael, would be willing to take your case pro bono. Especially considering who the victims were."

"He did, I swear. Just ask him. He said it was for a noble cause." Benny swooped his hand down toward his substantial midsection and bent in a mock bow.

Richard didn't even bother to hide his disgust. Being near Benny made his stomach turn.

Then why are you actually thinking of taking his case? his conscience fired.

As loathsome as he found the idea of working with Benny Johnson, he had to admit he was curious about the case. He remembered hearing about the trial when he was a kid and had been fascinated ever since. In fact, that case was what made him interested in becoming a lawyer one day. Getting involved in such a high-profile case, even this many years later, was appealing. Working with Benny Johnson was not.

But still…

"I'll think about it," Richard offered. "I will tell you this, though. You'll pay me something. I don't find you nearly as noble a cause as Carmichael apparently did. I'll get back to you in a few days with my decision." He rose from his chair and indicated to the guard he was ready to leave.

"Don't drag your feet too long," Benny warned. "I'm sure there are others who'd be more than happy to take my case."

Richard bit his tongue so he wouldn't give Benny the tongue lashing he clearly deserved. He thought he was done representing people like Benny Johnson when he quit his job as a public defender.

Now he was thinking of going right back to where he started. And for what? The intrigue?

One thing was certain if Richard did decide to take the case: he'd have to have a stomach of steel to work with somebody like Benny.

35

JOAN SHEPHERD EXHALED sharply and dropped her cell phone onto the counter. She was trying to be patient, but Alex was making it difficult. First, she'd called and it went straight to Alex's voice mail, then it took Alex hours to return her call. While she waited, Joan's mind wandered to a dozen horrifying scenarios that could be keeping Alex from calling her back. The hardest one to swallow, though, was that Alex just didn't want to talk to her.

When Alex did call back, she'd been so vague about what she was doing that Joan was certain she was keeping secrets.

All she wanted to talk about was sightseeing. Joan had fought the urge to snap at her. She was sure Alex was doing a lot more than driving around town looking at the horse farms.

From the way she'd talked, Joan was sure Alex was falling in love with Lexington.

Maybe she'll never come back. She shuddered as the thought intruded her mind. Joan pushed it away. This is her home, she belongs here. She'll be back, she assured herself.

When she finally asked Alex how the search for her birth

parents was going, she clammed up. Then, Joan thought, she had the audacity to get upset with me for telling Steven what was going on. I'm the only person left who really cares about her. How dare she talk to me the way she did!

She did ask you to go with her, she reminded herself. And you already know telling Steven about this was a mistake.

Joan sighed.

Alex had given her the opportunity to be involved, but she'd chosen to stay home. Now, rather than feeling at peace that she hadn't gone against the wishes of her daughter and son-in-law, she felt only regret for not helping her only grandchild.

On at least a hundred occasions, Joan wondered where Alex came from, but Carla and Robert were so adamant that no one ever speak of the adoption, Joan had managed to squelch her curiosity. Now that Carla and Robert were gone and Alex knew the truth, Joan's curiosity begged to be satisfied.

You could still go, she thought, then dismissed the idea. Alex was upset and seemed to be holding a grudge. No, Joan told herself. I won't go now. If she asks again, I'll agree to it. For now, I'll have to come up with another way to find out what she's doing.

Joan picked up the phone that was still warm from her conversation with Alex just minutes before, and dialed Steven's number.

This isn't a good idea, she reminded herself. Steven has problems.

Shaking off the doubts, she waited as the phone rang. Steven knew what it was like to lose Alex. She vowed that no matter what it took, she wouldn't lose Alex, too.

<h1 style="text-align:center">36</h1>

H OW DARE SHE have the nerve to call me like that again? Steven fumed. Without offering anything to me, she called just to vent about Alex. How Alex wouldn't tell her what was going on, that she only wanted to talk about the touristy stuff. The old bat even said she called me because she understood this must be what it felt like for me when Alex wouldn't return my calls.

How would she know what it's been like for me? Nobody knows.

It had been three days since Joan first reached out to him with her concern for Alex. Three days since she promised to do anything she could to get Alex to go back to him.

But Alex hadn't called. Even though she was in a new place and was probably scared, she hadn't called.

Steven threw the small bouncy ball in his hand against the wall and caught it as it came flying back toward him. He repeated the action again and again. Thump, thump, thump. Each time it met the wall, it bounced back a little harder.

I hope the people next door aren't here, he thought. The

last thing I need is some busybody calling the police for a noise disturbance.

With one last burst of anger, Steven tossed the ball, this time watching it ricochet around the small room, knocking over a picture and finally coming to rest under the sofa.

He carefully picked up the frame that had just been knocked over. It was the same one he'd shattered two days before. The glass was held together with scotch tape, leaving cloudy veins running all over Alex's body.

Using his thumb, he gently stroked her hair, then moved it down to her bare shoulder.

We would have had such beautiful children, he thought. A dull ache settled in his stomach. You should have become Mrs. Steven Dorset. Alexandra Dorset. What a beautiful name, he mused. Many times, he'd scribbled his last name as hers, each time sure she'd want it that way too someday.

Any hope he had of that happening was gone. If anybody could have gotten her to see what she was missing, it was her grandmother.

Perhaps the old broad hasn't even tried, he thought, anger returning. She'd have to be senile to make that mistake.

He put the picture back on the TV stand with enough force to make the mended glass rattle in its frame.

If that's the case, maybe me and grandma need to have another chat. This time, though, she'll know better than to try to understand what it's like when Alex decides she wants you out of her life.

And if she didn't take the hint, maybe she'd do better with a visual demonstration...

37

A LEX SWATTED A tree branch away from her face. She felt like she was going to jump out of her skin as she waited to find out more about her birth parents. After spending the morning at the park with Jackson and returning the phone calls to Gram and Jeannie, she spent most of the afternoon in her hotel room poring over the newspaper articles she'd printed at the library. She was treading water with the same information she'd gotten Sunday. Sure, dinner with Simon and his dad had helped tremendously, but what now? She'd been obsessing about her birth parents since she found her birth certificate and desperately needed to clear her head. That was why, when Simon called for a third time and suggested they go hiking when he left the office, she readily agreed. Anything to distract herself from the fact it was the anniversary of her parents' death.

The rain from late morning returned in the afternoon, making it feel cooler than the forty-eight degrees the weather app on her phone indicated. She wasn't used to weather this cold so early in the year. That coupled with the damp air chilled her to her bones. And to think yesterday had been so warm…

Growing more annoyed with every soggy step, she told Simon about her decision to visit Benny Johnson in prison.

"Are you sure you want to do that?" Simon asked.

"I am," she said as she stepped into a puddle. Water seeped into her boot, chilling her foot instantly. "He's the only one that knows for certain what happened that night. Maybe he knows what really happened to the baby."

Simon stepped over a fallen tree then extended his hand to help Alex over. "I don't think you realize how emotional it could be for you to sit across from the person convicted of killing the people you believe to be your birth parents," he cautioned.

She clenched her jaw and stared at the trail straight ahead.

Simon stopped walking and placed his hand on her arm. Alex paused to face him. "I want to make sure you realize exactly what you're getting yourself into," he said. "I've known a lot of people in your position. This has happened to a few of my clients. Granted, none of them were murderers." Simon looked down at the toes of his wet hiking boots. "I'm not proud of it, I once defended a guy who was charged with battery and attempted murder. He'd beaten his wife so badly he shattered the bones in her face. Reconstructive surgery was required to repair the damage. The victim's mother wanted to see him face-to-face, to look into the eyes of the person that hurt her daughter. She had to be escorted out of the visitor's room when she spit in his face."

Alex's eyes widened. Maybe Simon isn't as upstanding as I thought, she mused, disappointed in what she'd just heard.

Silence hung between them as they listened to a creek running somewhere in the distance.

"That case wasn't my finest moment," Simon admitted, "and I'm still ashamed I agreed to represent such a worthless piece of trash in the first place. He was a smooth talker and had me convinced she'd taken a tumble down the stairs. I think he had a personality disorder. I truly didn't believe he was guilty." Simon half smiled. "I lost the case and he's still sitting in jail, so that's some consolation."

The two began walking again. Simon continued, "All that to say, I do have experience with this kind of thing, which is why I don't think it's a good idea for you to meet Benny."

"Look," Alex said, her tone clipped, "I didn't even know Thomas and Sheila Stone. I'm not emotionally connected to them. They're complete strangers that I'll never meet."

"True," Simon said calmly. "But you are emotionally invested in your crusade to find out whether or not they were your birth parents. That alone could trigger anger, disappointment, sadness, fear—you name it. You're a mental health professional. Shouldn't you know this already?"

He's right, Alex told herself. She'd already become so invested and was much more vulnerable to disappointment than she cared to admit. "Then what do you suggest I do?" she asked, exasperated. "I'm not going to stop looking."

"Let's try to look at the police report in more detail. I'm sure Dad made a copy for himself when he retired. We'll start there. Then, if it turns out we have enough evidence that we feel certain they were your birth parents, I'll get you in to see Benny Johnson if you still want to. I don't recommend it, but you're an adult and can make your own decisions. From what

I hear, he's a real piece of work. I don't want you to be exposed to him if you don't have to be."

Alex stopped walking. "Your dad has a copy of the police report? Is he allowed to do that?"

Simon shrugged.

"And he wouldn't mind?" Alex asked and began walking again, her thoughts lured away from Simon by her foot squishing in her wet boot.

Shaking his head, Simon replied, "I doubt it. He said he'd do whatever he could to help you. When Sam Caldwell offers something, he means it."

Twigs snapped under their feet and water droplets dripped from the leaves above. Even though it was overcast and damp, the trail was beautiful. Alex inhaled the earthy scent of wet leaves and mud.

Simon spoke again. "Is that a deal?"

Alex nodded. "That sounds fair."

They turned on the trail and started the trek back toward the car.

"Thank you for helping me. I really do appreciate everything you've done. Your dad, too. I promise I'm usually easier to get along with," Alex said sheepishly.

"Maybe it's time to take a breath and gain a little perspective. You've been trying to move at breakneck speed since you found your birth certificate. You know, you remind me of the Doberman one of my neighbors had when I was a kid."

"Oh?" Alex said as she stepped in the same puddle she had on the way to the trail. The mud slurped as she pulled her booted foot from it.

"Yeah. She attacked me and took a chunk out of my leg.

They had to put her down." Though he didn't look at her, there was a mischievous smile curving his mouth.

Alex sighed. "Message received. I know I can be stubborn."

They walked in companionable silence until they emerged from the woods and crossed the parking lot to Simon's car. Once he started it, Alex took off her boots and socks and turned the heat on full blast.

Simon turned in his seat to face her. "Now, I know you said everything between us was strictly business, but I was wondering if you'd come to a benefit dinner with me."

Alex hesitated. "I'm not sure that would be a good idea. When I'm finished looking into this case, I'm going back to Charleston."

"I know. I just thought it might be good for you to go. It's for work, and people from the firm will be there. You haven't gotten to talk to John Carmichael yet, and you might get a crack at him. He was Benny Johnson's attorney for the past three decades."

Alex turned to see the naked hope on Simon's face. "I don't have anything to wear," she protested weakly.

"Then you'll go shopping." With that, Simon won the argument.

She waved a hand toward her mud-crusted boots. "I probably need to do that anyway."

Simon smiled broadly and backed out of the parking space. "It would also be okay if we had a little fun."

Alex leaned back in her seat and gazed out the window. She knew she'd have a good time with Simon, and it was possible that someone could help her fill in the blanks of her past.

Whatever it was.

38

JOHN CARMICHAEL GROANED inwardly at the realization that it was only Wednesday. Less than a week—four days to be exact—since his life began falling apart. If he was honest with himself, he'd have to admit that the trouble started long before now, but he'd never felt desperate before. Now Clarence was forcing him to make the trouble go away on his own.

When had they switched roles?

John had never taken care of these kinds of problems for himself before. There was always somebody around to do the dirty work for him; somebody he didn't mind getting hauled off to jail.

This time, he was that somebody. Clarence was calling the shots and he was on his own.

He'd heard through the legal grapevine that Richard Wade wanted to talk to him about Benny Johnson. What on earth would make an upstanding guy like Richard Wade want to get tangled up with someone like Benny? John wondered.

As he stared out the window over the kitchen sink, he

thought about the irony of his life. On top of the world one minute, flat on his face the next. He shivered when he thought of all the opportunities he'd had. His life had been carefully planned and executed. Nothing was left to chance. Shrewd in both his business and personal relationships, he only entered into them if they would benefit him in some way. This approach had served him well, advancing his career much quicker than most of his colleagues. He was married to the job and had never fallen out of love with the power it gave him.

Now he looked at that life, teetering on the verge of ruin, and wondered what he could have done differently.

Everything and nothing.

He was who he was. There was no changing that. But each decision had been built on another, and if that first one had been different, his whole existence would be a far cry from what it was now.

There was no going back, no undoing what had been done.

In the background, a clock ticked the seconds away. John stood listening to the *tick-tock* for several minutes, grasping that every tick of the clock was taking him closer to the end. Soon this life would be just a memory and he would be forgotten.

Just a little while longer, he promised himself as he watched the wind plaster the leaves to the soggy grass. When he first made the decision to retire, it seemed like a good idea to announce that he'd stay on until he finished his current caseload. Now the thought of spending even one more day feeling like he was walking on eggshells around his coworkers made him wish he could be anywhere else on the planet. He didn't want to pretend everything was fine. Nothing was, and he was sick of the charade.

"Not that I've done a good job hiding anything lately," John muttered.

The benefit tonight would be dreadful. At least when he was at work he could hide in his office and avoid his colleagues. Tonight he'd be out in the open with nowhere to hide. As if he needed another reason to want to stay home, he'd overheard some of the administrative staff talking about how they were going to honor him with a lifetime achievement award tonight. He promised to act surprised, but really he wanted to vomit.

Practicing his gracious-winner face, he smiled. It felt more like a grimace.

He shook the thoughts of the dinner out of his head and walked to the den. Sitting in his favorite recliner, he turned on the evening news. Expecting the usual stories about traffic accidents and gas station robberies, John only half listened.

An eager young reporter appeared on the screen with the lead story, eyes flashing with excitement. She effortlessly had John's undivided attention.

The lead story wasn't about an accident or robbery, but an attempted murder, and the words that followed made him sit up straight in his chair.

39

HE WATCHED FROM a bench outside the hotel as Alex moved around her room, then disappeared into the bathroom. Even the bathrobe she'd been wearing accentuated her slim figure. He shook his head sadly at the thought of this beautiful woman he'd loved so dearly having to become his victim.

She should have loved me back, he thought. He didn't want to have to hurt her, but she left him no choice. She'd rejected him time and time again. Nothing he did had ever been good enough for her. While her smiles lit up his world, his went unnoticed. Even the most embarrassing details of his life were offered, and yet she refused to share anything about herself. He now realized their relationship had always been one-sided. He was the only one who had ever tried to make it work.

Now she's moved on to this other guy, he thought angrily. I wonder if he knows she's just going to lead him on then drop him the minute he shows any sign of vulnerability.

"Oh, well," he muttered. "Soon it won't matter. For either of them."

As he watched her emerge from the bathroom, he straightened from his slouched position and inhaled deeply. She was dressed up and looked absolutely breathtaking. She was going somewhere nice. Probably with that guy.

Fury burned in his chest. She'd cast him aside and was offering herself to another man.

He tried so hard not to think about what might have been, but the thoughts still took over his life. If only she'd accepted what he'd offered her. If only she'd returned the love he'd given her.

If only…

Those two words consumed his every thought the last few months, each time making him more bitter than before. He knew she was too good for him, but it crushed him that she thought so, too.

Her movement held his attention. She bent forward to scratch the top of her dog's head. How he wished he could be that dog, to have her affection, to feel her fingers in his hair.

His body shook. Rage consumed him and he vowed she would pay dearly. Soon. Then she wouldn't be able to love her dog, or anyone else, more than him ever again.

40

LEX GRABBED HER keys and raced out the door. The benefit started in twenty minutes, and she was running late. Simon had planned to pick her up but phoned to say there was a family emergency and he'd have to meet her there.

A knot settled in the pit of Alex's stomach. *I hope it doesn't have anything to do with Sam,* she thought. She'd become very fond of him, instantly drawn to his quick wit and generous heart. In a small way, though he was fifteen years younger, Sam reminded Alex of her grandfather, Frank.

She punched the address of the Marriott, where the event was being held, into her GPS and reviewed her day. Most of the morning and afternoon was spent at Sam's house, going over the police report from the Stone murder case. He answered as many questions as he could, and her hand was still sore from taking so many notes.

Sam had been fine then, so maybe the family emergency wasn't about him. She breathed a small sigh of relief and continued rehashing her time with him.

According to Sam, the evidence from the crime scene was still in storage. Apparently evidence from murder investigations was kept indefinitely. He said it would be possible to take a sample of her DNA and compare it to the DNA left on the murder weapons, but she'd have to be able to convince somebody to take her suspicions seriously. He'd warned her that it was a long shot, but worth a try.

She agreed.

Alex planned to go to the police station tomorrow to request a DNA comparison and prayed she'd find favor with them. With his permission, Alex was prepared to drop Sam's name if necessary.

She'd discovered a bit about Sam today, too. He talked about all the things he and Betty did together after his injury forced him into retirement. Since she died a year and a half ago, he said his activity level had decreased substantially and he kept to himself most of the time. Without someone to help him, getting out of the house took too much effort.

He must be terribly lonely, Alex thought as she drove toward the benefit to meet Simon.

Sam had also opened up about his son. Though he was obviously proud of his son and his many accomplishments, Alex sensed that Sam was disappointed in Simon's chosen profession. It made sense, since Sam had dedicated his career to putting the bad guys behind bars and Simon tried to help them go free. In a way, she was surprised their relationship was as solid as it was.

Sam also briefly mentioned having another son, though he didn't say much about him. Alex got the impression he wasn't close to the rest of the family.

Pulling into the parking lot of the Marriott convention center, Alex noticed a few people hurrying inside.

At least I'm not the only one who will be making an entrance, she thought.

Quickly scanning the parking lot for Simon's car, she realized he wasn't there. After a few minutes, his car pulled into a spot adjacent to hers. He dashed out and began jogging toward the entrance. As the distance between them grew, she hurried as quickly as she could in her newly purchased high heels.

"Simon!" she called, when she realized there was no way she'd be able to catch him.

He turned and walked briskly toward her. As he got closer, Alex noticed how disheveled he was. The knot of his tie had been loosened and pulled down, his shirtsleeves were rolled up, and his hair looked as though it hadn't been combed in days. The stubble on his face was way past a five-o'clock shadow, which only deepened the purple shadows under his eyes.

She placed a hand on his forearm. "Are you okay?"

He looked down at the asphalt and ran his fingers through his already unkempt hair. The lights overhead revealed red fingertips and jagged fingernails, as though he'd chewed them until they were raw.

"Simon, what's wrong?" she urged.

"I can't stay for the benefit tonight. I wanted to tell you in person and see you all dressed up." He gave her a quick once over, his brief smile indicating she'd made the right choice when she selected the red gown. "You look beautiful."

Alex ignored the compliment. Simon was barely recognizable as the confident man she'd met two days ago when she walked into Hughes, Stone, and Bentley. The sight rattled her.

"What do you need?" she asked, hoping that in some small way, she'd be able to help erase the hurt from his face.

A tense smile tugged at the corner of his mouth. "Maybe a good therapist when this is all over."

"When what is over?" Alex asked over the lump in her throat. "What's going on? Is your dad okay?"

Simon nodded. "Dad's fine. It's my brother. He's been accused of trying to kill Benny Johnson."

41

ALEX BLINKED. "HE'S been what?"

Simon didn't answer. He stood still, looking over Alex's shoulder. The dim lights in the parking lot cast shadows on his face, making his eyes look hollow and turning his tanned skin into aged leather.

"Simon, I can't help you if you don't answer me."

He turned his face toward her, looking like he might pass out. She braced herself to catch him in case his knees buckled.

"My little brother, Tony, has been accused of trying to kill Benny Johnson," Simon repeated.

She felt her forehead furrow and said, "But Benny Johnson is in jail."

"Yeah."

A few beats passed before Alex connected the dots. "Oh…" That explained why Simon had never mentioned him and the reason Sam hadn't said much about having another son. With a father who was a police detective, a mother who was an investigative journalist, and a brother who's an attorney, Tony would have been a disappointment to the family when he went to prison.

"I know I talked you into going to this benefit with me tonight, and that you were really hoping to get a crack at John Carmichael, but I can't go in there." Simon's tone was somewhere between apologetic and anguished. "I just can't…"

His anguish erased any disappointment Alex might have felt. "Don't worry about it," she assured him. "You have bigger things going on right now than helping me track down my birth parents." She paused, then added, "What can I do to help?"

"Can we go somewhere to talk?"

"Me? Are you sure? Surely there are people you are closer to who you would rather talk to." In her experience, she knew very well the responsibility of hearing a person's story, of sharing their burdens. It wasn't something that Alex took lightly, and she wasn't sure she was ready for Simon to need her like this.

"There are, and they know the whole story," he replied. "They know it so well, actually, that I doubt they'd want to hear it. Please, Alex? I need a friend right now."

Alex took a breath and nodded. After all he'd done for her already, how could she possibly turn him down?

After only a brief objection, Simon agreed that he probably shouldn't be driving, and the two walked to Alex's car, silence broken only by the click of her heels on the asphalt.

Twenty minutes later, they were sitting at a corner table of a quiet coffee shot off East High Street. Every so often, she noticed the curious glances from other customers as they took in her red evening gown.

"Looks like you're the best-dressed one here," Simon said wryly.

She shook off the self-consciousness and turned her attention back to Simon. "Start at the beginning," Alex said gently. She eyed the barista behind the counter, trying to squelch the feeling that this conversation would require caffeine.

Simon started rambling something about his brother and drugs but wasn't making any sense. As he continued his disjointed narrative, Alex stopped him. She'd need coffee for this. If her hunch was right—and Simon's agitated movements suggested she was—he'd probably already consumed too much caffeine today.

This is going to be a long night, she thought, then excused herself.

"Large coffee, please. Black," she said to the barista. "And a decaf, please."

She looked back at Simon, who was tapping his fingers nervously on the table, and jiggling his leg under it.

"Actually, make that last one a chamomile tea," she requested. The smiling barista happily complied.

When Alex returned to the table, she scooted the tea in front of Simon and said, "Okay. Go on."

He frowned into his cup.

"You need to calm down," Alex instructed, not giving him a chance to voice his displeasure with the tea. "Now, tell me about your brother," she encouraged.

Simon took a small sip of the tea, grimaced, then inhaled deeply and let the air escape through his lips. "Tony is my younger brother," he began, making an obvious effort to slow down. "He's four years younger than me, so we weren't that close as kids. It wasn't until he was in his early twenties that we had any kind of relationship. Tony went to a community college for a couple years then went straight to work as a mechanic. It suited him well. Even as a kid he was always tinkering with things and figuring out how to fix them." He paused and took another sip. "We've been polar opposites our whole lives. I always had my nose in a book or was doing stuff outside. Tony, on the other hand, was always the life of the party and spent most of his time hanging out with friends. He was never a bad kid. Mischievous, but never bad. He got in trouble for normal kid stuff, toilet papering houses and things like that, but never any real trouble."

Alex nodded her encouragement, then, slipping into counselor mode, said, "Go on."

"Things started to change after he got out of school. He stopped being the fun-loving guy we all knew. Mom had just been diagnosed with breast cancer, so we all attributed the change in his mood and behavior to that. He and Mom were always very close—closer than he was to the rest of us. Looking back, I think he was probably very depressed. He withdrew from the things he'd always loved. After a while, his friends stopped calling or coming around. He turned into a very lonely person, which I'd never known him to be. Of course, I was already working sixty-hour weeks when all this was going on and probably didn't notice the change in him as much as I should have. I dealt with Mom's diagnosis by burying myself in work. I realize now that I was hiding, trying to distract myself from the reality that we were losing her. It wasn't healthy, but that's how I coped." Simon dropped his eyes to his cup of tea.

Guilt. Alex knew it well, and it was written all over his face.

"After a while, he started going out again. He'd made new friends and we were all relieved, especially Mom. Nobody knew these guys, but we assumed he'd know how to discern what kind of people would be good for him." Simon swallowed hard. "We were wrong. He and I were starting to get closer, but I always felt he was holding something back. I was still too absorbed in my work to really worry about it, but we started getting suspicious when he started giving Mom and Dad large amounts of cash to help pay for her treatments. He made a good living, but what he was giving them was way more than he should have been earning." Simon looked up at her, his eyes glistening with unshed tears. "Eventually, he was arrested during a sting operation while he was trying to sell cocaine to high school kids."

"Oh, Simon, I'm so sorry." She reached across the table and grasped his hand. She didn't know what to say. Her whole career depended on her ability to talk to people when they were having a hard time, and she was good at it. Tonight, though, she was at a loss for words.

I guess this is why therapists don't counsel friends and family, Alex thought. It was too hard to be objective.

Simon continued. "He was found guilty of possession and distributing illegal substances and sentenced to ten years in a federal prison. Dad pulled some strings and had him placed at the state penitentiary instead so he'd be closer and we could visit more often. As you can imagine, the whole family was heartbroken. We all had relatively public images—a cop, a journalist, and an attorney. Then we've got Tony, a convicted drug dealer."

One of these is not like the others, Alex thought. Instead, she said, "I can only imagine how difficult that must have been for your family." Alex wanted to bite her tongue. She *couldn't* imagine it. She didn't even know what it was like to have a sibling, let alone one who got himself on the wrong side of the law.

She did, however, know what it was like to have parents who were in possession of a forged birth certificate and a daughter who was adopted with no paper trail.

Simon didn't seem to notice how empty her words of sympathy sounded. Instead, he nodded and continued, "After his arrest and during the trial, Mom's health really took a nosedive. The stress of watching her son be convicted of something so awful took a toll on her. She'd been doing relatively well before that, but I think it's the stress that killed her. Almost a year into Tony's sentence, Mom died. He wasn't able to go to her funeral, and it really messed with his head. He already blamed himself for her death. Her prognosis was never good, and she was terminal, so it was ridiculous to blame himself for her death. She was a fighter, though. Even the doctors were surprised she hung on as long as she did. After he was convicted, the fight just sort of went out of her. She was going to die anyway, but the stress and despair just brought it quicker."

Alex pressed her lips together. So much hurt in one family.

"Then, when he couldn't even go to the funeral, he resigned himself to believing he was a worthless piece of garbage who deserved to be in jail and shouldn't have a family who loved him. That's the Tony we've been dealing with ever since. He's become a very bitter man." Simon raised the cup to his lips and took a small sip. "This stuff is truly awful," he complained and set the mug back on the table.

"It will help you relax," Alex affirmed, then said, "And he's in prison with Benny Johnson, I assume."

"Yes."

"I'm having a hard time understanding where Benny

would fit into all this. What happened to him, and why would Tony want to kill him?"

"Benny was stabbed with a shiv in the cafeteria. It missed all major organs, apparently, and the medical staff at the prison was able to get the bleeding under control and sent him to the hospital. After an assessment, the doctors sent him back to the prison infirmary. He's expected to make a full recovery. Otherwise, Tony would be facing a murder charge."

Alex took a big gulp of coffee. "Did someone see Tony stab him?"

Simon shook his head. "No. There were a lot of inmates around, and Tony was only one of them."

"If nobody saw him, why is he already being accused? They must have *some* kind of evidence," Alex objected.

"None that I know of." Simon rubbed the stubble on his face.

"But how can they charge him with attempted murder when they have no evidence and no eyewitnesses?" Alex was shocked that the system could be so broken.

Simon shrugged helplessly. "Tony and Benny had what they called an 'altercation' in the exercise yard over the week-end."

"Oh."

"Yeah. There were a lot of eyewitnesses to that. That is more than enough to make him the number-one suspect. In fact, if I didn't know Tony, I'd suspect him based on that," Simon admitted. He leaned back in his chair and stretched his legs out in front of him. He looked like he was finally starting to calm down.

"Thirty-two years in prison is a long time, though. Surely

Tony can't be the only one to have had a run-in with Benny. He's bound to have ruffled a few feathers over the years."

Simon snorted. "You can say that again. Almost everybody who knows Benny hates him. He thrives on knowing exactly what buttons to push to get people worked up."

"Including Tony's?"

"Including Tony's. Tony doesn't have a bad temper. Just the opposite, in fact. It takes a lot to make him mad, and even then he manages to rein it in. Benny works harder at Tony than anybody else. He hates Tony because our dad is the one who arrested him."

The pieces fell together. Of course! That would give Benny more than enough reason to bully Tony. Now things were starting to make sense. "And this altercation. It was physical, I assume?"

Simon shook his head tightly and leaned forward. "No. Some of the guys who saw it said Tony controlled his anger, but apparently he made some threats. Now everyone assumes he was just making good on those threats."

"What did Benny do?"

"He brought up Mom," Simon sighed. "That's the one thing that would set Tony off. If he did it again, it's possible that Tony could have snapped." Simon hesitated as though trying to picture the scenario in his head. "Not likely, but possible."

"If everybody hated Benny, there must have been plenty of others who would have wanted to see him dead," Alex challenged.

"I'm sure there are," Simon agreed, thrusting out his jaw in determination. "And I intend to find out who they are."

42

I T WAS AFTER midnight when Alex and Simon left the coffee shop. They'd been the only ones left, and the staff waited impatiently behind the counter for them to leave. She dropped him off at his car and watched him slide behind the wheel with his shoulders slumped.

She felt exhausted and helpless.

Sometimes one person's bad choices impacted multitudes, and this is a prime example, she thought as she drove away.

Back in her hotel room, Alex settled in at her computer. Her eyes burned with exhaustion, but there was no way she could fall asleep now.

Maybe I should have had chamomile tea, too, she thought, instead of that bucket-sized cup of coffee.

As she waited for her laptop to boot up, a plain white envelope lying to the left of it caught her attention. She only vaguely remembered taking it off the door of her room yesterday afternoon but forgot about it as soon as she put it down.

She carefully picked it up and opened the seal, wondering what could possibly be inside. She hadn't ordered room service, so it couldn't be a bill. Sliding her fingers into the envelope, she grasped something that felt like an index card. She pulled it out and read the words once, then twice.

It was a warning. A warning to stop looking into the Stone murders and a threat that if she didn't, she could end up just like them.

Alex shuddered.

With her hand shaking, Alex placed the card on the keyboard of her laptop and read it a third time.

"I'm making somebody nervous," she said aloud. "But who?"

43

A LOT OF money was raised the night before to help feed hungry kids, but other than that, the benefit had been as dreadful as John had feared. Before the speaker took the stage, John was presented with the lifetime achievement award. After saying how much he would be missed and that it would be impossible to replace him, the MC handed John the mic and he was obligated to say a few words. Boiling his life's work down to a three-minute speech seemed ridiculous, but now it was behind him and he could move on.

He'd been careful not to drink too much during dinner so his farewell speech would be clear and concise. He hadn't been clear and concise in weeks.

On a few occasions during his speech, he'd had to raise his voice to be heard over the sniffles coming from the audience. Try as he might, he couldn't figure out who would have been so upset about his retirement that they would cry about it, especially in public.

Probably Julia, John thought. She's been moping around all week.

He now looked at his award, a cheap plaque that was supposed to commemorate his entire career, lying on the passenger seat of his car. It seemed to mock him, a cruel reminder that the mighty still fall. All the money spent on school, the hours spent poring over his cases to ensure his clients' acquittals were boiled down to a thirty-dollar award.

Sitting in his car at Veterans Park on Thursday morning, he watched people go by. Mothers pushed strollers, elderly couples held hands on their leisurely strolls, people walked their dogs. Joggers were completely absorbed in themselves and the music coming from their ear buds. Occasionally a solitary walker ambled by, and John wondered if they were lonely. Never a people-watcher by nature, John always had little interest in the mundane lives of others. Now he was drawn to them. What were they like? Were they fulfilled? Had their lives gone the way they'd planned?

His cell phone rang.

"John Carmichael," he barked when he raised it to his ear.

"Hello, Mr. Carmichael. This is Richard Wade. I wonder if I might speak with you for a few minutes," the caller said politely.

Richard Wade.

John groaned inwardly. He wanted to hang up and get back to his musings, not talk to this guy.

"We met a couple years ago when I first began working as a public defender. My secretary contacted you earlier in the week," Richard continued, as though John had no idea who he was.

Of course I know who you are, John thought bitterly. You're the guy who won't let me forget about Benny.

John remembered being slightly impressed by Richard

Wade when they met at a conference a few years ago and didn't think he'd be a public defender for long. Apparently he'd been right.

"How are you, Richard?" John said with as much geniality as he could muster. The last thing he wanted right now was to talk to someone about Benny Johnson.

"I'm doing well, thank you. I hate to bother you first thing in the morning…" Richard began.

But you're going to anyway, John mused.

"… but I wanted to get your opinion on something." He paused. "A few days ago, Benny Johnson asked me to represent him. He wants to file an appeal, but I didn't want to take his case until I spoke with you."

"I don't work with Benny anymore," John said coolly, "and I would rather not discuss him. There's a reason we parted ways." That's an understatement, John thought.

"I understand he wasn't easy to work with, and from my brief interaction with him, I can understand why." He paused and John could hear him take a deep breath. "Even so, I'm considering taking him on, but I wanted your insight first. You know him better than anyone."

"Unfortunately, that's true," John agreed. Sometimes he wondered how much he really knew about the man. "What would you like to know?"

For three decades, John had been fighting a losing battle. Each interaction with Benny was worse than the one before, and over the years they'd grown to resent each other. The longer he knew Benny, the stronger John's dislike for him became. Now he downright hated the man. Though he'd never come right out and admit it, John was sure Benny was at least partially responsible for his increased drinking.

But how do I tell Richard Wade all that? John wondered. He seems like a nice enough guy. I guess I should just say it straight. Minus the drinking part. That's none of Richard's business.

After several minutes, John had given Richard his opinion of Benny, with the recommendation that Richard decline to take Benny on as a client.

"Thank you for your time, Mr. Carmichael," Richard said. "I will certainly take your advice under consideration."

When they disconnected the call, John was certain Richard Wade was going to disregard everything he'd just said and would agree to represent Benny anyway.

John shook his head. He'd tried to warn Richard. His conscience was clear.

About this, anyway.

He did regret that a talented lawyer with a bright future was about to flush it all down the toilet on someone like Benny, but there was nothing more he could do.

"Better him than me," John muttered. Now that someone had tried to kill Benny, he would be even more unbearable. Always proficient at playing the victim, Benny would use this to his advantage and con his new lawyer any way he could.

Lost in thought, John didn't notice the man approaching him. His head snapped to the right as he heard the passenger door of his car click open and his visitor slide onto the plush leather seat, knocking the plaque to the floor. The smell of stale cigarette smoke filled the car.

Clarence requested that John meet him at the park. At first, he'd suggested they meet in a secluded area, but John managed to convince him to say what needed to be said in his car. Knowing what he did about Clarence, a secluded, wooded area screamed "body dump," and he wasn't willing to be the body that got dumped.

"You're jumpy," Clarence stated, his voice flat. "Your nerves aren't getting the better of you, I hope."

"Not at all," John lied. "I was just thinking."

Clarence narrowed his eyes and studied John. "You're always thinking. That's the problem with you, and that's why you're in the mess you're in. You do more thinking than doing." The gruff voice mocked him. To Clarence, too much thinking showed weakness, a limitation of an otherwise successful person.

"I have everything under control," John said, feigning confidence.

"This is you having control? I'd hate to see what you're like when you're out of control." Clarence began laughing, showing a gap where his left incisor should have been. The chuckle soon turned into a sputtering cough caused by years of smoking.

"What's this about, Clarence?" John demanded. He had no patience for this today.

Clarence stared straight ahead, watching a squirrel hop toward a tree. He's probably thinking about popping its head off, John thought, sobered by the image. He reminded himself to watch his step around Clarence.

"There are some loose ends that need to be tied up," Clarence ordered without looking in John's direction.

John gulped. "Loose ends? Like what?"

"I think you know," Clarence said, turning his cold, snake eyes to John. "She's become a liability. Sooner or later, some pretty unsavory things about you will come out. You don't want that, now do you?"

"No," John admitted quietly.

"You have to take care of it," Clarence demanded.

"I know."

"Soon."

"I know." John stared at his hands, now gripping the bottom of the steering wheel. "Any suggestions?"

Clarence shook his head. "All that thinking you do, you should be able to come up with something. Do it however you want. Just take care of her."

John barely noticed Clarence getting out of the car or that the stench of stale cigarettes dissipated. He'd never expected to get in this deep. How could a plan that seemed foolproof years ago be going so horribly wrong now?

44

SAM LOOKED OUT the kitchen window early Thursday morning at the changing leaves while he sipped his coffee. It was already a beautiful day, and he was glad to be alive.

Since he'd been forced into retirement after a stray bullet lodged in his spine during a robbery, he often reflected on what a blessing life was. He celebrated each day as a gift he didn't deserve. Over the years he'd attended countless funerals for fallen officers, acutely aware that the next one could be his.

And it almost was.

Even though he'd lost the ability to walk, he gained so much more. He got to spend the last years of Betty's life with her. As her health declined, there were days they'd go to the park and sit for hours enjoying the sunshine. Both had been avid fishers in their younger days, and until helping him into the boat became too burdensome for Betty, they still occasionally found the time and energy to go out on the lake.

As Sam took the final drink of his coffee, he reminded himself he should be glad Betty wasn't around to know what was happening. Betty and Tony had always been very close, and when they found out he'd been selling drugs, she knew it was to help pay for her treatment. Although she never admitted it to him, Sam knew she felt a tremendous amount of guilt, blaming herself for the trouble Tony had gotten himself into. On several occasions, she'd say, "If I wasn't sick, Tony wouldn't have felt like he had to make extra money. If I wasn't sick, he never would have started selling drugs. If I wasn't sick…" Then she would burst into tears, her frail shoulders shaking as she sobbed.

Try as he might, Sam couldn't help but wonder if she'd still be with them if the guilt and stress hadn't eaten away at her. Even though, according to the doctors, she wasn't supposed to survive, if anybody could have beaten the cancer that ravaged her body, it would have been Betty.

She'd been tough when investigating a story, but she was all soft when it came to her family. Especially her boys, and especially her youngest.

What would she think of this? Sam wondered. She'd be a basket case. He could almost picture her pacing in the middle of the night or unconsciously wringing her hands at the dinner table, just as she had during the trial. She would probably say she just wished everything would go back to normal.

But nothing would be that kind of normal ever again. The past twenty-four hours had been anything but. Ever since he'd gotten word that Tony had tried to kill Benny Johnson, Sam bounced between disbelief and the notion that it could be true. He knew how much Tony despised Benny, but he also knew that in his heart, Tony was a gentle, decent guy.

But is he a gentle, decent guy who is capable of murder?

Sam had asked himself countless times since he'd gotten the call.

As a father, he had a hard time believing his son could do anything so terrible. As a former police detective who'd spent more than thirty years on the force, though, he knew people were capable of almost anything when pushed to their limits.

Had Benny pushed Tony past *his*?

At the sound of the door opening, Sam turned toward the living room. His heart ached when he saw Simon, rumpled and weary, emerge from his childhood bedroom.

Simon rushed right over to Sam's house yesterday when he heard what Tony had been accused of, and then that evening, after Sam assured him that he'd be okay, he went out to find Alex. When he returned a little after midnight, Sam was still wide awake.

They sat together for hours, neither uttering a word as they tried to process what the guards at the prison said happened. With no appetite for dinner and unable to sleep, Sam imagined Simon did the same thing he had—look back over Tony's life and wonder what went wrong, thinking they should have been able to stop it.

The family had endured enough pain the last few years, and as strong as they were, Sam wondered how much more he and Simon could take.

Last night, Sam realized something he wondered if even Simon knew. Simon and Tony hadn't been close as children, and it wasn't until Tony had already started dealing that they had much of a relationship at all. Sam was certain Simon took much of the blame for what went wrong with Tony because he hadn't made time for him when they were kids.

Just like Betty, Simon was probably saying "if only" to

himself over and over. So much like his mother, Sam thought as he watched Simon pour himself a cup of coffee and stare blankly out the window.

"You look rough," Sam observed.

"Thanks," Simon replied, looking down at his wrinkled shirt and gym shorts and mismatched socks.

"Did you sleep?" Sam knew better than to ask if he slept well. He knew he hadn't.

"Some. You?"

Sam nodded. "I took a sleeping pill. You should try one," he suggested.

Simon shook his head. "You know how I feel about those things. I don't want to wake up feeling hungover and foggy. I need my mind to be sharp. Especially now."

Sam waved his hand in Simon's direction. "And you call this being sharp?"

"Dad…"

"I know. I'm sorry. This isn't a good time," Sam apologized.

"How do you think Tony is?"

Shrugging, Sam said, "I wish I knew. We should be able to see him soon. That will help us all, I think," he said, hopeful. The truth was, if it was having the same effect on Tony that it was on him and Simon, seeing Tony depressed and hopeless would make it worse.

Sam narrowed his eyes and watched his son. There was something else going on. *He's worried about more than Tony's latest predicament. It's something that has nothing to do with Tony.*

"What else is on your mind?" Sam asked softly.

"What do you mean?" Simon asked, diverting his gaze. "I'm just worried about Tony."

"You know exactly what I mean, Simon. Something else is bothering you."

"It's nothing. Really."

Sam frowned. "Simon, do you remember what I was known for on the police force?"

"Yes."

"And what was that?"

"You were known for being able to read people as well as a lie detector. You could tell if someone was lying, even if no one else could."

"Then, are you really trying to tell me I'm misreading you?" Sam paused. "I'll ask you again. What else is bothering you?"

Simon ran a hand through his already disheveled hair. "I told Alex."

"You told Alex what?" Sam asked, extending his hands.

"Everything. About the drugs and Tony being in prison and what they're saying he did to Benny."

So that's it, Sam thought. He's ashamed. Ashamed that his brother was a drug dealer. Ashamed that his brother was now being accused of attempted murder.

"And?"

"And what if she won't have anything to do with me?"

Ding, ding. That's his real fear. He's told the girl he likes a deep, dark family secret and now he's convinced himself he's scared her off, Sam realized. "Have you tried calling her?"

"This morning, but my call went straight to her voice mail."

"What did you say in your message?"

Finally, Simon looked at his dad. "I didn't leave one."

"Then she has no idea you tried to contact her," Sam stated. "Isn't it possible she knows you're having a tough time and wants to give you some space? She's a mental health professional for pity's sake. She knows this stuff."

"I guess so…" Simon admitted.

"Then stop being paranoid. Does she strike you as the kind of person who would be scared off so easily? Think about it. Alex came to a strange city where she knew no one, walked straight into the office of someone she'd never met but thought they might be able to help her, and is stubborn enough to stay focused on what she's looking for, even though she knows she might not like the outcome," Sam challenged. "Does that sound like someone who would be scared off because our family has some skeletons in the closet?"

Simon shook his head and smiled a tired smile. "No, I guess not."

"Then stop worrying. Trust me, I've talked to my share of people, from saints to scumbags. She's one of the good ones." Then candidly, Sam added, "You really do like her, don't you?"

"Is it that obvious?"

"Yes, and not just to me. I'd bet good money that it's obvious to her, too. Especially if she's as good at reading people as I think she is."

Simon's mouth drooped into a frown. "She's made it perfectly clear that she doesn't want to have anything to do with me… in that way."

"Give her time. She's busy working through her own skeletons. My advice," Sam added, "as someone who's been around a few years, don't give up that easily. That one's a keeper." He winked at his son, who smiled in return.

Simon watched a bird hop around the backyard before he spoke again. "You're right. I don't intend to let her go back home without a fight."

"That's my boy," Sam said as the phone began to ring. He picked it up and greeted the caller with an enthusiastic "hello."

Simon could only watch as the color drained from his father's face.

Sam's hand trembled as he pressed the button on the cordless phone to disconnect the call.

"Dad, what is it?" Simon asked, his voice trembling as much as his father's hand.

"It's Tony," Sam said, his own voice shaking. "They found him in a pool of his own blood. He slit his wrists."

45

JULIA BURKE SAT at her desk late Thursday morning, doing her best to concentrate on her work.

This was one of the worst weeks of her life.

There was a long to-do list, but she didn't even know where to start. Since the news broke that Tony Caldwell tried to kill Benny, there had been palpable tension in the office. The only thing that made it easier to deal with was that John was no longer representing him. Everyone knew Benny probably had it coming, but the fact that Simon's brother was the one accused of trying to kill him added to the strain.

Simon left work yesterday as soon as he got word and hadn't returned since. Anybody would understand this must be terribly difficult for him, but she wondered what Simon knew that he might not be saying. He went to visit Tony every week, and Julia suspected he might have picked up on clues that Tony was planning to kill Benny.

That was her opinion, anyway. Not that her opinion mattered much around here. She was fully aware that everyone viewed her as "only an assistant." She knew what that meant; they thought she was no more than a glorified secretary.

With everything that seemed to be happening around the office, Julia had the feeling the rug was about to be pulled out from under her.

Then, there was that woman who came by the office on Monday. Julia didn't know who she was or why she was asking questions about the Stones, but the more she thought about it, the more certain she was that whatever was going on had to do with her.

Who is she? Julia wondered, and what could she possibly want?

Julia made a note in her own special shorthand to find out more about Alexandra Tucker. Should anyone happen to see it, no one would know what it meant. Her shorthand had been a source of frustration for John, who often left notes for her complaining that he could never tell what anything said because of her "nonsensical chicken scratch." Despite his annoyance, she continued using it. It was the perfect way to make notes about things going on around the office in case she ever needed them.

No one had been the wiser.

Her heart rate quickened at the thought of losing everything. She felt dizzy. She stood and rushed to the bathroom. Just before she reached the bathroom door, she heard a voice that seemed miles away ask, "What's wrong with Julia?"

What's wrong? she thought frantically as she rushed into a bathroom stall. What's wrong is that I'm about to lose everything I've worked so hard to build. I left my family, my friends, everything I knew because I was determined to be better than that. I wasn't going to spend my adult life going from one lousy-paying job to the next, freezing in the winter because I couldn't afford heat. I'm just weeks away from becoming everything I vowed I would never be.

She gasped for air. *So this is what a panic attack feels like?* Leaning heavily against the stall door, she was determined not to pass out.

Taking slow, deep breaths to regulate her breathing, she knew this had to stop. She was allowing what was only a possibility to interfere with her work and personal life.

Worrying will do nothing, she reminded herself. *I have to talk to John. He's the only one who can put my mind at ease. Besides, he was generous enough to give me this job in the first place and has been happy with my work. Sure, he's been a little moody lately and seems preoccupied, but I can still talk to him.*

What harm could that do?

46

JOAN SHEPHERD WAS enjoying a brisk walk around the neighborhood, feeling more at peace today than she had in a week. For the first time since Alex found out she was adopted, Joan was beginning to believe things were going to be okay.

She'd been pulling weeds around her mums when the phone rang. It was Jeannie Davidson, calling to tell her she'd talked to Alex this morning.

Jeannie reported that though Alex was clearly exhausted, she seemed to be in good spirits. Since Alex left on her little adventure, Joan had been picturing her depressed and lonely, chasing the ghost of her past. The news that Alex was doing fine encouraged her.

Before hanging up the phone, Jeannie spoke sincerely that although Alex was fine, she was concerned about the effect the whole situation would have on her relationship with Gram. Jeannie shared that Alex was worried Joan would think she wasn't enough family for her, and that Alex knew how painful this must be given her losses the past couple years.

"She loves you, Joan," Jeannie had assured her. "You don't have to doubt that for a moment. She's just confused." Jeannie had paused, then added, "And you know how stubborn Alex can be."

Joan was so grateful for the reassurance she nearly burst into tears before they ended the conversation. After they disconnected the call, tears of relief raced down her cheeks. Unlike the ones she'd cried because of guilt and fear, these felt as though they brought healing.

Buoyed by the encouragement Jeannie had given her, the sun shone a little brighter this afternoon.

Joan paused at her mailbox before turning off the sidewalk and onto her driveway. As she collected the stack of mail, an envelope slipped from her grasp and landed address-side down on the asphalt. She bent to pick it up, looking for the sender as she stood. There was no return address, but the postmark indicated it was sent from Lexington, Kentucky. Eagerly tearing open the envelope, she looked forward to seeing Alex's unique handwriting scrawled across the page.

Instead, she was greeted with words cut from a newspaper and arranged into a message.

Her fears were confirmed. Alex was in danger.

47

BENNY SHIFTED UNCOMFORTABLY in the bed in the prison infirmary. Right after he'd been stabbed, he was taken to the emergency room of a real hospital. After undergoing a minor blood transfusion, the doctors decided he was going to be fine and, seeing no need to tie up a bed for the likes of him, discharged him. He was taken directly to the infirmary, where he'd been the last two days. At least at the hospital he'd been taken care of by female nurses who had a little wiggle in their walk. Now he had burly men poking and prodding him.

Though he'd never been a physically active guy, he didn't know if he'd be able to handle lying in this bed much longer. The few short walks he'd taken up and down the hall every day with his male nurse escort wasn't exactly doing anything to cure his cabin fever. Even his cell was more appealing than being confined to this bed.

About an hour ago, most of the medical staff rushed from the infirmary. They all looked worried. Benny was miffed that no one told him what was going on. He already felt like an invalid and missing something exciting shortened his already barely existent fuse.

He stared at the institutional beige walls, listening to the constant beeping of a machine on the other side of the room, and wondered if there was this much commotion when Tony Caldwell tried to kill him.

Probably not, he thought harshly. They probably waited as long as they could before they called an ambulance, hoping I would die before they got to me. The other inmates hate me, the staff hates me. They all want me dead.

He'd expected to hear from John Carmichael. A note, a phone call, something. They'd been together for over thirty years, after all. But there'd been nothing. Benny was sure he knew about it. Maybe it's 'cause he works with Tony's brother and the office politics are too much for him to handle, Benny thought.

Even before Tony attacked him, Benny hated him. He couldn't put his finger on it, but there was something about Tony that rubbed him the wrong way. Maybe it's because he keeps acting like a Goody Two-shoes. Growing up in a family where his dad was a cop was bound to rub off on him. Then his older brother went and decided to be a lawyer. Poor kid never got to be bad, and when he was, he got caught and his own family showed him no mercy. His old man didn't try to get the charges dropped. His brother wouldn't represent him and left him with some crummy public defender who looked like he was about twelve years old. He didn't stand a chance.

Now he's spending his time in jail, the one place he's surrounded by people who all have the same thing in common—getting caught for doing something bad—and it's like he's seeking some kind of retribution or something. The one place he can be accepted for being who he really is, and he doesn't even have the guts to do it. He's nothing but a coward. Either that or doing something to get thrown in jail was out of character for him.

Benny found that prospect even more disgusting.

He'd never had any patience for people who thought they were better than they really are. Tony was one of those people.

A sneer found its way to Benny's face. *But now he's getting what he deserves. People are finally seeing that the son of the mighty Sam Caldwell is just like the rest of us, that he's not some model prisoner trying to redeem himself for his mistakes.*

Benny's fists clenched and unclenched. His disdain for Tony Caldwell was spiraling into something deeper.

"So, do they think you're going to make it?"

The voice pulled Benny from his rumination. He turned his head toward the door of the infirmary to see Richard Wade standing there.

Benny snorted his response. "Yeah, I'll make it. Isn't the world such a lucky place? If Tony hadn't been such a coward, the doc said he could have finished me off. Lucky for me he *is* a coward."

He watched Richard studying him. *That jerk is going to turn me down,* Benny thought. *The most interesting case he'll probably ever have and he's going to let it slip right by.*

Though he didn't pay any attention to the news, Benny knew that any movement in his case was sure to make headlines. Sheila Stone had been known in many of the elite circles in town, having come from a very wealthy Lexingtonian family. When she married Thomas, he gladly played the part of doting husband and quickly slipped into the role of a young, handsome, blue-blooded lawyer. Benny knew that much about the

Stones. Just the kind of exposure that could help this fellow's career really take off. If he uncovered any new evidence, or at least got grounds for an appeal, it would be all over the news. Richard would have more publicity than he ever dreamed of.

"Then be glad he was too much of a coward to rid us of you," Richard said hurriedly, crossing the room and settling into the chair at Benny's bedside. It was the first visitor Benny'd had since the attack. "Not only do you get to live another day, you get a new lawyer."

Benny's eyes widened. Maybe he'd misjudged the guy, after all. "Well then, welcome to the team. As soon as they let me out of here and I get to go back to my cell, we can start working on my appeal. Now, if you don't mind, he says I need to rest." Benny thrust his thumb in the direction of the scowling nurse who watched from across the room.

Rising from the chair next to Benny's bed, Richard slowly walked toward the door, pausing only once to take a backward glance toward his new client.

When Richard was gone, Benny settled in as comfortably as he could on the lousy excuse for a bed. A smug smile tugged at his lips as he thought about the information he would give Richard. Information he'd never shared with anyone, not even John Carmichael. He could almost see Carmichael's head exploding when he found out what Benny had been sitting on all these years.

48

RICHARD LEANED HIS head against the wall and fought the urge to go back into Benny's room to tell him he'd changed his mind. It had been a struggle to keep those very words at bay as he listened to Benny talk. Benny wasn't grateful to be alive, he was just annoyed that the person who tried to kill him didn't have the guts to finish the job.

Maybe Benny wishes he'd died, Richard thought. His reckless behavior could be part of a death wish.

He asked himself for the hundredth time what he was getting himself into, and what he hoped to accomplish.

It's not too late to back out, his conscience warned again. *You can step back in and tell him the two of you aren't a good fit. It's the truth. In a single minute, you could be free.*

I know, Richard answered himself, but to be part of a case with such a huge spotlight attached, even this late in the game, comes around once in a lifetime. This could be my only shot to get a case like this.

A case that is thirty-two years old and was put to bed three decades ago. The murderer is already in prison, probably congratulating himself for pulling the wool over your eyes. What do you possibly think you could gain from this?

Richard shook his head, trying to squelch the internal argument. Deep down he knew he shouldn't have agreed to take the case, and everyone he consulted warned him it could be a career killer. Even John Carmichael, who'd spent the better part of his career on this scumbag, recommended against it.

Take that as a sign, a small voice in Richard's head advised.

But John has already done the heavy lifting on this case, Richard countered. I probably won't even have to do much. There's no way we will ever have grounds for an appeal, so it'll just be smooth sailing.

After all, what new information could possibly come out after all this time?

49

THE AUTOMATIC DOORS at the entrance of the emergency room whooshed open as Alex rushed through, careful not to spill the two cups of coffee she was balancing. It was no longer sunny and mild as it had been that morning. Overcast and growing colder, Alex couldn't get inside fast enough. As she turned the corner and entered the emergency room waiting area, she was struck by the image of the two men sitting in the corner by the window, their grim faces an extension of the gloom outside.

She slowed her pace as she got closer and stopped a few feet in front of them. Simon was leaning forward in his chair, head resting in his hands, his long fingers flexed in his sandy brown hair. Sam had his wheelchair turned away from her so she could just see enough of his face to note that it was devoid of color. Her heart broke for the two men before her.

As though he sensed he was being watched, Simon looked up. Sam turned toward Alex. Both men had been so deep in thought they hadn't heard her approach.

"I brought coffee," Alex said, extending the cups toward them.

"Thank you," Simon said hoarsely as he took one of the cups. It seemed to take all the energy he had to say those two words.

"What are you doing here?" Sam asked.

She motioned toward Simon. "I called your cell phone. When you didn't answer I called your work number, thinking maybe you decided to go into the office today. I guess the calls from your direct line had been transferred to the secretary. She told me I could find you here." Alex turned toward Sam, motioned toward the cup, and added, "I thought you could use a pick-me-up, and I wanted to see if you needed anything else."

"Thank you," Sam answered as he took a slow sip of the coffee. "We're just in shock."

"I can't even imagine what this has been like for your family. The secretary said Tony was brought here for emergency care. From the looks on your faces, I guess it's serious…"

Sam and Simon looked at each other briefly before Sam spoke. "Yeah, it's serious." He took a deep breath before continuing. "Tony made a suicide attempt."

Alex backed up a few steps and lowered herself into a chair facing them and covered her mouth. She stood slightly and pulled the chair closer so others in the waiting room couldn't hear her. Resuming her seated position, she leaned forward. "That's awful," she whispered. "What happened?"

"One of the guards found him in his cell, lying in a pool of blood. His wrists were cut," Simon answered, his voice shaking.

Alex took one of Sam's hands in her right and Simon's in her left. "I'm so sorry. Did anyone suspect Tony might be suicidal?"

Simon pulled his hand from Alex's grasp. "Tony was *not* suicidal," he said firmly.

"What do you mean he wasn't suicidal?" Sam's voice was incredulous.

"I mean just what I said, Dad. Tony wasn't suicidal, just like he wasn't homicidal. I don't know what's going on at that prison, but somebody is trying to make Tony look like he's coming unhinged." Simon shot to his feet and took a step toward his father. "I can't believe you'd even think he could be capable of either."

Sam leaned forward in his wheelchair in an effort to close the distance between him and Simon. "I know you're angry and upset and scared, Simon. So am I. But you have to remember we're on the same side here. If I learned anything from my years on the police force, it's to never underestimate what people are capable of. If you'll remember, none of us thought Tony would ever sell drugs, either. We were completely floored when he was arrested, but he was guilty. Now, would you please sit down?" he hissed at his son.

Simon reclaimed his seat and leaned toward his dad. "He sold drugs to help pay for Mom's treatment. He knew what he was doing was wrong, but he did it to serve a purpose. He wouldn't have a good reason for trying to kill himself or anyone else. I just don't believe he would do it." Simon shook his head as he spoke.

The two seemed to have forgotten Alex was there, and she felt like an intruder in this sensitive and complicated family situation. She stood to leave.

Sam looked embarrassed. Simon's mouth formed a hard straight line.

They both looked scared.

"I think I should be going. I'm sorry for everything that's happening to your family. Please let me know if there's anything I can do," Alex offered, wishing she could snap her fingers and make everything better.

"You don't have to leave. Really. I'm sorry things got tense. As you can imagine, we're both on edge. Right now, they're pumping buckets of blood into Tony to try to save his life. You can see that it's taking a toll on us." The crack in Simon's voice as he spoke betrayed the intensity of his emotion.

"Of course." Alex indicated the chair she'd been occupying just moments before. "If you're sure?"

"Yes," the father and son said in unison.

"Sit," Sam commanded. "We could use some distraction. Tell us what you've been up to."

"Well," Alex began, "my friend Jeannie called this morning."

"I'm sure it was nice to hear a familiar voice," Sam said tightly.

Alex appreciated his effort to appear interested and squelched the urge to turn the conversation back to their problems. "It really was. We—" she began but was cut short by the approaching doctor.

Simon and Sam simultaneously drew a sharp intake of breath, bracing themselves for bad news.

Already feeling like an intruder and knowing whatever the doctor had to say was better said in private, Alex quickly excused herself and hurried out the door into the dreary cold. One quick look through the window revealed that the doctor had a grim look on his face, relaying the message those in the medical profession are loath to deliver.

50

SUSAN BENTLEY WAS tired. The past several days had been a roller coaster. She'd spent long hours at the office, but not because she had work to do. During the early days of her career, that happened almost every day. Now she stayed because she couldn't stand the thought of going home to her empty condo.

Since Alexandra Tucker had showed up at the office on Monday, Susan was only getting a few hours of sleep each night. The realization that the young woman could be Thomas's daughter hurtled her back to the past, and each night she felt like she was being chased by a ghost.

As if that wasn't enough to deal with, she was still reeling from John's impending retirement. Over the years, the two of them had joked that they'd have to be buried in their offices because neither would ever retire. Susan often had a funny image of a skeleton dressed in her sensible pantsuit sitting at her desk.

It wasn't so funny anymore.

Now that John was bailing, Susan wondered what it would

be like if she were to retire. By design, her caseload wasn't heavy. She'd intentionally been accepting fewer clients the past couple years, so it wouldn't be difficult to wrap up the cases she was working on and stop accepting new clients altogether. There were so many eager young lawyers out there who would be more than willing to buy her share in the firm, she could probably be gone within six months or so.

Then what? she wondered.

The logistics were easy enough. She'd saved more than enough money over the years to fund an early retirement. The financial aspect would be simple. She hadn't spent her money on a family or travel, so it was just sitting there, waiting to be used. It was when she began wondering what she would do with her time that she realized just how empty her life was. She had no husband to take post-retirement trips with, no grandchildren to spoil, and because she'd spent most of her career working a minimum of sixteen-hour days at the office, very few friends. Her colleagues served a dual role as makeshift family and friends, though she wasn't close enough to any of them to really call them that. Her career had been her life, and the thought of walking away from it into a gaping hole of loneliness showed her just how bleak and empty her future really was.

Her past was filled with so many mistakes, so many regrets that she often wondered if she would ever have the chance to live a happy, fulfilled life that didn't revolve around work.

People envied her when they looked at her success, but what did they know? On the outside, she had a thriving career, a nice car, and a condo in one of the most exclusive parts of downtown, but on the inside, she was empty.

The envy of others only served as another way to remind

her that no one really knew her. Her days dragged by, each one running into the next. She no longer enjoyed her work, the days becoming painfully predictable.

Until the day Alexandra Tucker walked into her office.

There was something so unsettling about her. It wasn't just that she undeniably looked like Thomas. Susan thought about the young woman's mannerisms: the way she carried herself, her firm handshake.

They were so familiar.

Is she that much like Thomas? Susan wondered. Or am I just looking for something that isn't there, reliving the past and wishing for what might have been?

She thought she'd buried that part of her life with Thomas. Allowing her mind to wander wouldn't help anything. The past was gone. Thomas was gone.

Despite the promise she'd made to Alex, she had no intention of contacting anyone involved in Thomas's murder case. There'd already been too much sorrow, too much pain brought to the surface by that woman's sudden arrival. Finding out the truth wouldn't stop the ache that had been Susan's constant companion the past thirty-two years.

Some things are better left unknown, she reasoned. Besides, what good could come out of that poor woman finding out her parents are dead?

Susan vigorously shook her head. No, she wouldn't look into the case, and though she'd deny it to anyone who suggested such an absurd thing, she was certain.

Alexandra Tucker was, indeed, Thomas Stone's daughter.

51

"I'M AFRAID TONY has suffered major blood loss," Dr. Reynolds said after introducing himself to Sam and Simon. "When they brought him in, his pulse was faint and erratic. We weren't sure if he'd make it long enough for us to get him into surgery to close the wounds, but he's a fighter. Based on his blood volume when he came in, we estimate he lost about three and a half pints. We gave him an infusion, but it may have been too late."

A low groan tore through the silence. Sam and Simon knew what that meant.

"He's still hanging on, but he's far from stable. The next few hours will let us know if the transfusion is working. I assure you that he'll be under constant supervision, and we're doing everything we can for him."

"Can we see him?" Sam croaked.

The doctor shook his head. "I'm afraid he can't have any visitors right now. Your son is incredibly fragile right now. We'll let you know when and if he stabilizes."

"What are his chances?" Simon asked, casting a sideways glance at his father.

Dr. Reynolds hesitated before answering. "If you're praying people, I suggest you start."

Sam buried his face in his hands as the doctor walked away. Simon sat motionless. Somewhere in the distance the scream of a siren announced an approaching ambulance—a reminder that they weren't the only family members wondering whether or not their loved one would pull through.

The two sat in silence as the minutes stretched on. Sam stole a glance at his oldest son. Simon looked as bad as he felt.

"He's not dead," Simon finally said.

"No, he's not," Sam replied.

"He's going to make it, Dad."

"We don't know that, Simon," Sam said, his voice holding a note of compassion. "He lost a lot of blood—almost half his entire blood volume. You've got to understand, Simon, I worked a lot of cases where people died after losing a lot less blood than that."

"But those people probably had trauma to their internal organs. Your cases probably involved people getting stabbed, or shot, or bashed in the head, right?"

"Yes," Sam acknowledged, pinching the bridge of his nose with his thumb and index finger.

"See?" Simon said and held his hands out in front of him. "Tony's only injuries are the cuts on his wrists. No internal organs were damaged, so he probably has a better chance of surviving than someone who lost a lot of blood because they were stabbed or shot. Right?"

Sam nodded and said nothing. Simon needed to convince

himself that his little brother would be okay, and Sam couldn't bear to bring him any more pain.

"This whole thing is so unbelievable. First he's accused of attempted murder, then he makes an alleged suicide attempt. Why?" Simon wondered aloud.

"Which one are you asking 'why' about?" Sam asked.

"Both. Why would Tony try to kill Benny? We both know he can be a real jerk, but what motivation would Tony have to want him dead? And if he did try to kill Benny, why would he then try to kill himself? It just doesn't make sense." Simon always worked through problems out loud, a habit he picked up as a kid after hearing Sam do the same thing.

"Maybe he figures he'll get a lot more grief because Benny survived, and that once he recovers, Benny will make his life even more miserable. From what we know about Benny, it's not a far leap. Maybe Tony just doesn't think he can take it," Sam suggested.

Simon shot his dad a look of disbelief and, voice growing louder with each word, said, "Why does it sound like you think Tony actually did it?"

"I *don't* think he did it. You were asking why he would have done it. I was giving you reasons, but that doesn't mean any of them are legitimate. Cops weigh different scenarios. I was just giving you one of them."

"Well, there's one scenario no one has considered yet," Simon countered.

"What's that?"

"That he didn't do it."

"Which one?" Sam rubbed his forehead. Between the stress and Simon talking in circles, his head was throbbing.

"Either!" Simon snapped. "Everybody is so sure he's the

bad guy in all this. Has anyone even considered the possibility that he might have been framed for the attempted murder?"

"You and I have," Sam offered, "but probably not anyone else." Sam paused, then said softly, "There was a witness."

"What? I thought the people at the prison said there wasn't one, that the assumption was made because of the argument between Tony and Benny over the weekend."

"A guard came forward and told the warden he saw the whole thing."

"He's lying!" Simon shouted as he bolted from the chair, oblivious to the attention he was drawing from others in the waiting room.

"Be quiet," Sam ordered. "And sit back down. I don't like it when you hover over me." He pointed firmly to the chair Simon had just vacated.

Simon dutifully obeyed and leaned toward his father, lowering his voice. "Why did he wait so long to come forward?"

Sam shrugged. "He said he didn't want to get involved. He's new to the job and hasn't figured out what he should be doing. Apparently he's trying to make friends with the inmates to get on their good side and trying to enforce the rules at the same time. He wants to play nice with the people that could hurt him but wants respect from the other guards. Evidently he's having a hard time finding the balance."

Simon snorted his disapproval. "That's stupid."

"You're telling me," Sam said, rolling his eyes. "But the guy is young. He'll find his way."

The two listened to the sounds around them. Magazine pages being turned, a bad reality show on TV, nervous whispers of family waiting for the news of how someone they love is doing.

It was surreal. How did they, of all families, find themselves in this situation?

"I still think the guard is lying, and I intend to prove it," Simon vowed, sounding like a perturbed teenager who was out to prove the world wrong.

Hours later, Simon and Sam were still in the waiting room. Simon paced constantly while Sam alternated between staring blankly out the window and trying to read the magazines that had been haphazardly cast aside by others in their position.

Just as they decided to go out and grab some dinner, Dr. Reynolds emerged from a door and walked into the waiting room.

Time seemed to stand still as father and son held their breath, watching the doctor close the distance between himself and the men who'd had their lives turned upside down.

52

ALEX WRAPPED HER jacket tightly around her body as she walked across the street. After seeing the pain on the faces of a family she was already beginning to care about, she needed a distraction. Now that Tony was in trouble, she wanted to be there for Sam and Simon.

Unfortunately, it wasn't the time, and it wasn't her place.

She'd come to Lexington for one reason, and she needed to get back to it.

Alex maneuvered her car into the parking garage off Main Street. Relieved to be out of the damp cold, Alex ducked into the Lexington Division of Police. Since she found the articles covering the Stone murders, she'd been wanting to make this visit. A positive DNA match would answer her questions once and for all. Sam had agreed to call ahead and let them know she'd be coming by, but with everything that had been going on the last couple days, she didn't count on it.

"After all," Sam had said, "I was the lead detective on that case, and I still have some pull at the department. If I have a hunch about something, they'll listen."

Maybe they'll listen to me if I drop his name, Alex thought hopefully. Otherwise, she risked looking like a crazy person.

That's a risk I'll just have to take, she reminded herself as she walked through the front door.

Never having been in a police station, Alex hadn't been sure what to expect. Using only the crime dramas she'd seen on TV as a point of reference, she wasn't prepared for the drabness that met her. The gray walls had the institutional feel of a standard government building.

"Can I help you?" asked a tall man with a barrel chest, the buttons on his suit jacket stretched to their limit.

"I hope so," Alex replied with as much charm as she could. Now face-to-face with someone who could take her the rest of the way in her search for her birth parents, her confidence wavered. "I need to speak with someone about a murder."

The detective's deep brown eyes narrowed under perfectly shaped eyebrows.

"Right this way," he said, motioning for her to follow him. They stopped at a cluttered desk in the far-left corner of a large room.

The smell of stale coffee hung in the air and the phone rang incessantly. She'd go crazy working in a place like this.

"Please, have a seat," he offered, pointing to a vinyl chair in front of his desk.

"Thank you." Another glance around as she lowered herself into the chair told Alex the room must still have its original furnishings.

After introducing himself as Detective Adam Bryant, he leaned forward, picking up a pencil and a pad of paper. "Tell me about this possible murder."

Alex winced. It hadn't occurred to her that the police must

get dozens of tips a day, mostly from wackos about crimes that didn't even exist.

He's not out to get you, she reminded herself.

Clearing her throat, she said, "Well, there was definitely a murder. I also think there might have been a kidnapping."

Detective Bryant cocked one of his perfect eyebrows. "And what makes you think there was a kidnapping?"

Composing herself and shaking off the feeling that he was judging her, Alex told him what she'd told everyone else since finding her birth certificate and her mother's journal. "My adoptive parents passed away last year, so they can't answer my questions."

"I understand this must be a very confusing time for you, but I'm afraid *I'm* a little confused about why you think a kidnapping has occurred," Detective Bryant said.

"I believe I'm the child of a couple that was murdered in Lexington thirty-two years ago."

"And who might that be?"

"Thomas and Sheila Stone."

Detective Bryant's forehead wrinkled in a frown under his receding hairline, which obviously didn't get as much care as his eyebrows. "You think you're the kidnapped daughter of Thomas and Sheila Stone?"

Alex was sure she heard skepticism in his voice that time. She looked around, and paranoia set in. She could have sworn people at other desks had stopped what they were doing and were listening intently at the bizarre conversation taking place at Detective Bryant's desk.

"Yes, I do," she said, forcing herself to sound confident. "Sam Caldwell suggested I come by and speak to someone."

That did it. Now she really had his attention.

Detective Bryant leaned back in his chair and laced his fingers together over his broad chest. "Go on."

Picking up where she left off, Alex continued her story, beginning with the vague birth certificate and the articles she read covering the murders. She ended with Sam's statement that evidence from the murder scene was still stored at the station.

She waited.

Finally Detective Bryant spoke. "Even though I was just a kid at the time, I know that case. And I know Sam Caldwell. The official report says their daughter was staying with relatives at the time of the murders, and that those same relatives immediately assumed legal guardianship. If I remember correctly, one of Thomas Stone's coworkers took care of the whole thing. From what I know about the case, there was no kidnapping."

Remembering Sam's own doubts about the fate of the infant, she lifted her chin in determination and said, "I know what the report says, but there are too many coincidences for me to believe that, without proof, I'm not the daughter of Thomas and Sheila Stone."

The lines on Detective Bryant's face had deepened in the last fifteen minutes. "What kind of proof are you looking for? That case has been closed for decades," he said wearily.

Her eyes met Detective Bryant's. "I want you to take a sample of my DNA and compare it to the DNA on the evidence from the murder scene," Alex insisted.

An hour later, Alex walked out of the police department building, satisfied she would soon know the truth, and mentally blessing Sam Caldwell for being such a legend. It was Sam's involvement in her crusade that persuaded them to take the DNA swab.

Seeing a Starbucks at the corner of Main and Broadway when she pulled into the parking garage, Alex decided to run across the street for a cup of coffee. Flipping the collar of her jacket up to shield her neck from the wind and rain, she stopped at a crosswalk and waited. The damp coldness of the day chilled her to the bone, and at this moment she wanted nothing more than the comfort of a cup of hot coffee.

Just before the light turned red, Alex heard a voice say her name as a hand wrapped around her arm while another one found the small of her back. In an instant, she was thrust forward into the path of a pickup truck speeding down Main Street. She turned just in time to have the image of a man burned into her mind. As her head hit the curb and darkness enveloped her, she wondered if she would live long enough to find out if her hunch about her birth parents was right.

53

H E'D WATCHED ALEX as she sat in the waiting room of the emergency room, trying to comfort the man he'd seen her with on Monday. He wondered what was going on. Not that he thought it had anything to do with her personally. She didn't look sick enough for that to be the case.

Not yet, anyway.

She looked worried, but not the same kind of worry as if someone she loved was sick or hurt.

Jealousy barely scratched the surface of what he felt when he watched her with the other man. He would give anything to make Alex be as concerned about him as she was for whoever she was waiting for in the hospital.

The dark circles under her eyes told him she wasn't sleeping enough, and the paleness of her skin communicated that she wasn't taking care of herself like she usually did.

If she'd let him, he would have taken care of her. He wanted so badly to put his arms around her and have her rest her head on his shoulder, even if it was only for a moment.

He'd gladly carry her burdens for her. He'd stroke her hair and tell her everything would be okay, that he was there to make it all better.

But that can never be, he thought, gritting his teeth. She was just another in a long line of women who had rejected him. Women he'd cared deeply for and dedicated his life to treating special, only to be turned down time after time.

He couldn't take it anymore. His patience had worn too thin.

No more, he thought as he watched her standing at the crosswalk. I won't keep letting her treat me as though I don't exist. I do exist, and soon she will have to admit it. Then she'll realize how powerful I really am.

He took a few steps forward, his lips parting to say her name for the last time.

54

"EXCUSE ME, MR. CALDWELL?"

Sam looked up at the smiling nurse standing in front of him. He was so exhausted he hadn't even heard her coming. "Yes?"

"Tony has responded extremely well to the transfusion. His vitals have stabilized, and you can see him now. He's still very weak, so you'll need to limit your visit to only a few minutes."

He nodded, and for the first time since he got the call that morning, Sam allowed himself to hope that Tony might pull through. He looked at Simon, who'd drifted off to sleep only a few minutes before. Seeing no need to wake him now, Sam wheeled past the reception area, and asked that Simon be given the news that Tony had improved if he woke up before Sam returned.

He followed the nurse's brisk pace into the ICU and caught the first glimpse of his youngest son through the glass wall of his room. Sam had been in hospitals dozens—maybe hundreds—of times. His own injuries, the injuries of fellow officers, and the many times Betty had been admitted at the end of her illness ensured he'd had plenty of exposure to the sterile environment that felt anything but comforting. Even so, he wasn't prepared for the sight of his son lying in a hospital bed. Tony's body looked so small, almost shriveled, beneath the blankets that covered him. His face was gray and ghostly pale.

The beeping of the heart monitor was slow and weak, no doubt reflecting Tony's own faint heartbeat. Thick gauze was wrapped around Tony's arms from his palms halfway up his forearms, bearing witness to the reason he was here.

Sam took a deep, steadying breath and moved his wheelchair closer to his son's bedside. When he stopped, he rested a hand on Tony's shoulder.

Tony slowly turned his head to face his father, eyes vacant and breathing shallow. "Hi, Dad," he said weakly.

"Hi," Sam said quietly. "How do you feel?"

"How do I look like I feel?"

"Like garbage," Sam said, forcing a lighter tone into his voice.

"That's about right," Tony agreed. "I'm so tired."

Silence hung between the two, thick with the tension of unasked questions.

How do I ask him what happened? Sam wondered. There's no good way to bring it up.

As though Tony had read his mind, he said, "I didn't do it, Dad."

"Do what?"

"Try to kill Benny. I didn't do it." Though his voice was weak, he was adamant.

Sam winced at how vulnerable and fragile Tony sounded, almost like a child.

"I know," Sam said, nodding his reassurance.

"Do you?" Tony challenged. "I know I've made a mess of my life, and I thought by now you'd be thinking I was capable of anything. Policeman's mentality and all that."

"We all know the reason you did the things you did. We also know you're not a killer." Sam listened to the machines beeping for a moment. "Is that why you tried to kill yourself? Because you thought nobody would believe you?"

Tony held his father's gaze before lowering his eyes to his bandaged arms. He looked again into Sam's worried eyes and said, his voice barely audible, "I didn't do that, either."

"What do you mean you didn't do it? How could that be?"

"I didn't try to kill myself, Dad. I'm not suicidal. Never have been."

Sam's mind whirled in circles. "Then what happened? Was it a plan to get out of prison for a while? Or maybe you thought you'd be found sooner?"

Tony's mouth drooped, his face flushed with color. "No," he objected. "I've never tried to hurt myself, or anybody else, no matter what people say."

A knot of tension worked its way into Sam's shoulders. "Then tell me what happened," he demanded.

Tony's eyes no longer vacant, they now held a look of panic. "I can't."

Sam tightened his grip on Tony's shoulder. "Tell me what's going on. If you didn't do this to yourself, who did?"

Tony turned his head away from Sam and looked at the far wall, indicating he wasn't going to talk anymore.

Always so hardheaded, Sam fumed.

As if on cue, the nurse who'd led Sam to the room announced that his time was up, and that Tony needed to rest.

Sam hesitated, looking at his son before turning to go back toward the lobby, his mind still reeling with questions.

When he reentered the waiting room, Simon was awake and sitting on the edge of his chair, a mixture of relief and concern mingled on his face. The two men looked at each other and Sam shook his head. Simon had been right.

Lifting a determined chin, Sam vowed to himself that he was going to get to the bottom of what was going on at that prison, and that somebody was going to pay for hurting his son.

<h1 style="text-align:center">55</h1>

ALEX CLOSED HER eyes tightly against the bright light overhead. She heard the humming and beeping of machines, hushed voices, and footsteps in the distance.

Where am I? her brain demanded.

Confused and disoriented, she forced her eyes open slightly and moved them slowly around the room. Her head pounded and a wave of nausea washed over her. Rolling to her side, she fought the urge to throw up.

What happened to me?

She reached up to rub her eyes, her hand grazing a bandage on her forehead. A blood-pressure cuff squeezed her right arm.

I'm in a hospital, she realized. But why?

The door of her room opened. A man wearing scrubs appeared. Doctor, nurse, janitor—she didn't care who he was.

"You're awake," he said in a soothing voice.

"Yes, but what am I doing here?" she asked.

"You took a bit of a spill and have suffered a concussion,"

the man said in the same soothing tone. "Can you tell me the last thing you remember?"

Alex inhaled deeply, trying to pull an image from her battered brain. Her mind worked backward the best it could until she was able to see a clear picture of where she'd been. "I was in a hospital. A friend's brother had gotten hurt, and I went to see if he was okay," she began slowly, closing her eyes to visualize what had happened. "A doctor came into the waiting room to speak with the family, so I left. It wasn't my business."

"And after that?" the man urged.

"I drove downtown to the pol—" She froze. For now, that part was better left unsaid.

"And?" he prodded gently.

"And that's it," Alex lied. "I don't remember anything after that."

"Okay," he said, bobbing his head as though he accepted her forgetfulness. "How are you feeling?"

For the first time since the man entered the room, Alex really looked at him. He had thin, sandy brown hair and wore oval, wire-rimmed glasses. The badge clipped to his scrub top said his name was Daniel Proth, M.D.

So, he's a doctor, she thought, relieved. He can help me feel better. "Like my head is going to explode and I'm going to vomit."

He smiled warmly. "I'm afraid those are symptoms of the concussion. I'll send a nurse in with some painkillers for the headache and something to help control the nausea," he offered.

"Thank you," she whispered, eternally grateful her doctor had a good bedside manner.

At the door, Dr. Proth paused. "There are two men who

are waiting to see you, whenever you feel up to it. Sam and Simon Caldwell. They're in the waiting room."

"Maybe once the meds kick in," she said, closing her eyes. She didn't stand a chance of having a coherent conversation without them. "And Dr. Proth? Nothing that will make me too drowsy, please?"

"Of course," he said, then left the room quietly. Minutes later, a nurse came in with medication and a small cup of water. After Alex swallowed the pills, the nurse left as quickly as she came.

A half hour later, Simon and Sam sat at her bedside. The medication helped tremendously at curbing the nausea, and though her head still hurt, the pain had decreased to a dull ache.

"How did you know I was here?" Alex asked, trying to sit up. Her head made it no more than a few inches before she dropped it back to the pillow. It wasn't worth the effort.

"We were leaving through the emergency room exit when we saw an ambulance stop and the paramedics pull out a stretcher. We saw it was you and that you were unconscious, so we stuck around." Worry lines creased Simon's face even though he tried to smile. His face became more serious. "What happened to you? Since we're not family, nobody will tell us anything."

Alex shrugged one shoulder against the pillow. "I have no idea. After leaving the hospital, I drove to the police station." She looked at Sam. "They agreed to run a DNA comparison, thanks to some name-dropping." She managed a wink and a weak smile. "Anyway, since the day had gotten so cold, I decided to run across the street for a latte. That's the last thing

I remember before waking up here. The doc said I took a spill, so I guess I must have slipped."

The three of them grew quiet. "You two really should go home," Alex urged. "You have spent too much time in a hospital already today. You don't need more time here. I'm fine here by myself. Go home, get some dinner and some rest, and try to forget everything for a few hours. It will do you both a world of good."

Sam and Simon nodded in agreement. Simon stood and they started toward the door. A woman carrying a dinner tray from the cafeteria entered her room and slid it onto the table, then positioned it over Alex's bed.

"Thank you," she said as the woman turned and walked out of the room.

"Oh, and have you heard anything about Tony?" Alex asked as she lifted the lid off her tray and scowled.

"I got to see him," Sam offered. With a relieved breath, he said, "I think he'll be okay."

"That's great! How is he? What did he say?"

"He said he didn't do it," Simon interjected.

"Try to kill Benny? You already knew that," she said, pushing the table holding her unappetizing dinner away.

"He also said he didn't try to kill himself," Sam added.

"Then what happened? He had the injuries. If he didn't do it, that would mean somebody else did and tried to make it look like a suicide attempt." Alex rubbed her temples. That didn't last long, she mused. Her headache was already coming back.

Simon pressed his lips together to form a hard line. "Exactly," he said. "I never believed Tony was suicidal in the first place. Homicidal either." He stole a sideways glance at his father. "From the time the prison called to tell us what happened, I knew there was something wrong." Simon took a step closer to Alex's bed and lowered his voice. "I think Tony's alleged suicide attempt is a cover-up for what really happened to Benny. Whoever tried to kill Benny also tried to keep Tony quiet about being framed. I'd put money on it."

"Does Tony know who it was?" Alex asked, still rubbing her head.

"Yes," Sam interjected.

"Who did it?" It was getting harder to focus through the pain.

"He wouldn't say. He's really spooked, though. He won't tell me anything, just that he didn't do it. Whoever did has really gotten to him, and I don't know if there's any way to get him to talk to us. We're the only ones who believe him, so I can see why he'd be afraid, but we're his family. No active law enforcement official is going to take the word of a convicted criminal over that of a prison guard who claims he was a witness to Tony's attack on Benny."

Alex narrowed her eyes, and this time it wasn't because the overhead light made her headache worse.

"You're on to something," Sam observed.

"It's probably nothing." She looked at Simon. "Didn't you tell me that pretty much everybody hated Benny?"

Simon snorted. "That's an understatement. Anybody who ever met him wanted to kill him. I'm actually surprised it took someone this long to try. Why do you ask?"

"Is there anybody Benny has confided in? Somebody who might know another reason someone might want him dead. Or who might want to see him killed?"

Simon shrugged. "I don't know. He's got a cellmate, so that

might be our best shot. I can try to find out, though. What are you thinking?"

"Just that if Benny treats everyone that badly, there might be someone we don't know about who could have tried."

A frown creased Sam's forehead as he weighed the possibility. "It's a thought, I guess."

"I'm probably wrong. I blame the head injury. Now, you two go get some dinner and relax," Alex ordered. "I could use some rest, too."

"Yes, ma'am." Simon's exaggerated bow brought a small smile to her lips. "I'll come back later and bring you something decent to eat."

Alex closed her eyes and, still smiling, said, "Make it Italian."

With that, Sam and Simon left, and Alex was alone again. She drifted off to sleep, only to be woken by a faint knock on the door. Forcing her eyes open, she saw a uniformed officer standing in the doorway.

As the officer approached, she introduced herself to Alex. "Therese DiVito, Lexington police."

"What can I do for you, Officer DiVito?" Alex asked. Being startled awake made her headache worse.

"I need to talk to you about your accident," Officer DiVito began. "Can you tell me what happened?"

Officer DiVito was strictly business, and whatever accent she had grated on Alex's already frayed nerves. There was definitely no melodic Southern drawl when she spoke.

"I can try," she offered, "but I don't know how much help I'll be. I remember going to get a cup of coffee and that I was cold and in a hurry. I guess I slipped. That's all I can tell you. I'm sorry I don't remember anything else."

Officer DiVito held eye contact for several seconds before speaking. "We have reason to believe your accident might not have been an accident at all."

"I don't understand," Alex said, trying to focus on the information instead of the splitting pain in her head.

"A witness has come forward. He claims he saw someone push you."

"Push me? Who would want to push me?" Alex asked. This was ridiculous. She had no enemies.

She pressed the button to call for the nurse. If she was going to be able to make sense of what Officer DiVito had just said, she'd need more painkillers.

Therese DiVito pressed on. "Have you had an argument with anyone recently? A disagreement?"

"Not really. I don't even live around here. I've been here less than a week."

A different nurse than before came in. Alex asked for more pain meds, and when the nurse returned, Alex downed them with the water in one gulp.

"Can I have a few minutes before you ask me anything else? The pain makes it hard to concentrate."

Officer DiVito agreed, and after a long stretch of silence, the pain started to subside. "You're not from around here, are you?" Alex asked when the hammering in her head stopped.

"New Jersey transplant," the officer offered, then went back to business. "What brings you to Lexington?"

Alex considered the question and decided to be straightforward. She'd already been to the police station, so Officer DiVito would find out eventually. She gave an abbreviated version of the story, content to let the officer find out the rest from someone else.

"So you started looking here?"

Alex nodded, the back of her head still pressed against the pillow. "I didn't know what else to do. I spent my first day here at the public library, poring over old newspaper articles beginning with my birth date. That's when I found articles about two murder victims who had an infant daughter. I thought it was worth a shot, so I started there."

"You believe you're the daughter of the couple who were murdered," Officer DiVito clarified.

"I do."

She pulled out a pen and paper. "Who were the victims?"

"Thomas and Sheila Stone."

A knowing look crossed the officer's face. She pointed her pen in Alex's direction. "You're the one who came into the station today asking for a DNA comparison." Noticing Alex's frown, she added, "People talk."

"I guess they do," Alex said in a flat voice, wondering how many jokes she was the butt of around the police department.

"If you'll excuse me, I need to step outside and make a call," Officer DiVito said as she rose from the chair and stepped into the hall, pulling the door shut behind her.

Alex laid still, trying to regain her equilibrium. The room spun, but not because of the head injury. Someone had deliberately pushed her off the curb, intending to kill her.

But why?

She swallowed another wave of nausea, this time because somebody wanted her dead.

56

WITHIN THE PAST two days, Tony Caldwell had been accused of attempted murder, then his wrists were cut to make it look like he was trying to kill himself. If he'd had a worse week in his life, he couldn't remember it. Even when he was arrested for dealing drugs it hadn't been this bad.

Only losing his mother came close.

He wasn't as tough as most of the guys in prison, but he kept to himself and didn't say much. Over time he'd learned to look at people in a way that made them think he was more dangerous than he really was.

He owed his survival behind bars to his ability to adapt.

Except now people thought he was full of rage and took it out on Benny Johnson. Failing, of course.

Prison life was about to get a whole lot harder. Other inmates would see him as weak, and he'd be forever branded a coward.

His pulse crept upward.

Only his father had been allowed to see him in the ICU, and he'd said too much.

Why did I have to open my mouth? Tony berated himself. Why did I tell him I didn't do this? The cop in him is going to start wondering how someone else could have pulled off a staged suicide attempt—and why somebody would even want to. He's going to start poking around to find out who's behind it, and I'll be in big trouble.

Tony hadn't lied to his father when he'd asked who did this to him. He honestly didn't know. All he knew was that someone had grabbed him from behind, whispered a threat in his ear, then hit him on the head with something. He remembered the hot breath on his ear and the smell of nervous sweat on his attacker, but that was it. The next thing he knew, he was waking up in the hospital, bandages halfway up his arms. It wasn't until he heard the hospital staff talking when they thought he was still unconscious that he put everything together.

He'd almost told them what happened, then remembered the threat and kept his mouth shut. Now somebody watched him constantly, making sure he didn't find a way to hurt himself in the hospital room. He couldn't shake the feeling that if it wasn't for the injuries on his wrists, he'd be in restraints right now.

A soft knock at the door interrupted Tony's thoughts. He recognized the man as Dr. Gray, the psychiatrist he met shortly after regaining consciousness. He'd been pretty out of it when they spoke and wondered what he'd said to warrant another visit.

"Good evening, Mr. Caldwell. How are you feeling?" Dr. Gray's greeting was pleasant enough, but for some reason

Tony got the impression he'd rather be anywhere else other than talking to him.

He never knew how to respond when that question came from a mental health professional. Were they really concerned with his well-being, or were they hoping he'd tell them the voices in his head made him do it?

"I guess I'm doing okay, considering…" Tony waved a bandaged arm around the hospital room, careful not to tug the tubes running from his arm.

"I'm sure it's not very comfortable to be stuck in that bed all the time," Dr. Gray said.

Tony shook his head. He was an active guy, and would be completely miserable if he wasn't so tired.

"Have you had any more thoughts about harming yourself?"

"Just that I'll need to try harder next time, Doc," Tony said dryly.

Alarm flitted across the psychiatrist's face, and Tony mentally kicked himself for trying to joke with someone who could order him to be put in a straitjacket.

Eyebrows still raised, Dr. Gray said, "So, you're going to keep trying until you succeed?"

The statement hung between them.

"No, I'm not," Tony ground out. Why wouldn't this guy just let him sleep? "I'm not going to do anything to hurt myself." He'd heard from other inmates that a lot of these guys just want a verbal commitment or a signed paper saying you agree not to hurt yourself. As if that would really stop someone who was determined to end it, Tony thought, wondering if the agreement was meant to protect the client or if it was to keep the shrink out of trouble if the client happened to be successful.

"You're having second thoughts about whether or not you really want to die. That's very good." Relief flooded his words, as though he'd just had a major breakthrough with Tony. "You know, sometimes we get overwhelmed with life. Everybody does. It can seem like the situation we find ourselves in is too hard and we don't see a way out. Many people use suicide as an escape hatch so they won't have to face their problems. Unfortunately, they don't realize that things will get better if they just hang on."

Tony fought an eye roll at the psychobabble, and instead nodded in agreement.

Let this guy think he's getting through to me. Maybe then he'll leave me alone.

A few months ago, an inmate and one of the few friends he had on the inside, Alan O'Brian, was found hanging by a bedsheet in his cell. Tony'd noticed that Alan seemed a little down but hadn't even considered it could be anything more than him just being sick of prison. He found out after the fact that Alan had been struggling with depression since he'd been found guilty of manslaughter a year earlier after causing a traffic accident that claimed the lives of two children. Apparently he'd never forgiven himself and believed death was a more fitting punishment for his crime than sitting in a cell for fifteen years.

Tony was genuinely upset when he learned of Alan's death. Like Tony, Alan was an otherwise decent guy who'd made a few stupid mistakes and would be paying for them for the rest of his life. Only Alan decided the rest of his life didn't mean much and decided it wasn't worth living. That was where the similarity to Alan O'Brian ended.

That, and Tony's bad decision hadn't resulted in someone ending up dead. Maybe if it had, Tony would have given the whole suicide idea some thought.

"I'm not overwhelmed with life, Dr. Gray. I'm managing just fine," Tony said. Better than a lot of guys, anyway, he added to himself.

Dr. Gray looked briefly at the folder lying in his lap, then back at Tony. "I see there have been some issues between you and another inmate."

Great, Tony thought. He knows about Benny. Now this guy probably thinks I'm a homicidal maniac. "There have been, yes," Tony agreed. "He has issues with everybody."

"I also see you tried to kill him," Dr. Gray said, the color draining from his face as though he was suddenly aware he might be in the room with a killer.

"That's what the file says." There was no point disputing it now. No one would believe him. He just needed to play the part of the reformed sinner and let the whole thing blow over.

"Tell me more about that."

"What does the file say? How can I possibly tell you more when I don't know what you already know?" Tony bit his tongue. His mouth was going to get him in trouble again.

Dr. Gray cleared his throat, shifted uncomfortably in his chair and read over his notes. Tony took a sick pleasure in watching him squirm.

"It says you and the victim had an altercation in the exercise yard the weekend before the incident. You made some threats, then several days later an eyewitness saw you stab him in the stomach with a shiv."

The silence that followed told Tony that Dr. Gray wanted him to fill in the gaps.

He didn't.

After several minutes of listening to the hospital sounds interrupting the silence in the room, Dr. Gray finally spoke. "Is there anything you'd like to add?"

"Nope. That pretty much says it all." Tony was getting tired and wanted to be left alone.

"Would you mind telling me your motivation for trying to kill this man?" Dr. Gray prodded.

"I would mind. Now if *you* don't mind, I'd like to get some rest. A near-death experience really takes it out of you." Tony inhaled deeply, settled his head deeper into his pillow, and closed his eyes.

Finally, he heard the chair squeak as Dr. Gray stood. Before exiting the room, he said quietly, "I'll be back tomorrow. I believe we have more to talk about."

"Whatever you say, Doc," Tony mumbled to the empty room through clenched teeth.

He should have cooperated with the psychiatrist's questions, he knew that, but he was just so tired of everyone thinking he was guilty of things he didn't do.

So much for being presumed innocent until proven guilty. Everybody already assumes I'm guilty and won't believe me when I tell them I'm not.

Tony sighed. Maybe he was just fooling himself and everyone was right about him after all.

57

S IMON HURRIED DOWN the hall toward Alex's hospital room carrying a bag of takeout from his favorite Italian restaurant. At the sound of a woman's voice, he stopped just before turning the corner and walking down the corridor that led to Alex's room.

"I know you thought she was a nutcase, but you need to have that DNA run ASAP," the woman hissed into her phone.

Simon waited while she listened to the person at the other end of the call. "I don't buy that," she said. "We have a witness claiming she was pushed into oncoming traffic just minutes after coming to the station requesting to have her DNA compared to evidence from an old murder case. There is something to her hunch, I know there is," she urged, then listened again as the other person spoke. "Thank you! I owe you one."

It wasn't an accident. Somebody meant to hurt Alex, Simon thought frantically.

"Yes, sir. I know you won't forget. Call me as soon as you get the results," she requested, then pressed the button to disconnect the call.

Simon waited several seconds, then turned the corner to Alex's room. He knocked lightly on the door and pushed it open just in time to hear the woman who'd been on the phone—a police officer, judging by her uniform—say goodbye to Alex and make the promise to let her know if she learned anything else. She nodded briefly in Simon's direction, then left the room.

"You were pushed?" Simon blurted once the officer was out of earshot.

Alex ignored the question. "Do I smell Italian food?"

"Don't try to change the subject, Alex," he admonished. "You were pushed."

Alex cleared her throat. "Apparently a witness has come forward claiming they saw someone push me, yes."

"How can you be so calm about this?" Simon shook his head in disbelief.

Taking a deep breath, then wincing, Alex said, "I'm not convinced anybody actually did push me. It's much more likely that I slipped. Who would possibly want to kill me? I don't know anybody here except you and your dad, and unless I'm really getting on your nerves, I'm not aware of anyone who'd want me dead. Really, I'm not sure it was anything more than an unfortunate accident."

He shook his head firmly. "That police officer seems to think something different. I heard her on the phone, and she made it perfectly clear to whoever she was talking to that she's convinced your 'accident' is directly related to the fact that you went to the police station today asking them to run your DNA. Are you seriously going to try to make me believe it's not related? She's pretty sure it is." Simon hooked his thumb over his shoulder in the direction that the police officer left.

"Simon," Alex said quietly, "Please settle down. You're making too big a deal of this."

"And you're not making a big enough deal of it!" he countered, his voice rising with each word. "You come to a new city and start poking around in an old murder case, one that has had question marks around it from the beginning, and now there's a police officer claiming to have a witness that saw you intentionally pushed into traffic. How can I not make a big deal of this?"

"What do you expect me to do?" She held her hands out in a gesture indicating she was willing to take any advice he could offer.

"Be more careful. You're making somebody nervous, and they've already gone after you once. What if they don't stop?"

"I'm not giving up, Simon," Alex said, a determined thrust to her chin. "I came here to find out where I came from and I'm not leaving until I have answers."

Simon dropped into the chair at her bedside and grasped her hand. "I'm not asking you to give up," he said softly. "I'm just asking you to be careful. If something happened to you…"

Alex's eyes met Simon's. He was sure she could see right through him and see that he was falling for her. "I'll be careful, I promise," she said, her tone gentle. Her gaze wandered to the bag of takeout sitting at Simon's feet. "So, what's in the bag? The nausea is mostly gone and I'm starving."

Simon reluctantly let go of her hand and reached for the bag. "Your choice of chicken Parmesan or fettuccine Alfredo. I didn't know which you'd prefer."

"Alfredo." She paused and chewed her lip for a moment. "Will you join me?"

Simon was buoyed by the hope in her eyes. "I'd love to,

if that's okay. I called ahead and ordered the food, then Dad and I picked it up. I dropped him off at home with his dinner, then I came here."

"Is he okay by himself tonight? This has been such a hard day for the two of you, maybe it would be best if you were with him," Alex suggested.

Hearing the disappointment in her voice, Simon smiled. "He insisted I eat dinner with you. I think he's trying to play matchmaker." Not that anybody has to work that hard on me, he thought. Instead, he said, "Besides, nobody tried to kill *him*. I am starting to feel like everybody is just trying to get rid of me, though."

Alex ignored the remark. "Can I ask one more favor of you?"

"Another one?" Simon joked. "I already brought the Italian food you asked for."

The corners of her mouth lifted in a smile. "You did. Thank you. Jackson has been cooped up at my hotel all day. Would you be able to stop by tonight and take him for a short walk and feed him? He's bound to be going stir-crazy."

"I'll do better than that," Simon said over the crinkling bag and the squeak of the takeout containers. "I'll take him back to my place tonight. He can keep me and Murray company."

Alex's face lit up at the suggestion. "Are you sure you wouldn't mind watching him? I think they're just keeping me overnight for observation, so I should be out sometime tomorrow."

"Don't worry about us, we'll be fine. You'll know he won't be lonely so you can just focus on healing."

Alex nodded. "Okay. Thank you for that."

"No problem," he said as he divvied up the plastic utensils

and napkins. Balancing his chicken Parmesan on his knees, he took a bite. It was the first thing he'd eaten since they got the news about Tony late that morning.

"The doctor probably wouldn't approve of this, given the state of my head and the nausea I had earlier," Alex said with her mouth full of fettuccine.

"Probably not," Simon agreed, his own mouth full of food. "Have you called your grandmother?"

"Oh no," Alex moaned and set her fork down. "I completely forgot. Between the pain, the police officer, and you, I've been so distracted I didn't even think about it." She looked around the small room. "I don't know where my stuff is. Do they keep personal belongings somewhere when a person is admitted?"

"I'll check." Simon wiped his mouth on his napkin. "While I'm looking, try to enjoy your pasta and figure out what you're going to say to your grandmother. She's going to be upset, and you'll try to minimize the situation like you did with me. You might want to come up with a more convincing argument than you had earlier." With a quick smile that communicated she wasn't fooling anybody, he left the room.

58

A LEX BARELY NOTICED when Simon left the room. He was right, of course. She hadn't been convincing when she protested the idea that someone had deliberately pushed her into traffic. Add that to the fact that Gram was already so worried about her, and it was a guarantee that this news wouldn't go over well.

What should I say? she wondered as she absently took another bite of pasta.

I'll tell her exactly what I told Simon, she decided. I'll tell her that it was an accident. It had been raining and I lost my footing on the curb. Since there was no actual proof that her tumble onto Main Street had been anything other than an accident, there was no need to make her grandmother more worried than she already was.

Simon returned a few minutes later holding a plastic bag with her name scrawled across the front. She took the last bite of fettuccine and reached for the bag. "Sorry I didn't wait for you. That's the best Alfredo I've ever had."

Simon released the bag into her hands. "It's one of my favorites, too."

Breaking the seal on the plastic bag, Alex pulled out her purse, opened it, then gasped. The index card containing the warning that had been taped to her hotel room door was stuck to the back of her phone.

"What's wrong?" Simon asked, already digging back into his dinner. A string of melted cheese hung from the corner of his mouth and stuck to his chin.

"Nothing," Alex lied. "Just worried about how Gram will react. This is the last thing she needs."

When did I put that note in my purse? she wondered as she selected her grandmother's number from her list of contacts. As it rang, she said to Simon, "I'll only be a few minutes."

Joan answered on the fourth ring, just before her answering machine picked up.

"Hi, Gram," Alex said, forcing her greeting to sound cheerful.

"Alex, are you okay?"

"Yes. Are you?"

"Not in the least. I got a call from the police telling me you'd been in an accident, then I haven't been able to get through to you all day. I thought you might be dead. Why didn't you call sooner?" Joan scolded.

Once again it struck Alex how closely tied fear and anger were to each other.

"The hospital staff had my phone. I just got it back."

"What happened? I want you to tell me the truth..." Joan ordered.

Alex sighed. This was her one shot at convincing Gram that there was nothing nefarious going on. "I fell off a curb and hit my head. They said I have a concussion and are keeping me in the hospital overnight for observation. It's just a precaution and standard protocol, from what I've heard. I'll be out tomorrow, so there's no need to worry."

"Maybe I should come up there," Joan suggested.

"No, don't," Alex said too quickly. "I'm okay, really. Please, try not to worry."

"How can I not be worried? You're in the hospital!"

Alex started to roll her eyes, but it hurt. "I know, Gram, but I'm fine. I've got somebody to take care of Jackson tonight. He even brought me dinner so I didn't have to eat the horrible hospital food." She glanced at Simon, who wiggled his eyebrows at her.

"He?" Joan said, the worry in her voice being replaced with curiosity.

Alex could almost see her grandmother's radar going up. She'd been on Alex to get married and give her great-grandkids for the past couple years. She'd even suggested to Alex that she should marry Steven.

"Yes, Gram, he. I met him on Monday. He and his father have been helping me sort some things out."

"Did you find something?" Gram queried.

She glanced at Simon. The corner of his mouth twitched, and she had to keep from chuckling. "Maybe. It's too soon to tell," Alex said, hoping her noncommittal answer would curb her grandmother's curiosity about the male company she'd been keeping the last couple of days.

"Alex?" Gram said after several long moments of silence.

"Yeah?"

Hesitation. "Please be careful."

"I will, Gram," Alex promised. "I love you."

Alex disconnected the call with the nagging feeling that her grandmother had been about to tell her something, then changed her mind.

59

J OAN BRACED HERSELF against the arm of the sofa. She hoped she made the right decision by keeping the letter she'd received earlier in the day to herself.

The whole time Alex was talking, Joan couldn't bring herself to sit down. Since the police called late that afternoon, she hadn't been able to stop pacing. It was too much of a coincidence that Alex had that kind of accident so close to the time Joan got the letter. Frank never believed in coincidences, and Joan found herself thinking he might have been on to something. Whoever sent the letter demanded that Joan stop Alex from looking into who her birth parents were, and that if she didn't, Joan would never see her again.

From the looks of things, whoever sent that letter was making good on the threat. Though Alex insisted her fall was an accident, Joan suspected differently.

The letter was a warning, and no matter what Alex said, the so-called "accident" was a deliberate attempt on Alex's life. It had to be.

Joan's chest clenched. She gasped for breath.

Alex had come so close to dying.

When the police called to inform her that Alex had been in an accident and that she was in the emergency room, Joan's thoughts immediately drifted to the letter before settling on the possibility of losing her only grandchild.

A knot of dread settled in Joan's stomach. If whoever sent the letter was responsible for Alex's accident, would he keep trying until he succeeded in killing her?

Even Alex's upbeat assurance that she was okay and that her overnight stay in the hospital was just a precautionary measure didn't ring true. She could tell Alex was rattled.

Does she know it might have been premeditated? Joan wondered. If she does, that would explain the strain in her voice. Or maybe she's just trying to protect me.

Alex's brief pause when Joan asked if she'd found anything was all the answer she needed. She had, and it was important.

Important enough to make someone try to kill her.

But what did she find? Joan wondered. And why would it make someone feel threatened enough to want her dead?

60

STEVEN SLAMMED THE shot glass down on the bar. The fourth one never burned as much as the first, and the seventh never burned as much as the fourth. He slid the glass toward the bartender, who was looking at him with disapproval as he refilled it.

Up yours, Steven thought as he grabbed the glass and in one quick motion downed the amber liquid. I don't need you passing judgment on me.

Again, Steven slid the glass forward.

"I think you've had enough, buddy," the bartender said. "Go on home and try to sleep off whatever's bothering you. And take a cab."

Steven narrowed his eyes and stared at the man behind the bar. A hulking guy of about six feet four inches and an easy two hundred pounds, he dwarfed Steven's five-nine but stocky frame. Deciding it wasn't worth the trouble, Steven smacked down a twenty and slid unsteadily off the stool. "Keep the change," he slurred as he stumbled toward the door and out into the cool evening air. He plopped down onto a bench, wallowing in self-pity.

Joan had called a few hours ago to tell him about Alex's accident and that she was nearly killed. Bouncing between tears and anger, Joan all but accused him of having something to do with it.

"How could I have possibly done anything to her?" he'd asked. "You told me she was out of state."

"She is," Joan confirmed, "but I got a threatening letter in the mail today, Steven. With the way you've been acting since I agreed to help you get back together with Alex, I've been wondering what kind of person you really are."

Despite his protests, Joan didn't waver. She'd even had the nerve to threaten him if he hurt Alex in any way.

Like you could ever hurt me, old lady, he'd wanted to say.

If she knew what kind of man I am, she wouldn't have even tried to threaten me, Steven assured himself. *But she might be starting to suspect who I am,* his subconscious warned. *Be careful.*

A cab pulled up to the bar. Figuring the bartender called it for him so he wouldn't try to drive home, Steven rose on wobbly legs and, teetering like he was just learning to walk, went over and got in.

"Take me anywhere," he mumbled to the cabbie, then leaned his head back and fell asleep.

The scene that played out in his mind when he drifted off was the image of Alex, tumbling forward into traffic, barely escaping death.

61

"HAVE YOU TAKEN care of our little problem?"

"I'm working on it," John hissed. First thing Friday morning and Clarence was already hassling him.

"Well, you better do it soon. Otherwise, our little problem is going to turn into a big problem."

"I said I'm working on it," John growled. Clarence had pushed his last button. His plan to lay low until he decided what to do wasn't panning out.

"I hear you. Just make sure—"

John slammed the phone down before Clarence could finish his sentence. Elbows resting on his desk, he dropped his head into his hands and began planning his escape. He inhaled deeply and tried to calm himself while considering the irony of his life. He was desperate to get away from everything that used to matter most.

A soft knock at the door interrupted his thoughts. Julia's concerned face appeared. "Is everything okay, John?"

He had no way of knowing if she'd been listening to his

conversation with Clarence or not. He held his breath, waiting for her to give him some indication she had.

"Can I talk to you about something?" she continued when John didn't respond.

I guess she didn't hear, he thought. "Sure," he said and motioned to one of the high-backed leather chairs in front of his desk.

As Julia sat, she took a deep breath. Looking at her hands, she said, "I'm worried about my job."

"What about it?"

"When you retire, what will happen to me? You hired me, someone else might fire me. Our arrangement won't work if you're not here."

Who cares? John thought impatiently. My life is falling apart, and you want me to care about your *job*? Instead, he said, "I understand your concern, Julia, but as I've told you before, all I can do is recommend to my replacement that they consider keeping you. The rest will depend entirely on him or her. I'm sorry I can't do more."

"Try," she demanded coldly.

"Julia," he began calmly. "I've told you what I can do. As you just said, our arrangement is between us. If someone else doesn't want to have the same one with you, I can't help that. I'm sorry."

"You're not going to get out of this that easily, *Mr. Carmichael*," Julia spat. "You forget you're not the only one with power. I know a thing or two that could bury you, and all the prestige you've enjoyed would be gone. Poof." She opened her hand as if she was releasing something.

"It would be wise to keep what you know to yourself," John warned.

"Then I need a guarantee. If I don't keep my job, I'm going to need money. I'm not going back to flipping burgers. Not now, not ever." She shook her head emphatically.

"And what do you presume I do about that?"

"Think about it, Mr. Big Shot. If this little—" she wiggled her fingers, "arrangement between us falls through, we might just have to consider making a new one. One where you agree to help me keep the life I've become accustomed to, and I keep my mouth shut about anything and everything that's ever come out of this office." Julia's words were pure venom.

John glared at her, regretting his decision to hire her despite what he knew about her. He hadn't felt this kind of disgust toward another person since he was the guy all the popular kids picked on.

Finally, he looked away from her and let his gaze rest on the globe in the back corner of his office. Julia's triumphant smile told John she thought she'd just won the stare down. The fact was, he just couldn't stand to look at her.

"Fine," John agreed. "I'll make sure you're taken care of. If I were you, though, I'd start looking for a new job anyway. You have no business working in a place like this."

"You're one to talk," she mocked. "All these decent, law-abiding citizens would drop dead if they knew who you really were."

"Ditto." John felt like a child on the playground, but he'd reached his limit with Julia.

He'd reached his limit with everyone.

Julia got up and stalked toward the door, then turned to face him. "We do make a good pair, John Carmichael. It would be a shame if all this had to come to an end." With that, she pulled the door open and walked back to her desk. She hadn't closed the door all the way, and from where he sat, he could see her smiling and talking to one of the other assistants.

If she knew what I know about Julia, he thought, she would think twice about telling her anything.

Out of his anger came a moment of perfect clarity. He'd somehow thought of a solution to his problem. Clarence would finally get off his back, and he could go anywhere in the world he wanted.

But before that, he reminded himself, I have unfinished business to take care of.

62

ALEX WOKE FRIDAY morning feeling sore but refreshed. She gathered the few personal items she'd had with her when she was admitted to the hospital and dressed in yesterday's clothes, shuddering at the streak of dirt on the front of her sweater.

That must be where I hit the asphalt, she thought.

A chill raced down her spine at the fact that someone might have intentionally pushed her. Despite an apparent eyewitness, denial was a powerful coping tool.

A nurse came into Alex's room carrying discharge paperwork. She signed it quickly, ready to be away from the smell of disinfectant and the cold, white walls. Officially homesick, she longed to be home in her own apartment with her own things.

She'd had enough adventure.

After briefly telling Alex what symptoms she should be watching for and which ones warranted a visit to a medical professional, the nurse told Alex she was free to go.

Remembering her car was still in a parking garage downtown, Alex called a taxi. Twenty minutes later, when she was in her own car, she finally began to feel herself relax. The familiar smells and feel of the upholstery she'd sat on thousands of times comforted her.

Simon had been planning to go to the office today, so he'd given Alex a key to his apartment before he left the hospital last night. Double checking the address he'd written on a scrap of paper, she pulled into the parking lot of his apartment complex.

Still sore from the impact of hitting the curb, Alex slowly climbed out of the car and shuffled across the parking lot.

Inserting the key into the lock, she turned the knob and announced her arrival as Simon had instructed. She was greeted by an excited bark.

As she entered, Jackson bounded across the living room and nearly knocked her over. Murray was close behind.

She knelt gingerly to pet the dogs, paying extra attention to Jackson's favorite spot behind his ears.

"I've missed you, too," she whispered into his fur as she pulled him close. "What would I ever do without you?" A tear pooled in the corner of her eye. Jackson loved her as much as she loved him. If she'd died yesterday, he would be devastated. He'd rescued her just as much as she'd rescued him.

A quick glance around the apartment confirmed that a bachelor lived there. The decor was minimal, at most. Though Alex suspected that with Simon's long hours at the office, he probably didn't spend much time here anyway.

Alex gathered Jackson's things and took him to the car. After dropping him off at her hotel, she picked up lunch for Simon to thank him for taking care of Jackson last night. Knowing he wasn't alone and was having play time with another dog gave her one less thing to worry about. The least she could do for Simon was to treat him to lunch.

Forty-five minutes later, she parked in the parking garage adjacent to Simon's office and lifted the bag of takeout from the passenger seat. She brought her favorite comfort food to him, thinking that after the week he'd had, he'd need it, too. Grilled cheese and tomato soup always made her feel better when she was upset.

Hoping he didn't mind the intrusion, she reached for the handle to open the car door. As she did, her cell phone rang. The number wasn't one she recognized, and she debated about whether to answer. Just before the call rolled to voicemail, she tapped the screen to answer the call.

"Hello?"

"Hi, is this Alexandra Tucker?" The voice was familiar, but Alex couldn't place it.

"It is," she said, carefully getting out of the car. Her back popped with the effort.

"This is Officer Therese DiVito, Lexington PD. Do you have a minute?" She sounded pleasant enough but was still all business.

"Sure. What's going on? Have they gotten the results of the DNA test already?" Alex asked, hopeful.

"Not yet," Officer DiVito began, "but we did learn something else that was very interesting…"

63

JULIA TOOK A bite of the frozen burrito she'd heated up for lunch and scowled. Never much of a cook herself, she was sure she could still do better than those people. Even so, she usually preferred takeout or frozen dinners to her own attempts in the kitchen.

It doesn't have much flavor, she thought, but at least I didn't almost burn the place down.

Several months ago, she accidentally caught her stove on fire. As usual, Mikey had been no help as she frantically tried to smother the flames leaping from the burner. From that moment on, she'd sworn off cooking for good and decided to leave it to the pros.

Like the people who created this burrito, she thought sarcastically and tossed it into the garbage.

So far, the day had been awful, but Julia knew she only had herself to blame.

What was I thinking? she scolded herself. John has been in a foul mood for weeks, and I had to go in there first thing this morning and threaten blackmail if he didn't arrange a way for me to keep my job, or at least pay me for my silence.

The disgust on his face made her want to find a hole to crawl into. No matter. It was too late now. There was no way she could take back the words she'd said.

He'd been so kind when he offered her the job as his assistant. With no previous office experience, the closest she'd ever gotten to legal matters was the time she filed a restraining order against her mother's boyfriend when he showed her too much "affection." She'd known she wasn't qualified for the job but was so thrilled to finally have respectable employment that she jumped at the opportunity. Now she wondered if she would have been better off staying in the low-end retail store she'd been working at when she applied for this job.

The day she came in for the interview, she thought she looked pretty good. The clothes she wore were much nicer than the ones she'd grown up wearing. She thought she looked the part, but when she walked in the front door, she immediately felt frumpy and out of place. Even the secretary who'd greeted her at the front door was dressed in quality business clothes. At that moment, she'd nearly turned around and walked out before the interview. Fortunately, she'd been promptly taken back to John's office where he conducted the interview and offered her the job on the spot. She remembered how warm his smile had been and, sensing how nervous she was, went out of his way to make sure she felt comfortable.

That was the John Carmichael I came to work for, Julia thought, but somewhere over the past several months he's turned into someone else.

Even so, how could I have been so ungrateful and threaten

to tell people some of the things I've found out about him over the past two years?

The first time she walked into his office without knocking was a couple weeks into the job. She was still getting used to working in such a formal environment. He'd been so forgiving of her mistakes up to that point, she hadn't thought it was a big deal, but when she heard his end of the hushed conversation, Julia realized she'd just learned things she was never supposed to know. John's back had been toward the door, and she tried to leave the office before he noticed she was there but bumped into a small table by the door on her way out.

She'd thought it odd at the time, but he never tried to explain what he was talking about. Maybe he thought it was none of her business, or maybe she'd made a bigger deal of it than it was. Either way, she hadn't been able to forget the things she heard that day, or the things she'd learned since then.

And she never forgot to knock again.

John was always such a good boss, never giving her more than she could handle and almost always sensitive to her limitations. He'd even given her generous Christmas bonuses out of his own pocket when the other partners in the firm voted not to give secretaries and assistants bonuses from the company's profits.

The first one went toward a new wardrobe more suitable for her working environment and a small down payment on a used car.

More than once, she'd wondered if the bonuses were closer to hush money than generosity, but until now she'd always managed to push the thought out of her mind and focus on the money.

Like boss, like assistant, she thought ruefully.

The job had given her so many things she could have never dreamed of having. As a child, she vowed to have a better life than her mother had. She wouldn't keep parading new boyfriends in front of her kids, leaving them to wonder if this one would be as bad as the last. Her children would have more stability than she'd had.

Now there wouldn't be any stability, and with the way things were going with Mikey, she began to doubt if there would ever be a family.

Pushing her pride aside, Julia decided she'd go to John's office and apologize as soon as he got back from lunch. Even though she couldn't make him forget what she'd said, she could try to convince him that his secrets were safe with her. There would be no need for him to worry about her ever telling anyone. If he could persuade his successor to let her keep her job, she'd tell him she wouldn't expect any financial assistance from him, either.

Surely that will help smooth things over, she assured herself. That and a bottle of his favorite scotch.

She glanced at her watch and noted she still had twenty minutes left of her lunch break. Knowing she'd be cutting it close, she went back to her desk and grabbed her purse. There was a store nearby that carried his favorite brand, and she'd give it to him when she apologized.

It cost nearly as much as her monthly car payment, but it would be worth it if she got back on his good side.

If he still had one…

Turning quickly, she almost ran into someone.

That's the woman who was in here on Monday, Julia thought. What does she want now?

Julia remembered the woman's bright eyes and warm,

albeit nervous, smile. Now she was ghostly pale, and her eyes looked sunken.

I wonder what's gotten into her, Julia wondered as she quickly left the office and headed toward her car.

64

"I WAS PUSHED!" Alex cried as she walked, unannounced, into Simon's office. It was just as stark as his apartment. Aside from the painting of a mountain-scape hanging on the wall across from his desk, it was completely devoid of personal touch.

Startled, Simon looked up. "You already knew that. Is it just now sinking in?"

Alex took in a gulp of air. "I knew what they said, but I honestly didn't believe it. I mean, who would want to hurt me? Despite what you've seen this week, I'm actually very easy to get along with."

Simon nodded. "Then what made you finally believe somebody pushed you off that curb?"

She slouched into the chair opposite Simon's desk. "I got a call from Officer DiVito just after I parked. I brought lunch." She held out the bag containing the soup and sandwiches, then leaned forward and plopped it on his desk.

"Thank you," Simon replied, "but right now I'm more interested in knowing what Officer DiVito had to say."

"They've identified the eyewitness."

"Is that bad? Wouldn't it mean that they're one step closer to knowing who's gunning for you?" Simon winced at his choice of words as soon as they left his mouth.

"You don't understand," Alex said slowly. "They've identified the eyewitness, and he's one of my clients."

"A client? From Charleston?" His eyebrows knitted together as he processed what he'd just heard. "What would a client of yours be doing all the way up here?"

Alex slumped deeper into the chair. "Apparently he followed me."

Why is this happening? Her thought was so loud, Alex wondered if she'd actually voiced the question.

Simon leaned back in his own chair and pressed the tips of his fingers together. "Why would he follow you? And how can you be sure it's him?"

"He was assigned to Jeannie's caseload while I've been gone, but he missed his appointment on Monday. It's the first appointment he's ever missed."

"But how would he know you were coming here? I still don't understand."

Alex shrugged. "It wouldn't be hard for him to follow me home after work. If he was watching my apartment, he could have seen me pack up and leave. He has no job or family, so it would be easy for him to disappear for a week or so without anyone noticing. Except maybe his therapist."

Simon extended an index finger in her direction. "Which is you."

Alex nodded and repeated, "Which is me."

"But why? What would be the point of following you?" Simon sounded as confused as Alex felt.

She took a deep breath and released it, looking out the window over Simon's shoulder.

Her mood was a direct contradiction to the sunny day. "I think he's become fixated on me," she said, matter-of-fact. If she was going to hold it together, she'd have to be clinical, as though she was discussing a case, and in a sense, she was.

Simon raised an eyebrow. "What do you mean 'fixated'? What does that even mean?"

Alex sighed. "Over the past month or so, he's been saying things about how nobody else understands him and how he thinks we're a good pair. Nothing overly suggestive at first, just a few red flags. In the last session, though, he said I was the most important person in his life and he couldn't imagine living without me. I wanted to believe he meant in a client-therapist capacity, but I've started to doubt that's what he meant. Especially now. I've also seen him out in public, places I wouldn't expect him to be. My dry cleaner, the grocery store. It's just… odd."

"And now he's here," Simon stated.

"Apparently so. The police are trying to locate him, but at the moment they don't have any clue where he is. Officer DiVito wanted to know if I would have any idea where he'd go in a strange town, but to tell you the truth, I'm so rattled I can't even think straight."

"So, there's somebody walking around this city who's obsessed with you, may want to see you hurt or dead, and nobody knows where he is." Simon's words hung in the air like a lead balloon.

Alex nodded. Could Simon tell just how uneasy she felt about Jeffery Anderson? Or how many times she'd thought about requesting that Jeannie assign him to another therapist, only to remind herself that she couldn't turn her back on him? Or the fact that there was something about him that had always bothered her?

"Do *you* think he's the one that pushed you?" Simon asked.

Alex had been turning the same question over in her mind since the call from the officer. On the one hand, he was overly attached to her, and there's no question that he's a very sick man. On the other hand, he had a gentle streak that wouldn't allow him to hurt her. She shrugged. "Maybe. I think it's a possibility."

Alex slid her hand into her purse and pulled out the note that had been taped to her hotel room door and slid it across the desk to Simon.

As he read it, his face went white. "When did you get this?"

"Tuesday, I think. The truth is, my days are running together so I'm not really sure," Alex confessed.

Simon rubbed the stubble on his face. "Tuesday? You've had this three days and didn't feel like it was something you ought to mention?"

"I only remember taking it off my hotel room door on Tuesday," Alex said defensively. "I didn't read it then."

"Well, when *did* you read it?"

"I read it Wednesday night, when I got back from the coffee shop. Then I put it in my purse. I had every intention to show you, but with everything that was happening with your brother, I forgot. I remembered it at the hospital when I got my phone out of my purse to call Gram."

"And you didn't think he was worth mentioning last night when you found it? Especially on the heels of somebody almost splattering your brain all over Main Street?"

Alex shrank deeper into the chair and away from Simon's rising frustration.

"That means somebody tried to warn you two days before your so-called 'accident,' and you still thought you just *slipped*? What were you thinking, Alex?" he chastised.

"I'm sorry, I just—"

"What else aren't you telling me?" he interjected. "I'm trying to help you, Alex, but I can't do that if you don't tell me what's going on, and I certainly can't do that if you're dead."

"Would you please keep your voice down?" Alex snapped, reaching her limit on how much scolding she was willing to take. "Do you want the whole office to hear you? I said I was sorry, and this is the only thing I haven't told you about. I promise."

Simon's eyes darted around his office as if he was looking for danger to spring out of any corner. "You can't stay at that hotel anymore." He held up the note. "Whoever sent this knows where to find you. You aren't safe there."

"And where do you suggest I go?"

"To Dad's," he said, already reaching for the phone on his desk. "Just check out of that hotel and get yourself over to his place as soon as you can. And whatever you do, please make sure you stay alert."

Alex nodded like an obedient child and listened as Simon made arrangements for her to move to Sam's house.

Simon hung up the phone and turned his attention back to her. "Everything's settled. Go get your stuff and head over there now."

She nodded again and rose from the chair, for the first time feeling scared and alone in the strange city. Even though she knew Sam and Simon relatively well by now, they were still new acquaintances. As she walked out of Simon's office, she completely forgot about the cold soup and soggy sandwiches sitting on Simon's desk.

Instead, she thought about how vulnerable she felt having to depend on people she'd known less than a week to keep her safe.

<h1 style="text-align:center">65</h1>

HE WAS SICK of waiting. It should have been done by now, but as he watched Alex walk into that guy's office building, he wondered if she had some kind of guardian angel.

It was a miracle she survived being pushed into traffic. Even though it hadn't been rush hour, there had been a steady flow of cars on Main Street.

He'd made sure of that.

Whoever was driving that pickup swerved just in time to miss running over her. But even then, the impact of her head hitting the curb would have killed most people.

Stroking the stubble on his unshaved chin, he wondered how he could make sure she didn't survive the next time—guardian angel or not.

As she'd toppled forward, she'd turned her head just enough for him to see that her eyes were wide, stricken with terror. A zip of adrenaline shot through his stomach. She was paying penance for all the hurt, all the anger she'd caused by not wanting him.

Just remembering the sickening thud of her head meeting concrete and the way it bounced off the curb caused his mouth to twist into a wicked smile.

The smile quickly vanished at the thought that something else would have to be done. He couldn't risk it this time. There was no way to account for every variable that could interfere with his plan unless he was there while she left this life behind.

Karma wasn't doing its job. She'd have to die by his own hand.

But how?

The smile returned as an idea shot to mind. It would be perfect. Symbolic, even.

And this time, no guardian angel in heaven or earth could help her escape.

66

JOHN FINALLY HAD a plan, one that was foolproof. Never before had he been the one to get his hands dirty, but this time he was out of options. Clarence wouldn't tolerate his stalling any longer, and John knew that for his own well-being, he needed to make Clarence happy.

Not that Clarence was capable of being happy, John decided.

He picked up his jacket and walked out of his office. Despite her apology and peace offering, he couldn't bring himself to even look in Julia's direction. She'd seemed truly sorry for the things she'd said, but the fact that she said them at all told him more about her than her heartfelt apology could.

Assuming there actually is a heart beating inside that chest of hers, he thought.

The corner of his mouth twitched as the irony struck him that she probably thought the same thing about him.

Avoiding eye contact with her, John flicked his wrist as he walked past her desk. Knowing Julia, she would have waved back. She didn't ask where he was going or when he'd be back, and he didn't offer. It was none of her business and irreversible damage had already been done.

As he walked quietly down the stairs to the first floor of the building, he solidified the scheme in his mind. If everything went according to plan, the issue would be resolved by morning.

If it wasn't, Clarence would make sure he paid dearly for the screwup.

John squelched the guilt that nagged at him when he realized that others would have to be hurt in the process. Just collateral damage, he reminded himself. A sacrifice that must be made for the greater good.

In this case, the greater good was John's own self-preservation.

He slid behind the wheel of his Lexus and rested his head against the plush leather seat. Exhaling slowly, he shifted the car into drive and mentally checked off everything he needed to complete the looming task. The disguise and necessary tools were in the trunk of the car, to be discarded in the Kentucky River when the job was done.

He drove quickly, but at the same time was careful not to draw the attention of law enforcement as he made his way across town to his intended victim.

"I bet she never thought it would end like this," John mumbled as he pulled into a parking spot one street over from his destination. "Or that it would end when she was so young."

Glancing around quickly for cameras on the outside of the surrounding buildings, he mused that sometimes things just didn't go as planned. I never thought I'd resort to murder, either.

❧

John walked the four flights of stairs back up to his office, confident that within the next twenty-four hours she would no longer be a threat to him. He'd finally be able to get Clarence off his back and disappear for good. He could get on with his life without worrying that one day everything would come crashing down around him.

Breathing a sigh of relief, he picked up his pace and walked into his office, ignoring Julia's pleasant but forced greeting.

I guess she thinks I forgive easily, he thought. Unfortunately for her, she couldn't be more wrong.

Just before he closed his office door, his cell phone rang. His mouth went dry when he looked at the number on the screen. When would Clarence stop calling him?

Breath coming in short bursts, he debated whether he should answer. Deciding it was in his best interest to take the call, he quickly closed his door and tapped the button on the screen to accept the call.

"Where are you?" the gruff voice asked.

"In my office. You know better than to call during working hours. That's gotten us into trouble before. What do you want?"

"And you know better than to question me. Give me an update. Have you taken care of our little problem?"

"As a matter of fact, I have. By this time tomorrow, we won't have a problem," John said confidently but still feeling a little sick about what he'd done.

"Congratulations. How's it feel to be a big boy? I hope you didn't do something stupid to screw it up," Clarence chided.

"I didn't mess up. It will look like an accident," John growled through clenched teeth. He was sick of playing second fiddle to a man like Clarence, and the sooner he could disentangle himself from the man, the better.

"Let's just hope you don't grow a conscience or anything."

John snorted. "No need to worry about that. If I haven't managed to grow one by this stage of my life, I doubt I ever will."

"I hope not, for your sake," Clarence affirmed. "Doesn't it feel good to get some dirt on your hands every now and then?"

"No, it does not," John contradicted. "I haven't gotten where I am by getting my hands dirty. Not like this, anyway."

"Relish the thought that by this time tomorrow, we'll be home free. Maybe we'll even head to sunny Mexico." Clarence laughed and launched into a coughing fit.

"You really should give up smoking, Clarence," John suggested flatly. "Those things will kill you."

As if I'd ever get that lucky, he thought.

Clarence laughed even harder. "Right. Nothing can kill me, John. Remember that."

"We'll see about that. Now, I really have to go. Never call me at work again. Understand?" John warned.

Clarence's voice was deadly quiet. "John, you know better than to try calling the shots. Never speak to me like that again. We'll talk soon." Clarence disconnected the call.

A chill raced down John's spine. What was that "we" business Clarence was talking about? To him, finishing this job meant finally being rid of Clarence. Now it sounded as though Clarence had every intention of leaving his wagon hitched to John's. Despair crept over him and smothered the relief he thought he'd feel.

For the rest of his life, it looked like he'd be stuck doing the bidding of the most dangerous person he'd ever known.

67

TONY LOOKED AROUND his cell at the all-too-familiar surroundings. "Home sweet home," he muttered.

This place had been his home for the past two years, and though he hated it, he took some comfort in knowing he was back where he belonged. As horrible as it was, he'd become accustomed to life on the inside.

His time at the hospital had been a vacation of sorts, and it was nice to be alone. Nobody spoke to him, other than nurses and the occasional doctor. Each time, he only said what he had to and let his silence convey his message: I want to be alone.

It had been difficult to play that game when his dad visited, since Tony had been truly glad to see him. If he'd started talking, though, he knew he might have told his father what happened just before he went unconscious.

No matter what happened, he couldn't tell anyone. In his mind, there was already enough blood on his hands, and he didn't want to be the cause of any more.

"You should know Benny is out of the infirmary and has

been making a lot of noise about you," the guard escorting Tony back to his cell said.

"I'm sure he is," Tony acknowledged.

"Most everyone knows he's just blowing a lot of hot air, but he's got a few converts. It would be wise to consider this a hostile environment."

"Because it was a five-star resort before?" Tony retorted.

"Just watch your back for a while. You know how Benny can be," the guard warned.

That's some kind of welcome, Tony thought as the cell door slammed shut and the lock snapped into place.

Tony knew it must have taken some string pulling to keep him out of solitary confinement. That's where somebody would normally be after trying to kill a fellow inmate. He'd stake his life that his dad made a few calls to keep that from happening.

Another reason for Benny to hate me, Tony mused.

Lying on his bed, Tony placed his hands behind his head and stared at the ceiling.

Would Benny really try to get revenge?

Even though a jury convicted Benny and there had been a mountain of evidence against him, Tony had always been skeptical of whether or not he was actually guilty of murdering the Stones. Sure, he was unpleasant and started more than his share of fights, but deep down he didn't believe Benny was violent enough to kill someone. That was part of the reason Tony was less concerned about his well-being than the guard seemed to be. He could get everyone riled up and make Tony's life miserable, but he couldn't make himself believe Benny would actually hurt him.

The fact that his own father had been the one to arrest Benny almost made the whole situation laughable.

Almost.

The biggest reason Benny lashed out at him so much was because he held a grudge against his father, and the harassment hadn't started until he found out that Tony's father was Sam Caldwell.

Still weak from the blood loss, Tony spent the late afternoon reading a book he'd started before he was taken to the hospital. He was interrupted by a guard announcing dinner.

"Warden suggests you take your dinner in your cell," the guard suggested.

"No way," Tony protested. "I'm not eating in here by myself."

Had Benny really been that successful at turning the other inmates against him?

Eventually the guard escorted him to the cafeteria, where several inmates shouted at him that he'd have been better off dead. Some shouted obscenities, others merely glared at him. A few ignored him altogether.

"Well, look who it is," Benny said sardonically as he strode up to Tony. "You must be feeling brave."

Tony tried to step around him, but Benny moved his round body sideways so he couldn't pass.

"Come on, Benny. I don't want any trouble. I just want to eat," Tony said.

Benny lifted his lip in a sneer. "You can eat when I say so, and right now we have an important matter to discuss."

Again, Tony tried to step around Benny's wide frame, and again Benny blocked his path. "I don't have anything to say to you," Tony said.

"Oh!" Benny shouted. "He doesn't have anything to say

to me!" He turned toward the tables and raised his hands, eliciting a response from the others.

"I said I don't want any trouble. Let me by." Tony managed to keep his voice even, though he was starting to feel weak. He'd wondered if it was too soon for him to leave the hospital. Now he was certain it was.

"He doesn't want any trouble!" Benny yelled theatrically, then lowered his voice and pointed a beefy finger in Tony's face. "You should have thought about that before you shivved me."

Tony looked away and said nothing.

"You don't have anything to say to me?" Benny jeered. "You scared?"

"Of course I'm not afraid of you, Benny," Tony said, for the first time looking directly at Benny's eyes. He didn't feel fear. What he felt for the man was pity.

"You should be. Don't you know I'm a coldblooded killer? That I've killed better people than you?"

Tony narrowed his eyes and studied the face of the man he despised most in the world. He saw through the façade to the lonely, scared man who tried to mask it by acting tough. "I don't actually believe that," Tony said, for the first time in two years feeling like he had the upper hand against this guy.

Benny's stony expression crumbled. He stumbled backward as though Tony had struck him. The face that had been twisted in anger just moments before was now frozen in disbelief. "Now one has ever believed me. Why would you?"

"Because I can see right through you. You talk a big game, but you don't have it in you to kill anybody. You're in here because your attorney couldn't make a jury believe that, not because you actually did it." Tony waved toward the food line. "Now, if you don't mind, I'd like to eat," he said, stepping past a dazed Benny and walking as briskly as his wobbly legs would take him.

After he settled at a table by himself, Benny took the chair opposite him, eying the guard.

"He has to stay here," Tony said, jerking his head toward the man in uniform and then taking a bite of meatloaf. "Apparently you started a coup against me and I need to be protected," he said dryly.

"You talk weird," Benny said, plucking a fry from Tony's plate and cramming it into his mouth.

"Huh?" Tony asked, doing the same.

"You don't talk like the rest of us. Who uses the word 'coup'?"

"My mother was a journalist. She made her living with words. I guess some of it rubbed off on me," Tony said, then mentally kicked himself for mentioning his mom. He braced himself for Benny to pounce on the opportunity.

Instead, Benny asked, "Why do you think I'm innocent?"

Tony shook his head. "I said I don't think you're guilty of murder, not that I think you're innocent. There's a difference."

"Whaddya mean?" Benny helped himself to another fry.

"I don't think you killed the Stones, but you did break into the house to rob them. You're not a killer, but you are lazy. It just makes sense that you would try to make a living by not actually working."

"Hey, breaking into someone's house *is* work," Benny protested.

Tony cocked his head to the side. "Benny…"

"Fine. How come you know that just from watching me and my own lawyer didn't know that from years of talking to me?" Benny's mouth hung open, bits of chewed up French fry clinging to his teeth.

Tony shrugged. "I'm just good at reading people, I guess."

"Like father, like son," Benny quipped, then added, "It's true, though. I broke into their house, rummaged through the jewelry and other valuables, then went to the library. A little birdie told me Thomas kept some rare first editions in there. Not that I care about the books, but I could have unloaded them for a fortune. Anyway, that's when I found the bodies. It was gross. I couldn't call the police because I'd broken in. Why didn't Carmichael try to make a stronger case about that?" Benny asked, more to himself than Tony.

Tony and Benny finished the meal in silence, and Tony wondered if Benny was thinking the same thing he was: What exactly had John Carmichael been doing the past thirty-two years?

68

J ACKSON RAN AROUND the house, smelling everything and inspecting each room. Alex had arrived at Sam's
house only a few minutes earlier, giving her just enough
time to drop her bags inside the front door and tell Jackson to
get out of the trash a half dozen times.

It struck Alex that the way dogs get to know their hosts
was genius. If you really want to know who someone is, look
at what they keep hidden from the world.

The thought made Alex uneasy. She racked her brain about
everyone she'd come into contact with since arriving in Kentucky. It only took five days for somebody to try to kill her.

What was her subconscious trying to tell her? Somebody
was hiding something—obviously—but who was it? Was it
more than one person? And what were they hiding? Did it
really even have anything to do with her?

At the sound of Sam clearing his throat behind her, Alex
turned, feeling her tension ease.

"I hope you'll make yourself at home. Your suitcase is in

Simon's old room. The bathroom is right across the hall and is all yours while you're here."

She looked at the floor where she'd left her suitcase. It wasn't there. Somehow Sam had managed to wheel himself over to it, pick it up, and take it to the bedroom without her noticing.

"Thank you so much for this," she said, waving her hand down the hall. "I feel a lot better knowing someone else will be nearby." She wrapped her arms around her waist. "Knowing for sure that somebody deliberately tried to kill me has me a little shaken up."

"It would have that effect on anybody," Sam affirmed, then remarked, "Simon tells me the eyewitness is a client of yours."

Alex nodded. "I still can't believe he'd follow me here."

"Is he dangerous?" Sam asked, the corners of his mouth turning down.

"He can be when he's upset, yes."

"What can you tell me about him?"

Alex lowered herself to the sofa across from Sam. She rested her elbows on her knees and put her head in her hands. How much could she tell Sam without breaching client confidentiality?

"He's in his thirties and was diagnosed with schizophrenia at eighteen," she volunteered. That was a safe answer.

"Aren't there different types of schizophrenia?" Sam asked.

"Yes." Alex was sure Sam already knew the answer to his question, and that during his years as a cop he'd become familiar with each one. Still, she was grateful for the conversation. "He has the paranoid type. He suffers from delusions of persecution. He thinks others are out to get him, and in his mind, everyone has mistreated him in some way. This is particularly true if he views someone as being in a position of power or has authority over him. Typically, he likes people at first, but then thinks they're turning their backs on him. He takes it very personally and gets extremely angry when that happens." Once again, Alex caught herself slipping into clinical mode.

"Do you think he'd hurt you?" Sam asked, his eyes fixed on hers.

Alex looked straight ahead, her line of vision passing through the living room and out the window over the kitchen sink. "I honestly don't know. If you'd asked me that question any other time, I'd say no, but now I'm not so sure. He's been hospitalized three times when he's gone off his meds, and each time has gotten into some pretty serious confrontations with other patients. In one instance, he beat a female patient's head into a wall until she was unconscious. Apparently, he was sweet on her but she didn't return his affection. Poor thing had bipolar disorder and was in the middle of a major depressive episode. She wouldn't have returned the affection of George Clooney at that point."

Sam chuckled.

"Anyway," Alex continued, "when he's on his meds he functions very well. He's witty and charming and extremely intelligent."

Sam nodded as she spoke. "Is he on his meds now?"

"He says he is, but recently I've suspected otherwise. During our last two sessions he seemed irritable and made comments about how I didn't appreciate how hard he was working to make something of himself."

"So, now you're the one who isn't returning his affection," Sam ventured.

Alex sighed and pinched the bridge of her nose. "It would

seem so. If that's how he perceives things, I could be in a lot of trouble," she said, moving her hand to unconsciously rub the bandaged spot on her forehead.

Sam exhaled. "So, this client of yours, he's the one the police say claims to have seen someone push you? Is it possible he's the one that pushed you and wants recognition for it?"

"Anything is possible, I suppose. Assuming he really is trying to hurt me, he might want me to know about it. If he wants to shift the power in our relationship, he might do something to let me know he's taking control. In his mind, if I've used my position against him, he'd want to even the playing field. Making sure I know he's trying to kill me and that he's loose out there..." Alex waved her hand toward the front door. "Well, that would do it."

The two sat listening to Jackson explore while both considered the gravity of the situation. The paleness of Alex's face contrasted the deepening red of Sam's.

"I don't want you leaving this house," Sam ordered. "You are to stay here at all times until this mess is taken care of. Understand?"

"I understand," she agreed.

His air of authority probably made him an excellent cop, Alex thought, and his compassion probably makes him an excellent father and friend.

"I don't want you taking Jackson for a walk, or even standing at the door while he plays out back," Sam continued. "You must keep your visibility to the outside to an absolute minimum."

Alex nodded. She had a feeling this wasn't Sam's first time protecting someone, and for that she was glad.

"Now, go unpack your bags. We don't know how long

you'll be staying here. Keep your curtains closed. Simon will be here with Murray after work and will be staying until this is resolved," Sam said as he maneuvered his wheelchair from the living room toward the kitchen.

"Simon's staying here too? I hate to inconvenience him."

"Are you kidding? Nothing on earth could keep him away." Sam winked at her and with a twinkle in his eye said, "Besides, you didn't think you'd have to rely only on an old guy in a wheelchair for protection, did you?"

"I hadn't thought about it, actually. I just hate that the two of you are rearranging your lives for me."

Sam held up a hand against her protest. "It's no problem. Simon will still be going to work during the day, but he'll be here to help keep an eye on the place at night. He'll take Tony's old room, right next to yours."

"Sam?" Alex asked just before he disappeared into the kitchen. "Will I be okay?"

With a sharp nod, Sam assured her she would. "I might spend my life sitting down, but I'm still a crack shot. Now, come get something to eat. My neighbor, Ruth Cline, made banana bread this morning and brought it over. You slice it while I put on a pot of tea."

She dutifully obeyed, hoping the task would distract her.

Even though popular opinion was that Jeffery was up to no good and was a danger to her, her subconscious warned her that there was someone else she needed to be even more afraid of.

69

EANNIE LISTENED AS Alex described the last thirty hours.

She has certainly gotten herself into a lot of trouble, Jeannie thought as Alex told her about being in the hospital.

When Jeffery Anderson missed his appointment on Monday, Jeannie couldn't have imagined it was because he'd followed Alex to Kentucky with the intention of hurting her. As far as Jeannie knew, Jeffery had been taking his medication for months and was showing a marked improvement in his functioning. Since Alex hadn't told her anything different, Jeannie had no reason to question it. She and Alex even considered referring him to an agency that helps people with mental illness enter the workforce. He was intelligent and could be a good employee if given the opportunity.

Now this.

Jeannie's grip on the phone tightened as Alex told her she was staying with an ex-cop who would protect her if Jeffery showed up again.

As her boss, Jeannie had always been pleased with Alex's

ability as a counselor. Even straight out of graduate school, Alex showed a discernment and maturity most people have to work years for. She'd considered recommending that Alex take over running the counseling center when she moved on to a larger one.

Not after this, though, Jeannie thought with her teeth clenched. Had she been wrong about Alex, even after all this time?

She shook her head. Before this, Alex had never given her a reason to doubt her ability. But this lack of communication about a potentially dangerous situation gave her pause about what kind of leader Alex would be.

"Jeannie," Alex was saying, "I know I should have told you about my suspicions. Clearly, I didn't use my best judgment, and now I'm in trouble. Put yourself in my position," Alex said, a defensive edge to her voice.

Jeannie didn't respond. When she was younger, she very easily could have been in Alex's position. The truth was, Jeannie saw more of herself in Alex than she'd ever admit.

"Obviously I'm sure now," Alex continued. "Jeffery has been making excellent progress. He was showing me he's ready to get out there and do something. Our treatment plan includes ways to make that possible for him, including how he should deal with stress and disappointment. We'd even discussed cutting his appointments back to three times a month instead of every week. Tell me honestly, what would you have done if I told you he might be becoming fixated on me?"

"I would have assigned him to another counselor," Jeannie said, more sharply than she meant to.

"Exactly," Alex countered. "I couldn't let him start over with someone new. Not when we were so close to getting him back on his feet. Not if I wasn't sure he posed an actual threat. Clearly, he did and still does, but his progress wasn't something I was willing to risk if I wasn't sure. I know the supervisor in you has to be upset, but I also know the counselor in you would have done the same thing."

Jeannie relaxed her grip on the phone and tapped her desk with a pen. "You're right," she conceded. "I would have done anything I could to help the client. Once I made a commitment to him, I wouldn't walk away."

"Am I in a lot of trouble?" Alex asked quietly. Listening to her now, Jeannie couldn't shake the image of a dog with its tail tucked between its legs.

"You're in trouble, Alex. I wish I could say you weren't, but you disregarded your own safety. I have to question everything now." Jeannie rubbed her eyes.

"I understand you have to discipline me. There won't be any hard feelings," Alex promised.

"Two weeks unpaid suspension, and when you return to work, we'll meet weekly to discuss your clients and treatment approach," Jeannie said quickly. This was the awkward part of being friends with an employee.

To her surprise, Alex said, "That seems fair."

Jeannie wasn't sure, but she thought she heard a sigh of relief from the other end.

"You remind me of myself, you know," Jeannie confided.

"Oh yeah? Did you almost get murdered by one of your clients, too?"

Jeannie laughed. "Oh no, nothing like that. Ten years ago, I was just like you. It was all about the client, and I ignored a lot of subtle signs that something could be wrong. There were things I should have reported that I didn't—all for the same reasons you didn't report this to me. The difference is, I didn't get caught." Jeannie sighed. "Sometimes it's easy for me to forget what it's like to only be responsible to clients. Now it seems I've always got to watch out for my employees and the good of the center. I miss the simpler days." Switching from supervisor to friend, Jeannie said, "When your grandmother called to tell me you'd been taken to the emergency room, my heart almost stopped. Do you have any idea how worried I was about you?"

"Sorry about that. I won't let it happen again," Alex teased.

"So, do you remember anything that happened?" Jeannie asked. "Other than what the police told you, are you sure it was Jeffery that pushed you?"

"I'm not sure of anything. At first, I didn't remember anything," Alex offered. "I just remembered standing on the curb, waiting to cross the street, then waking up in a hospital room. But now… I don't know. I feel like something is tugging at my subconscious, trying to get me to pay attention to it. I don't know what it is, though."

"A face, maybe?" Jeannie suggested.

"No. It's more of a feeling I'm trying to remember. I remember feeling surprised then scared, but I don't know why."

"Maybe you saw something, or someone, you didn't expect to see, then realized you were in danger?" Jeannie urged. Eventually Alex's memory would come back, and she knew she shouldn't push her to remember, but she needed to know if it was Jeffery.

"Hello?" Jeannie asked, realizing Alex hadn't responded. "Are you still there?"

Voice shaking, Alex said, "It's Jeffery."

"You remembered? Jeffery is the one you saw?"

"No!" Alex shrieked. "I see him now. He's standing outside the house!"

Adrenaline shot through Jeannie's body, sending her to her feet. "Is anybody with you?"

"No." Alex's voice trembled as she spoke. "Sam went to his neighbor's house for a minute. Jeannie, he's walking toward the house. How did he find me? What do I do?" Alex pleaded.

Remembering her training in crisis intervention, Jeannie forced her voice to be calm. "Alex, I want you to—"

She looked at the phone as the line went dead. Frantically she dialed Alex's cell phone again, getting a busy signal.

Fear squeezed her chest, and Jeannie paced around the office as the realization settled on her that all she could do was wait.

70

S AM SMILED AS his neighbor, Ruth Cline, launched into another one of her stories about her grandson, the kid genius. As thankful as he was for the banana bread she baked for him at least once a week, he wondered if she always brought it over in the pan so he'd have to keep bringing it back.

He'd suspected for years that she had feelings for him, but for the last year and a half since Betty died, she'd really turned up the heat. It began with bringing meals over after Betty died and quickly escalated to bringing baked goods several times a week. A widow herself, Sam knew she was lonely. He was lonely, too.

But not that lonely.

It seemed as though any time he was outside, she miraculously appeared. It had gotten to the point that he dreaded even going to the mailbox.

Ruth was droning on about how little Hubert was the captain of his elementary school academic team because he always got the questions right when flashing lights caught

295

Sam's attention. He shifted in his wheelchair so he could get a better view over the hedge that separated their properties.

The blood drained from Sam's face when two police cruisers screeched to a halt in front of his house.

Something was wrong with Alex.

"I'm sorry, Ruth," he said as he quickly wheeled himself away from the front door and down the wheelchair ramp she'd had built for her late husband. "I've really got to go."

"But you haven't even heard the end of my story," Ruth protested, completely oblivious that anything out of the ordinary was happening on their street.

"Another time," Sam called, already halfway down the front walk. "Thanks again for the banana bread. It was delicious, as always."

Once he turned onto the sidewalk and was past the shrubs, he hurried toward the scene unfolding before him. A thin man with greasy hair hanging just past the tops of his ears and an unkempt beard lay face down on the pavement with his arms twisted behind his back. A uniformed officer was placing handcuffs on the writhing figure.

"Stop it! You're hurting me," the man protested. "I'm trying to help her!"

Sam looked toward his house and saw a curtain pulled back slightly in Alex's bedroom. A pair of fear-stricken eyes peered out of the opening.

Turning his attention back to the officers, Sam wheeled himself closer and caught the attention of the officer who'd just placed the suspect in the back of the car.

Sam extended his hand to the burly policeman. "Detective Sam Caldwell, retired. Mind if I ask what's going on here?"

"Officer Beck," the man in uniform replied, returning the handshake. "Do you live around here, sir?"

"This is my house," Sam said, waving a hand toward the small, ranch-style home.

"Well, sir. We received a call from someone inside the house saying a man was stalking her and she believed she was in danger. Can you tell me anything about that?"

"I could, but I think you should hear it from her. Excuse me." He moved toward the house, preparing himself for Alex's mental state.

Once inside, he knocked softly on Alex's bedroom door. "Alex, it's Sam. Everything is okay. The police are here, and they have the situation under control," he said calmly. He grasped the doorknob. It was locked. "One of the officers would like to speak with you. Can you please unlock the door?" Sam had worked enough home-invasion cases to know how vulnerable and violated the victims felt.

The doorknob rattled as she unlocked it and swung the door open. The image saddened him. The lights were off and the curtains drawn, her ghostly pale and tear-stained face a stark contradiction to the dark background.

Reaching for Alex's hand, he noticed it was cold and clammy and that she shook uncontrollably. "The police officer needs to talk to you," Sam said again, more slowly this time. "They'll talk to you here so you don't have to go down to the station. You need to tell him everything," he instructed. "I'll make you a cup of tea."

Alex's head bobbed as though she didn't quite have control of it.

As he made his way to the kitchen, Sam noticed the car holding Jeffery Anderson was gone and Officer Beck was standing on his doorstep. Sam motioned for him to come inside and said, "She'll be out in a few minutes."

When Alex emerged, Sam was just setting the tea on the coffee table. He gave her an encouraging nod as she began telling the story to Officer Beck. She spoke slowly, almost detached.

She's in shock, Sam thought, regretting not being there to stop this from happening. Of all times for him to take Mrs. Cline's loaf pan back to her…

He listened to Alex tell the police about Jeffery, his background, and the possibility that he'd pushed her into traffic the day before. A gnawing feeling that something just didn't add up nagged at him.

A cop's instinct never died, after all.

True, Jeffery followed Alex and had a history of violent behavior, and he *had* been there when she was pushed into traffic, but was he really as big a threat as everyone seemed to think?

71

S IMON'S HEAD SNAPPED up. "What are you doing here? You look terrible."

"Thanks," Alex said through a half smile. "Just what every girl wants to hear."

"No, I didn't mean… It's just that…" Simon stammered.

"I know what you mean, and you're right. I do look bad."

The corners of Simon's mouth lifted. He doubted she could ever look bad. "What are you doing here? You're not supposed to leave Dad's house." Worry knitted his eyebrows and the smile that had been present only seconds ago had disappeared.

"They got him," Alex said, sighing deeply and sinking into the chair across from him, just as she'd done earlier in the day when she brought lunch.

"That's great," Simon exclaimed, jumping out of his chair and circling the desk. He perched on the edge in front of her.

"Yeah, great," Alex mumbled half-heartedly. "He was outside your dad's house. I was so scared." She dropped her gaze to her hands and picked at her thumbnail. "I had to call the police."

The look on her face tore at his heart. "You feel guilty," he observed after studying her for several long moments.

She nodded. "I do. I know I shouldn't because he was a danger to me, but I do. I'm supposed to help him, not get him arrested." Tears sprang into Alex's eyes, and she quickly blinked them away then swiped at them with the back of her hand.

"Alex," he said as he reached out for her hands and bent to look into her eyes. "You didn't let him down. If he really has gone off his medication and is a threat to you or anybody else, you helped him by calling the police. If you hadn't, he could have gotten himself into a lot more trouble. You kept that from happening."

Alex shrugged. "I guess so."

"You did. Now," Simon clapped his hands together and stood. "I need you to perk up, because I'm taking you out to dinner tonight. We're going to celebrate."

Alex forced a smile. What was there to celebrate? Anybody could see she didn't feel much like celebrating, but she nodded in agreement. "Dinner would be nice."

"By the way, I forgot to ask you if you've heard anything from the police about the DNA comparison. I know it's just been a day, but maybe dropping Dad's name helped," Simon asked as he let go of her hands and went back behind his desk, settling into his chair again.

Shaking her head, Alex said, "Not yet. Officer DiVito said she'd call when she knows something. She asked them to rush it, but who knows how long that will take? Hopefully I'll know something soon. My gut keeps telling me Thomas and Sheila Stone were my birth parents, though."

A sound from the doorway of Simon's office caught their attention. As they both looked in that direction, the person standing there said, "You're not the daughter of Thomas and Sheila Stone. I am."

72

"EXCUSE ME?" ALEX and Simon asked in unison.

"You can't be the daughter of Thomas and Sheila Stone, because I am," Julia said, matter-of-fact. "Now you can stop poking around this office and bothering everybody."

"How's that possible?" Simon wondered aloud.

He grew up hearing about this case, Alex thought, and if Sam's hunch about what happened to the baby was right, everything about the case just changed.

"The official record states I was staying with relatives at the time, and that I just remained there. That's not what happened, but with a family like the Stones, of course there was a cover-up." Julia placed her hands on her hips, clearly ready for an argument. "An anonymous tip was called in a few hours after the police discovered the bodies. Someone left me outside a fire station—one of the ones marked 'Safe Place.' I was unharmed and placed with a distant relative. We moved across the country until I came back a few years ago, looking for a job and the inheritance that was rightfully mine."

"Can you prove any of this?" Alex challenged.

"Not that I need to," Julia huffed, "but yes, I can. I have my birth certificate and a DNA match. I'd say that's enough proof. Wouldn't you?" Julia's chin was angled upward, her voice defensive. "Unfortunately, there was nothing to inherit. It seems that my father had quite the gambling problem."

She understood why Julia seemed so confrontational. She'd responded the same way when she found out about her adoption.

"I hope that answers your questions about the Stones. As I said before, you don't need to come to this office with your pointless questions again." With that, Julia spun on her heel and stalked out of Simon's office.

Alex and Simon exchanged glances.

"What now? Are you going to stop looking for any connection you might have with the Stones?"

Alex shook her head. "Not a chance. I still have my original birth certificate, too. Though my parents' names might not be listed, my name is, and it says my last name was Stone and that I was born in Lexington. The fact that there's no other information on it just confirms to me that something else is going on here. I don't believe in coincidences."

"What are you going to do?"

Her gaze met Simon's. "I want to talk to Benny Johnson."

An hour later, Alex and Simon sat across from the man tried and convicted of the gruesome double homicide thirty-two years earlier.

"I know I'm a fascinating client to have, but in case you

haven't heard, I already have representation," Benny said smugly, motioning toward Richard Wade, who was sitting to his right.

Alex had heard what a piece of work Benny was, but being near him made her stomach roll. He's a bit too cocky for someone looking at finishing out a life sentence in this dump, she thought.

"I'm afraid I find you anything but interesting," Simon replied. "But that's not why we're here."

"I see you brought a friend," Benny said, turning his attention to Alex. "We don't see many pretty ladies around here. Is she your gift to me to make up for your brother trying to kill me?"

Benny's eyes slid up and down Alex's body. She cringed inwardly but forced herself not to react. She needed to find out what he had to say, and if she had to withstand a little sexual harassment to make that happen, she would.

Simon opened his mouth to speak, but Benny cut him off. "So, what do you want with me?"

"I have a couple questions about the night Thomas and Sheila Stone were murdered."

Benny sighed and crossed his arms over his thick chest. "Of course you do, but I got nothing to say about it. Anything I say will just get twisted and used against me. I know how you people work."

"First of all, I'm not a prosecutor. Second, that's why I called Richard. I wouldn't dream of asking you anything without your attorney present."

"I've got to admit, Simon, I'm beyond curious about what you want with Benny. This thing was closed three decades ago.

Most people just want to forget it," Richard said, lacing his fingers together and leaning toward Simon.

"Except you, apparently," Simon said, an edge to his voice. "I just wanted to ask a couple questions about that night. First though, I'm going to tell you what I already know." He held up his hand and ticked the facts off on his fingers. "Your fingerprints were found all over the first floor and on the jewelry box in the master bedroom, as well as on the safe in the library where the murder occurred. The alarm went off when you broke into the house, and you were arrested two days after that. I also know a large sum of money was deposited into your bank account the day after you broke in. The Stones had a baby, and there has always been speculation about whether or not the baby was in the house when you broke in." Simon dropped his hand to the table. "What I want to hear from you is your story about how the baby might have gone missing, and if it had anything to do with the money you came into just after the break-in." Simon leaned back in his chair, folding his arms, and waited.

Alex shifted her eyes from Simon to Benny, impressed at Simon's ability to stay civil with such a repugnant man.

Benny's face flushed and he shifted uncomfortably in the chair. "No, no, no! You've got it all wrong. Look, I was there. I admit that. I've always admitted that. You have my fingerprints so it would be pretty stupid of me to try to deny it. I'm a thief, yes, but not a killer and definitely not a kidnapper. I stole money and jewelry, not babies." Benny's voice had become high-pitched and whiny.

Simon narrowed his eyes as Benny spoke. "Benny, you have to admit the money makes you look pretty guilty. It looks like it was a payment to either commit the murder or kidnap the baby. Maybe both. Fifty grand is a lot of money."

"How many times do I have to tell you people?" Benny shouted, slapping the table with his thick hand. "I never had fifty grand in my life. I never made that deposit. Somebody framed me and they're still doing a bang-up job. Nobody seems to be able to get past that deposit." Benny's anger had flagged and was replaced with a look of hopelessness.

Simon turned his attention toward Richard and said, "How much of Benny's file have you had a chance to look at?"

"None, actually," Richard admitted. "John was supposed to send it to me but hasn't gotten around to it yet. I figured he was busy and would get it to me when he had the time."

Simon thought for a moment, then stood. "I need to go. Richard, I'll be calling you again tomorrow after I have a chance to look at something. I might need to meet with the two of you again."

"That sounds fine," Richard agreed.

Benny gave Alex a solicitous look. "Just make sure you bring your friend."

As Simon and Alex left the interview room, she struggled to keep up with him. The meeting with Benny and his lawyer had triggered something in his mind.

Now she just had to find out what it was.

Once they were a safe distance from Benny and Richard, Alex whispered. "You're onto something. What is it?"

"I'm not sure," he replied, never slowing his pace. "But I have a feeling something very important has been left out of this case."

"Does it have to do with the money?" Alex asked, quickening her step so she fell in stride with him.

"Yes."

"You know what it is, don't you?" Alex asked, breathless from the effort to keep up with Simon.

When Simon answered, his words were clipped. "I think so. I need to check something first, though."

Alex stopped and grabbed Simon's arm, forcing him to stop walking. "What is it?"

Simon turned to face her and lowered his voice to a whisper. His wrinkled forehead was a testament to his stress. "It's just a hunch, but I believe it's possible that John Carmichael manufactured evidence so Benny would be convicted of murders he didn't commit."

73

J ULIA SLIPPED HER key into the door of her apartment, cursing herself for being so careless about sharing her connection to Thomas and Sheila Stone to a coworker, not to mention the total stranger who was with him. One thing she never anticipated was telling anyone was that she was the daughter of two murder victims. After finding out there was no inheritance to be had because Thomas had gambled it all away, the last thing she wanted was people to find out who she really was.

Only Edna and a few other family members knew her story. Well, them and John Carmichael.

Julia often wondered how different her life would be if she'd been raised by her biological parents. Despite her father's gambling problem, she'd heard that at one time they'd been very wealthy and belonged to the most exclusive clubs and social circles. Instead, she'd been raised by Sheila's cousin, Edna, a woman who'd been addicted to both booze and men. As a child, she'd wished she could have been adopted by a different family, one that took care of the kids and cared about each other. Instead, she spent summer days sitting outside in the blistering desert heat waiting for whatever man Edna was seeing at the time to get what he wanted from her and leave the run-down old house where she'd spent her childhood.

Sighing heavily, Julia prepared herself to face the unhappy life she was destined for. She and Edna were more alike than she cared to admit.

We certainly seem to pick the same kind of men, anyway, Julia thought bitterly as she walked through the living room. The scene was nothing unusual. A pizza box lay open on the floor and a beer bottle was clutched loosely in Mikey's hand. He was asleep on the couch and didn't even stir when she walked by.

Just like every other day, she thought, rolling her eyes. He's such a slob.

Disgusted with herself and with Mikey, she went straight to the bedroom and closed the door. Leaning against the dresser, she caught her reflection in the mirror hanging on the opposite wall.

I'm not a bad-looking woman, she thought, though she had to admit her rough start in life made her look older than her thirty-three years. Her dark blond hair was already show-ing traces of gray, her brown eyes held a haunted look from a lifetime of sorrow and disappointment.

"There has to be more to life than this," Julia said quietly. "There just has to be."

The apartment was furnished with secondhand and hand-me-down furniture, much of it faded and torn. The couch was stained, and the stench of stale beer hung in the air like a cheap bar. More than once she'd wished the whole place would burn down—with Mikey in it.

I have to talk to him tonight, Julia decided. I can't go on living like this. After my wretched childhood, I deserve more than this.

She stifled a yawn and changed quickly into a pair of old jeans, a sweatshirt, and thick wool socks. The temperature outside had dropped steadily throughout the afternoon and as she drove home from work. The meteorologist on the radio said she expected snow overnight.

I must be coming down with some kind of bug, Julia thought as she rubbed an achy muscle in her back. Either that or the stress of the week is taking a toll on me.

Exhaustion settled in once she'd gotten home from work. A wave of nausea washed over her.

Maybe I should put off talking to Mikey until I feel better. No, she admonished herself. Get it over with.

She took a deep breath and opened the bedroom door. The sooner she told him she wanted to end things, the sooner he'd be out of her life. The lease was in her name and she paid all the bills. Legally, there was nothing he could do to stop her from kicking him out.

"Hey, Mikey," she said walking from the bedroom into the living room. "We need to talk."

No response.

"Mikey, would you please get up so we can talk?"

Again, he didn't answer.

She was so tired.

Gathering all her strength, she moved to the end of the sofa where his head was resting. "Mikey!" she shouted, allowing her fatigue to fuel her anger. "Get up, you worthless piece of—"

The ashen pallor on Mikey's face stopped Julia's tirade

mid-sentence. Something wasn't right. As lazy as he was, Mikey never slept this soundly.

She bent over to check on him, and, dizziness overcoming her, she lost her balance and fell forward. When she extended a shaky arm to catch herself, her hand grazed his face. It was cool to the touch. A wave of panic washed over her.

Mikey was dead, she was sure of it, and she was getting weaker and sicker.

Stumbling across the room toward the kitchen table where she'd dropped her cell phone, she picked it up and dialed 911.

"Please, help me," Julia begged the dispatcher. "My boyfriend. I think he's dead." She quickly gave the woman her address, then said weakly. "Hurry... I think..."

With that, Julia succumbed to the darkness waiting to pull her under.

74

SIMON HELD THE penlight in his left hand while he picked the lock with his right. When the lock gave, he put the light between his teeth to cast a beam on the filing cabinet, using his hands to pry the drawers open. Sweat coated his palms. Even though he had a good reason for doing so, if he got caught, he could be suspended, or worse, disbarred.

Over the past several weeks, he hadn't been able to shake the feeling that something strange was going on with John. His behavior had become erratic, and more than once, Simon noticed alcohol on his breath first thing in the morning. From the day Simon joined the practice, something about John made him uneasy. He'd never considered that John could be doing anything illegal, but Simon had questioned his ethics many times in the past.

Ironic that I would be questioning *his* ethics, Simon thought as he scanned the tabs on the file folders.

Never in his life did Simon think he'd ever resort to what amounted to breaking and entering, but he didn't know what else to do. Going on nothing more than a hunch, Simon doubted anyone would believe John would do anything as serious as intentionally losing a case so his client would be found guilty and be sentenced to life in prison.

The beam from the penlight illuminated the file he was looking for. He took a deep breath, conceding that even though what he was doing wasn't necessarily illegal, in his mind what he was about to do was nothing less than robbery.

Sometimes at night, when he couldn't sleep, he wondered how somebody like him even ended up representing criminals, anyway.

He pulled Benny Johnson's extensive file from the cabinet. Fortunately, it was eleven o'clock and even the workaholics had gone home.

Quickly scanning the main area of the office, he exited John's and carried the files to his own. He'd already decided he wouldn't dare take the files out of the office and was prepared to spend a long night poring over every inch of Benny's defense.

Or, if his gut was right, lack thereof.

Three hours later, Simon's eyes burned and a dull ache had begun at the base of his skull. The clock read two a.m., and he still had hours to go before he'd be satisfied that he'd covered every inch of the case. In most circumstances, it would take days, maybe weeks, to be as thorough as he intended to be. He didn't have that much time—and wouldn't need it—with this one since he knew exactly what he was looking for.

At five a.m. he carried the file, flagged with post-it notes, to the copy room. His time was running out and there were several pages he wanted to take a closer look at. People would start trickling into the office soon. Even on a Saturday, some of the younger attorneys would get there as early as six-thirty, others coming in around eight if they were working on a big case. Simon had to be sure he'd have time to get the files back in John's cabinet and clean up any trace that he'd been there.

This must be the same adrenaline rush criminals feel, Simon thought, suddenly sheepish that he saw the appeal.

Satisfied he'd gotten copies of all the suspicious pages in the file, he returned the files to their drawers, stuffed the papers in his bag, and switched off his office light. Just as he was about to step through the door, he heard someone walking through the main office area. Simon glanced at his watch. Six-thirty on the nose. He peeked out long enough to see John taking long strides toward his own office, fumbling with his key ring. His gait was unsteady, indicating he'd spent a good portion of the night with a bottle of scotch.

Simon ducked back into his office, moving as far into the shadows as he could, praying John wouldn't notice anything amiss.

From his post in the darkest corner of his office, Simon heard the heavy thump of a file being dropped onto the desk, followed by the sound of tearing papers.

He's destroying Benny's file! Simon thought frantically, hoping he'd gotten all the evidence he needed to prove John threw the trial.

Simon's pulse quickened at the sound of the paper shredder erasing any hint of John's involvement in Benny's conviction.

As quickly as he'd arrived, John snapped off his light and left the building.

Realizing he'd been holding his breath, Simon exhaled and rushed into John's office. Again, he jimmied the lock and jerked the drawer open. He grabbed the file he'd been looking at just minutes before. Flipping through the pages, he noted that most of the missing pages were ones he'd taken time to copy. Certain he had what he needed, he replaced the files and slammed the drawer closed.

Doing a cursory glance around the office to make sure he was still alone, he rushed to his car with the bag containing parts of Benny's file and pulled out of the parking space a hundred feet from the building that housed his office.

An hour later, Simon sat in his father's favorite leather chair, long legs stretched across the matching ottoman. A cup of coffee in hand and the copied pages from Benny's file in his lap, he hoped to get another uninterrupted look at them.

He looked up from the papers when he heard his father come into the living room.

"You look awful," Sam said after taking a moment to study his son.

"Thanks, Dad. We don't all wake up looking ruggedly handsome like you," Simon said through a tired smile.

Sam flipped the switch on the wall and a fire roared to life in the fireplace. "What are you doing? You usually research your cases at the office."

"This isn't exactly an official case."

How can I possibly bring up the subject with my ex-cop father? he wondered. Attorney-client privilege is a big deal, and he'd never condone me breaking it, no matter the reason.

"Surely you're not working this hard on a freebie."

"Dad," Simon said, then paused. "I have a suspicion about one of my colleagues. I think there's some dirty business going on."

Sam arched an eyebrow. "Oh?"

"Yeah. I was at the office all night gathering paperwork to see if I could make some sense out of my hunch."

"And have you?"

"Yes, but I don't have solid proof yet. I'm still trying to find links between this person and a client our firm represented," Simon said, then took a slow drink of coffee.

Sam thought for a moment. "John Carmichael?"

"Yes," Simon admitted. "But how did you—?"

Shrugging, Sam said, "I've always thought there was something off about him. I couldn't put my finger on it, but he's always bothered me. Not just because he made me look like a fool on the witness stand on multiple occasions, either."

So I'm not on a witch hunt after all, Simon thought, relieved that his dad had the same feeling about Carmichael.

"I'm looking into the Stone murder case. Alex and I met with Benny Johnson today." He glanced at his watch. "Well, yesterday. I've been up all night trying to piece things together."

"Come up with anything?"

"When I mentioned to Benny the fact that fifty thousand dollars had been deposited into his account the day after the murders, he went berserk. Said he'd never had that much money in his life and that somebody had been using the deposit to frame him all these years. That got me thinking, what if John had something to do with his conviction? I know it seems far-fetched, but it's possible. Why else would he have agreed to represent somebody like Benny, who couldn't pay him a dime and had been arrested for killing one of his own coworkers? John won't do anything for free." Simon took another sip of coffee. "And answer me this—"

"Simon, slow down," his father ordered.

Simon ignored him and forged on. "Why weren't his fingerprints on the murder weapon? The police lifted them from all over the house, but the shovel and the poker were clean."

He leaned over the arm of the chair to close the gap between him and his father. "And another thing. John's notes don't mention that he used that fact during the defense. If Benny was my client, I'd be sure every juror knew about it and was sick of hearing me bring it up."

The more Simon spoke, the more sure he became that John was involved in something bad, and that whatever it was had something to do with Benny needing to go to jail to cover it up.

"I've talked to people who knew him back then, and from what I gather, even then he probably wouldn't have done something for someone out of the goodness of his heart. He always expected something in return. The question is: what did he get from Benny that made representing him worthwhile?"

"John's notes? Is that what you're looking at?"

Simon swallowed hard, anticipating his father's reaction. "Yes. I got these from Benny's file. I was at the office all night scouring the file and making copies of the pages that raised red flags. I'm hoping to connect a couple things that will answer some long-standing questions about the case."

Sam looked intently at his son, eyes expressing disappointment. "Simon, did you get John's permission to go into his office in the middle of the night and look through his files?"

"No, I didn't."

"Did you find the filing cabinet unlocked?"

"No."

"Do you have a key?"

"No."

"How did you get into the filing cabinet?"

"I picked the lock," Simon admitted.

So this is what it feels like to be cross-examined, Simon thought. The adrenaline rush wasn't worth it.

Sam sat, looking at his son, his disapproving expression reaffirming what Simon already knew.

"I think you're going to want to see what I found," Simon finally said.

After one last disappointed glance to communicate that he didn't take lightly what his son had done, Sam rolled his wheelchair closer to Simon and began looking at the pages Simon handed him.

Simon highlighted the things he'd noticed when he went through the file at the office. Now, the look on Sam's face as he read the sentences in glowing yellow told Simon his father was seeing the same connection he'd found hours ago.

Sam studied the paper in his hand. "How did nobody notice this?"

"I have no idea. Everybody knows John is good at what he does. The best, probably. But apparently nobody knows what he's actually been up to."

"What do you plan to do about this?" Sam asked, handing the papers back to Simon.

"I guess I'll ask for a favor down at the police station. I've got a buddy that owes me one."

Sam crossed his arms over his chest. "What do you think he'll find?" he asked, watching the flames dance in the fireplace.

Simon followed his father's line of vision in the direction of the flames licking the ceramic logs before answering. "I think he'll find John Carmichael is the one that deposited fifty thousand dollars into Benny Johnson's bank account the day after the murders."

75

AFTER A QUICK breakfast of pancakes, fruit, and three cups of coffee with his dad and Alex, Simon made his way into the office a little before ten. It didn't take long to realize something was wrong.

He stuck his head in Susan's office before walking to his own. "What's going on?"

"You haven't heard?" Susan replied, turning her attention away from the file lying open on her desk. "Julia was rushed to the emergency room last night. The paramedics found Mikey, her boyfriend, dead on the sofa and she was unconscious on the floor beside him."

"No, I hadn't heard," Simon said, shaking his head. "What happened?"

Susan shrugged. "We don't really know. I called the hospital but couldn't get many answers from them. John just left to go down there and find out. The hospital staff was having some trouble getting in touch with her family," Susan offered.

I would imagine so, Simon thought, remembering his

conversation with Julia yesterday. Her family situation was probably complicated, at best.

"Please let me know if you hear anything," Simon requested, then turned to walk back to his office.

"Simon?" Susan called after him.

He stopped mid-stride and turned back toward her. "Yeah?"

"How is your friend? I heard she was being stalked. Is she okay?" Susan's concern was awkward, but sincere.

Simon still couldn't shake the fear that something would happen to Alex. When her life was in danger, he realized just how much he was beginning to care about her. The thought of losing her nearly choked him.

"She's fine, just shaken up," he managed to say over the lump in his throat. "They caught the guy yesterday outside my dad's house. She's staying with him until she goes home."

"Good. I can't imagine how frightened she must be. She seems like a nice person; I'm glad she's okay."

Simon was surprised at Susan's empathy. Why her interest in Alex? he wondered.

"I'll pass your concern on to her," Simon promised, then walked to his office.

Settled behind his desk, he phoned the weekend secretary, asking not to be disturbed unless there was an absolute emergency. After hanging up, he retrieved the contents of his briefcase and looked over the pages from Benny's file one more time.

Forty-five minutes later, satisfied he had enough cause to ask for a favor, he made the call to Jimmy Boone, a close friend from high school with a rebellious streak whom Simon had bailed out of trouble more than once.

And now he's in law enforcement, Simon thought, smiling at the irony. And I'm still trying to get people out of trouble.

Simon greeted his old friend. "Hey, Jimmy. Still locking 'em up?"

"Yep," Jimmy answered. "You still setting 'em free?"

"Still trying to. Listen buddy, I've got a favor to ask."

As he laid out his suspicions, he could hear Jimmy's pencil scratching notes onto a pad of paper.

"Are you switching sides, Simon? You usually try to find a way to keep the bad guys *out* of jail."

Simon winced. He didn't like the way that sounded. "Only the ones that aren't guilty," he said, the pit in his stomach reminding him that he'd done his share of keeping the guilty ones out of jail, too.

"This is a big favor to ask, but I'll do my best," Jimmy agreed. "When do you need this?"

"As soon as possible. And whatever you do, keep this quiet. If John knew what I was up to he'd bury me, and relish doing it."

"I'll see what I can turn up," Jimmy assured him. "If it turns out to be something, this could be a huge collar for me. They might even give me a raise."

Simon chuckled.

Relieved that he was able to find somebody to help, Simon tried to focus on his cases. The more he looked over them, the more his mind wandered. The discontentment with his job had been growing steadily over the past year, and it was getting harder and harder to make himself go to work every day. The career he thought would be perfect for him wasn't fulfilling him anymore. In fact, he grew more frustrated with the entitled clients that called him each day.

Besides, he reasoned, I'm tired of being so busy that I have to be at the office on Saturdays.

Even though he'd been at the firm for five years, he still hadn't put his personal touch on his office. Other than a painting he picked up at an art show featuring local artists and a family photo, the office could have belonged to anybody. Now he knew why. He didn't really want to be here.

Simon tried focusing on the case he was working on. An administrative assistant at a major department store had been accused of embezzling funds.

She deserves to be in jail, Simon thought ruefully. Nearly all of them do.

He rubbed his temples as his thoughts again drifted to Alex. What on earth had she stumbled into? Since she arrived in Lexington, she'd almost been murdered, and he was digging into a case that was closed three decades ago. Somebody tried to kill Benny Johnson, and Tony barely survived what everyone at the prison was calling a suicide attempt.

Were each of these incidents just bad luck, happening all at once, or was something bigger going on?

If they are all connected, Simon wondered, who's calling the shots?

76

JULIA TRIED TO wake up. She was swimming in a dark ocean, and each time she came close to breaking the surface of the water, something pulled her back under. The light seemed to be just out of reach, and no amount of struggling got her any closer.

Her subconscious told her something didn't make sense. Something didn't add up. There had been something off about the apartment when she got home, but her brain was too tired to make any sense of it. Frustration had been weighing heavily on her when she'd gotten home, so whatever it was hadn't been committed to memory.

Something pricked the corner of her mind as she felt herself drifting closer toward the light. Almost able to reach out and touch it, she saw a face on the edge of the darkness surrounding her. Using all her energy to focus her blurry eyes, she was relieved to see that the face was familiar. She'd looked at it every day for the past two years, but now it wore an expression she didn't recognize.

Her brain struggled to make sense of the images floating

in front of her eyes. The familiar steel-gray eyes, sharp features, and athletic build belonged in a suit. Instead, he was wearing scrubs and a white coat.

Her brain warned her that she was in danger. Panic willed her to move, but she couldn't. She was too weak to pull the hand away that suddenly clamped over her mouth and nose. Nearly silent whimpers were the only defense she had against the strong hand pulling her back, farther away from the light and down into the darkness she'd never escape.

77

ALEX RUBBED THE knot on the side of her head. Though smaller, the spot that hit the curb when she was pushed into traffic was unmistakable.

"Pushed," Alex whispered. Even with everything that had happened in the last forty-eight hours, she still couldn't wrap her mind around it.

Even now it was hard to believe Jeffery would want her dead so badly he was willing to travel more than five hundred miles to make it happen. They'd had such a good rapport throughout their working relationship, and he was making substantial progress.

What would make him turn on me like that? she wondered.

The only way to know would be to ask him, she reminded herself.

It had snowed overnight, so she dressed quickly in a heavy turtleneck sweater and jeans and stuffed her feet into heavy wool socks and boots. Once dressed, she dialed the number for the Fayette County Detention Center and waited patiently to be transferred to the correct department. The grim voice that answered the phone told her Jeffery had been transferred to the psychiatric hospital for evaluation.

A quick search on her laptop yielded the phone number and address of the hospital. The information page told her visiting hours would last another hour and a half.

Before she could change her mind, she grabbed her purse and keys and dashed out the door.

Thirty minutes later, she sat in a small interview room on the unit Jeffery was assigned to. The clock on the wall behind her ticked the seconds away. Any time she visited a client who'd been admitted to a hospital, she came away feeling depressed. Most of the time, the environment wasn't conducive to healing; it was just a place people went when things got too hard for them or their families.

Alex had her own ideas about how places like this should be run, but so far no one had asked her opinion.

The door of the interview room opened slowly. Alex inhaled as the hinges creaked softly. Only seconds away from looking into the face of her would-be killer, Alex's flight instinct kicked in and she wanted to bolt.

Having no way out but the door that was opening, she gathered her courage and clamped her hands on the edge of her chair, willing herself to stay put.

Jeffery entered the room accompanied by a frail-looking security guard. Jeffery settled into a chair across the rickety table from Alex while the guard took his post in the corner of the room behind her. With his slight build, Alex took little comfort in his presence. His small frame would be no match for an angry psych patient in the middle of a psychotic break.

"Alex," Jeffery began. "It's so nice of you to visit. How have you been?" Though cordial, his tone was chilly.

Alex's voice mirrored his. "I've been better. What about you?"

His shoulders slumped. "Well, they locked me up because I tried to tell them what happened to you, so I guess I've been better, too."

"Jeffery, they locked you up because they think you're the one that pushed me into traffic," Alex said, leaning back in her chair to create distance between them.

"I didn't push you. I saw who did, though. I tried to describe him to the police when I called, but as soon as I told them who you were and that I was one of your clients, they automatically thought I was the one who did it. Apparently just because I have a mental illness, I'm also a killer," Jeffery said, the pain of the stereotype written on his face.

She'd suspected he'd stopped taking his medication weeks ago, but he sounded so lucid now. If the meds were out of his system, it would take at least a couple weeks for them to fully take effect again. Two days' worth wouldn't make this big a difference.

This raised a whole new question in her mind: If he hadn't stopped taking his medication, was it possible that he really didn't push her but saw who did?

Her voice softened. "I know how hard it is for you that people automatically assume you're violent because of your illness. You do have a history of aggression, though. It's not a far leap to suspect that you'd do something to hurt me."

Jeffery reached a hand across the table toward her then pulled it back and folded his hands together. "Never when I was taking my medicine, though. Why would I hurt you?

You're helping me get my life together. You can help me get a job and my own place to live. Why would I jeopardize that?"

It was true. They were so close to reaching his goals. That's why she hadn't mentioned her suspicions about him to Jeannie.

"How do you explain the way you've been acting? And why did you follow me here?"

He leaned back and dropped his hands in his lap. "I showed up for my appointment on Monday and heard some people talking about you not being there, so I didn't stay. I heard them say where you were going, so I decided to come here and ask you not to leave me. I was afraid you wouldn't come back. I needed you to come back." He sounded so hurt and vulnerable.

Alex's heart twisted with compassion. "Can you tell me why you've been so quiet the last few times I saw you? I was beginning to think you stopped taking your meds."

Jeffery raised his eyes to meet hers. The sadness and shame in his eyes tore at her. She'd dedicated her life's work to helping people like Jeffery, but instead felt like she was turning him into another victim of a flawed system.

Finally, Jeffery spoke. "I was afraid if it seemed like I was doing really good, you'd cut me loose. I didn't want you to think I didn't need you anymore. The only reason I can do anything is because you believe I can. Nobody else does."

Leaning forward to close the gap she'd created between her and Jeffery, Alex said, "I wasn't going to get you back on your feet and cut you loose. I told you I would help you, but I can't do that if you won't talk to me." Alex hesitated briefly before asking the next question, unsure if she really wanted to know the answer. "Jeffery, did you really see who pushed me?"

Jeffery nodded, shaggy hair swinging around his ears.

She released the breath she'd been holding. "Can you describe him?"

He perked up. "I can do better than that." He reached into his pocket and pulled out a folded piece of paper and pushed it across the table to Alex. "I drew a sketch. I wanted to get it on paper while it was still fresh in my mind."

With trembling hands, Alex took the paper and unfolded it. The sketch was amazing. The detailed facial features would give any police department sketch artist a run for his money. She told him that.

A smile that lit up his face was Jeffery's only response.

"Do you know him?" the guard asked from his station in the corner.

Alex had forgotten he was there.

She narrowed her eyes and held the image closer to her face. "I'm not sure."

The face was vaguely familiar, but many of the features were so general they could have belonged to almost anybody. The man in the sketch definitely wouldn't stand out in a crowd.

Maybe that worked to his favor.

"Do you mind if I keep this?" she asked Jeffery.

"Of course not," he said. "And Alex? Would you please tell the police I didn't try to hurt you so they'll let me out of this place?" He leaned forward, smiled, and in a conspiratorial whisper said, "The people here are crazy."

Alex nodded, a smile tugging at her mouth. Jeffery did have a good sense of humor. "I'll talk to them. And I'm glad to see how well you're doing despite the circumstances. I'm very proud of you, Jeffery."

Again, a smile lit up his face.

On the drive back to Sam's house, she thought about the

face staring back at her from the sketch. The thing that bothered her about the day she'd nearly been killed tried to force its way into her consciousness. She was certain Jeffery had nothing to do with the attempt on her life, and that his sketch held the key to identifying the person who did.

Fumbling with the key to Sam's front door, bits and pieces from Jeffery's sketch floated around in her mind. She pushed the door open and closed it behind her, engaging the deadbolt.

Suddenly, the pieces fell together and formed a familiar face. The eyes, devoid of warmth. The mouth forming a hard, straight line. The forehead and heavy eyebrows that formed a V when he was angry.

It wasn't the face from the sketch that troubled her, it was the one she saw just before she fell. The face that was watching, twisted into a sneer as someone else tried to kill her. He'd seen it happening and didn't try to stop it.

"Steven was there!" she gasped.

She whirled around as a voice from across the room said, "I guess you finally had no choice but to notice me."

78

"SIMON, IT LOOKS like your hunch paid off," Jimmy Boone said when he returned Simon's call later that day.

"You got something?" Simon grabbed a pen, then wedged the phone between his shoulder and ear, ready to take notes. "That was fast."

"Yeah, and I charge extra on weekends," Jimmy jabbed at his old friend. "Truth be told, I did have a little help."

"Jimmy, I asked you not to tell anybody about this. If John finds out, I'm toast." Simon's palms were suddenly sweaty.

"Don't worry, buddy," Jimmy reassured him. "I had a friend that owed me one, so I got her to help me out. We'd get in big trouble if anyone knew she was involved, so nobody will ever find out. Got it?"

Jimmy's assurances did little to squelch Simon's mounting anxiety. "You're sure?" The knot in Simon's shoulder told him he did need to worry. Just like old times, Simon thought, Jimmy could get him into a lot of trouble.

"Positive. Look, she's a hacker. If anybody knew I had her hacking into bank account records, we'd be sharing a cell."

"You're working with a criminal?" Simon didn't know why he was surprised. Jimmy's ability to get himself mixed up with illegal activities never ceased to amaze him. Even as a law enforcement professional, most of Jimmy's methods were questionable at best. Simon wondered if one day he'd be trying to keep Jimmy out of jail.

"I prefer the term 'informant,' and let's just say we had a chance encounter at a bar. I actually find her quite fascinating."

Simon rolled his eyes. Always a soft spot for the ladies, he could practically see Jimmy beaming from ear to ear. "I'm sure you do. Tell me what you and your *associate* found."

"It's interesting. I hope you're ready."

"Oh, I am. Just get on with it." Simon knew he sounded impatient, but he felt like the well-being of his whole family rested on his shoulders. Not to mention Alex, who he'd already grown too attached to.

"I could do without the attitude," Jimmy snapped. "I risked a lot to help you, so the least you could do is show a little gratitude."

Simon sighed. "I know. I'm sorry. I've just got a lot on my plate right now. I really do appreciate everything you've done. I'm listening."

"We didn't find John Carmichael's name attached to any deposit made into Benny Johnson's bank account, now or ever. When we looked into *Carmichael's* bank records over the past thirty-five years, though, they were all squeaky clean, except for one thing. Every so often he deposited large amounts of money into his account. That raised a red flag for us, but there was no record of the bank flagging it as suspicious activity, so apparently it has been going on a long time. Maybe he'd already alerted the bank that he'd be making the deposits. I don't know."

Simon put the pen down and rubbed the back of his neck. "That's the opposite of interesting. Plus, it shows my suspicions were wrong. Those large deposits were probably from big cases he's won." Simon shook his head and muttered. "I broke into the man's locked filing cabinet for nothing."

"I'll pretend I didn't hear that," Jimmy said, then quickly moved on. "My computer genius friend did find, however, that the account used to transfer the money to Benny Johnson was opened years before he was arrested. The statements for the account are mailed to a post office box in a shady part of town. When I asked the clerk who came to pick up the mail, the man he identified sounds remarkably like Carmichael. Said the guy stuck out like a sore thumb in that neighborhood with his fancy suits. I doubt that's a coincidence. He also said for the past couple years, a woman who looked to be about thirty years old with dark blond hair and a sour disposition occasionally came to pick up the mail. Apparently, the guy at the desk tried to hit on her and she brushed him off. If you want my opinion, he's holding a grudge and wants to get this chick in trouble."

Simon's heart rate sped up. It was very likely he'd just stumbled onto something huge. Manufactured evidence, deliberately throwing a case to keep his client behind bars, possibly murder. In addition, the woman Jimmy described sounded a lot like Julia Burke. John and Julia's relationship always seemed like it was more than a simple boss-assistant one. Nothing romantic, of course, but definitely different. Now it looked like they were both involved in something illegal.

"Go on," Simon encouraged, hoping against hope that there would be more.

Jimmy took a deep breath before continuing. With a feeling that Jimmy was about to say something huge, Simon held his. Jimmy had hardly taken a breath between sentences before.

"I ran headfirst into an FBI investigation," Jimmy finally said.

"Did you say FBI?" That would mean Simon wasn't the first to suspect John was up to something dirty. Not by a long shot.

"Apparently the FBI has been using a forensic accountant to build a case against Carmichael for quite some time," Jimmy offered.

"A forensic accountant? Do they suspect some kind of fraud?" Simon asked, lowering his voice. Despite the fact that his office was tucked away, he couldn't help but worry that somebody might be listening.

"No idea. They wouldn't tell me. It's a federal case and they weren't exactly forthcoming with a local boy like myself."

Simon was sure he sensed resentment in Jimmy's voice.

"Anyway," Jimmy continued, "since I didn't exactly get clearance to be looking into Carmichael, I didn't push for info."

"They didn't give any indication about why they're looking at him?"

"Nope. The agent I talked to must have taken mercy on my poor soul, though, because he did tell me they're planning to make an arrest soon. He also told me not to do anything to screw it up for them. He didn't even try to hide the fact that my knowledge of it was a real pain in the rear, either. Made me swear to keep my mouth shut and not tell anybody else on the force; it was almost like they're afraid we'll steal their thunder or something," Jimmy snorted.

Simon sat back and ran his hand through his hair, reeling

from the news that his coworker was about to be arrested following a federal investigation.

Just when Simon thought Jimmy was finished dropping bombshells, he dropped the biggest one yet.

"Oh, and Simon? You might be interested to know two big withdrawals were taken from that other account in the fake name earlier this week. They were deposited into the account of someone named Danny Jones. I did a little digging, and it turns out he's a guard at the state prison where Benny is serving his sentence. I haven't been able to find out anything else, so I don't know what the money would have been for."

Adrenaline surged through Simon. "I do," he growled and hung up the phone.

I knew Tony wouldn't try to kill anybody, Simon thought. And I knew he wouldn't try to kill himself. But now I know who tried to kill them both.

And why.

79

ALEX'S HAND FLEW to her mouth. "Please, God. No," she moaned through her fingers.

Her blood turned to ice as she scanned the room. Sam's limp body slumped to one side in his wheelchair at the kitchen table. From a distance, she couldn't tell if he was alive or dead. Turning her attention away from him, she looked at Steven, who sat in a chair in the darkest corner of the room. His legs were crossed, his left ankle resting on his right knee. In his hand he held a scarf—the one she'd refused to accept from him just two weeks ago.

Her heart beat wildly at the realization that no one was there to protect her. Sam was unconscious and maybe dead; Jackson and Murray were nowhere to be found. She strained to hear any kind of movement from the dogs, only to be greeted by silence punctuated with her own ragged breathing.

"What's the matter, Alex?" Steven asked as he rose from the chair and moved slowly across the room. "Aren't you glad to see me? Do you feel uncomfortable being this close to me?"

Alex looked away from the menacing face. Bile rose in her

throat. She was disgusted at him for being such a worthless excuse for a human being and even more disgusted at herself for being afraid of him.

"What did you do to him?" Alex demanded, pointing at Sam.

"Don't worry about him. He's just napping." The sneer on Steven's face communicated that he had no concern about whether Sam lived or died.

"What do you want from me?" Alex asked. Her hands were going numb from fear. She flexed her fingers in an effort to regain some feeling.

"Just you. That's all I've ever wanted, but you don't think I'm good enough for you. That's why you've already replaced me with some guy you just met. I can tell by the way you look at him that you think he's everything I'm not."

The numbness in her hands spread toward her elbows. Steven had seen her with Simon. He'd been watching her all this time, waiting for the perfect moment to kill her. Now he was standing three feet away, wrapping the scarf around his hands.

"So, you plan to kill me because I broke up with you?" Alex asked, taking a step back and at the same time painfully aware that with each movement in that direction, she was running out of room.

"Not just because of that. Because you're no different than anyone else who has cast me aside. You toyed with me for a while, then got bored and broke my heart for your own entertainment. Now I have to make an example out of you—a warning to anyone else that thinks I can be thrown away like a piece of trash." His lip curled in a sneer as he took another step in her direction.

Just keep him talking, Alex told herself. You get people to talk for a living. Make that skill work for you now.

"How did you find me?" she asked, taking another step backward.

Steven laughed, a high-pitched cackle that chilled Alex to her core. "You can thank your sweet old grandma for that."

"What did you do to her?" Alex demanded, a flash of anger surging through her. She might be mad at Gram right now, but she was fiercely protective of the only family she had left.

"I didn't do anything to her. She called me, if you can believe that. She wanted me to keep you safe up here. Ironic, isn't it?"

Alex's eyes slid toward the scarf. Gram had told him where to find her? In an effort to protect her, Gram had unknowingly delivered her into the hands of a psychopath.

Steven took a small step forward. "What she didn't know was that when she called, I was already following you. It did make me feel a little better that she practically gave me permission to do it. You won't believe me, but I did feel a little bad about invading your privacy. That is, until I realized what you were doing with your privacy." Beads of sweat glistened on his forehead. "I knew you'd already forgotten about me, and the look on your face when I called you that first day you were here told me exactly how much I meant to you."

Alex's eyes widened. She could feel perspiration dampening her armpits.

A smile stretched across Steven's maniacal face. "That's right, Alex. I was watching you. I have been the whole time. I've seen you with that other guy, too. I can tell by the way you look at him that you like him. It's just too bad you'll never be able to be with him. If I'm not good enough for you, neither is he." Another step forward.

Desperate to buy more time, Alex began rambling. "We just didn't work out, Steven. Haven't you ever been in a relationship that just didn't work? We're two different kinds of people, that's all. There's somebody out there much better suited for you than I am."

She'd have to be completely deranged, Alex thought, but self-preservation kept her from voicing it.

"It was more than that," Steven said angrily. "You might not think I noticed, but I saw the look on your face each time I reached for your hand or tried to stroke your hair. You were disgusted and couldn't get away fast enough. The excuses you came up with not to see me were laughable, really. If I hadn't been so hurt, I might have thought they were funny. Your car was at the mechanic's? You had to work late? You thought you might be coming down with something? They were lies, all of them. I'm surprised you didn't tell me you had to wash your hair, too. But now… Now you're going to have to pay for those lies, and all the other ways you've hurt me."

He'd been moving slowly as he spoke and was now standing just inches away. He could grab her any time he wanted, and she knew he relished that power.

She knew the profile. Watching her squirm would give him almost as much pleasure as the kill itself. The thrill of the hunt, she guessed. His prey was backed into the corner with nowhere to go and was completely at his mercy. For the first time in his life, he felt powerful, like he had control of not only his own destiny, but the destiny of someone else, too.

Alex took another step back and bumped into the wall. She was officially trapped.

Steven licked his lips in anticipation before his mouth formed a twisted smile. She took a deep breath, preparing herself to fight. She caught the scent of nervous sweat. He was too close. Taking a step to the side, she bumped into the end table next to the sofa. The thought occurred to her that this must be the way a gazelle feels when it can't get away from the lion that's been chasing it.

Except there was nothing majestic about Steven that demanded admiration.

In one quick movement, Steven looped the scarf around her neck. Alex put her hands up to protect herself and he adjusted it so her hands would be pressed against her throat.

"Don't worry, my love," he whispered, his breath hot against her ear, "it will only hurt for a minute."

The more she struggled to get away, the more he tightened the scarf. The room began to spin as she became weaker with each passing second.

A burst of panic mingled with a sense of resignation. She couldn't save herself.

"Isn't it funny?" Steven said softly in her ear. "Your own hands are killing you. That's fitting, don't you think? You've been slowly killing me for months."

His voice sounded so far away. In a few moments she'd slip from consciousness. Gathering all the strength she had left, Alex made a final attempt to free herself from Steven's grip.

Just before darkness enveloped her, she heard another voice, then a crash. The scarf loosened. Fireworks exploded before her eyes as oxygen rushed to her brain. The sounds from the living room grew closer. As her eyes refocused, she saw Steven crash into the wall while another man grabbed him by the throat with one hand and lifted a lamp over his head with the other. The lamp met Steven's skull with a sickening crack and his body crumpled to the floor.

In a matter of seconds, Simon knelt beside her.

"Stay with me, Alex," he urged. "Breathe. Slow and steady. You're okay now. I've got you."

Alex obeyed the command, and within a few minutes she'd mostly regained her equilibrium. "I'm okay," she croaked, her voice hoarse from the trauma.

Simon smiled and brushed the hair away from her eyes. "You really can't keep yourself out of trouble, can you?"

80

JOHN KNEW THE end was coming. He'd become reckless. For the first time in his life, he felt trapped with no way out.

No one ever suspected he lost Benny's case on purpose. Benny was a lowlife who'd been easy to get convicted. His quick temper and sarcastic remarks on the witness stand for his own defense only made the jurors hate him. John knew by looking at them which way they would vote. Since he was representing Benny for free, he played the part of the generous attorney with a heart of gold while simultaneously helping Benny look more guilty every time he opened his mouth.

John had been confident no one would ever find out the truth.

Until now.

When he went to his office early this morning, it was obvious from the faint scratches on the lock and the fact that some of the pages in Benny's file were out of order that someone had broken into his filing cabinet. Even hungover, he'd known instantly someone was suspicious of the case.

Were they suspicious of *why* I had to make sure I lost the case?

John wondered. Nobody could possibly know, he quickly assured himself. I've been careful for more than three decades, and nobody has had a reason to go looking into my bank accounts.

Except the Feds. The thought slammed into the forefront of John's mind.

He'd gotten wind several months ago that Clarence suspected undercover agents were trying to place bets on everything from horse races to college basketball games. Fortunately, they'd been made and any evidence that could have been used against John and Clarence had been destroyed.

A loud knock startled him. He placed the nearly empty glass of Scotch on a coaster on the small table next to his chair. He stood, crossing the room to his wall safe. There, under his pistol, was all the information needed to convict him and everyone else in the operation, including Clarence. He withdrew the weapon, leaving the door of the safe open so the information would be easy to find.

He wouldn't go down alone. For all his threats, Clarence would go down with him. That almost made what he was about to do worth it.

"This is it," he said, as though he was a soldier going into battle.

He swung the door open and two FBI agents rushed inside. Taking note that he was armed, they leveled their weapons at his chest, ready to fire.

"John Carmichael, you're under arrest. Drop your weapon," shouted the agent closest to him.

I guess they have all the evidence they need now, he thought wryly. Raising his pistol, he pointed it at the agent's chest. He's young, John thought. Probably has a wife and kids at home that worry every time he goes to work that he won't come home.

Perfect.

"Drop your weapon!" the older agent shouted.

John flicked his eyes toward the safe. If he gave himself up, one of the agents would rattle off the charges against him: racketeering, bookmaking, operating a business without a license, tax evasion. Soon they'd tack on Julia's murder. His plan to get rid of her had been genius, but her boyfriend certainly hadn't been. He believed John when he said he was there to fix the fireplace. Instead, he tampered with the gas line, causing a leak that filled the ratty apartment with carbon monoxide.

He was the best criminal defense attorney around, but even he wouldn't be able to beat the charges if they took him in. Especially since it wouldn't be hard to prove that he'd been the one to suffocate her with his bare hands at the hospital.

As the investigation went on, the prosecutor would likely add manufacturing and tampering with evidence to the current charges. He was looking at life in prison. There would be no worry-free retirement, no traveling around the world. There would only be a cell, an orange jumpsuit, and the fear that a fellow inmate would at some point have a vendetta against him. He would always be looking over his shoulder.

Waiting.

That's not the life for me, John thought.

As the FBI agents inched closer, John cocked the pistol and slid his finger onto the trigger. He shivered slightly at the thought of what was about to happen. Mentally bidding farewell to the power, money, and prestige, he readied himself to pull the trigger. The sound of a gun firing echoed through the room as the bullet ripped through John Carmichael's chest, erasing the possibility of a life in prison.

81

"I HEAR THEY'RE letting you go home today," Alex said, squeezing Sam's hand.

"They are. And not a moment too soon. I'm sick of being poked and force-fed my weight in pills every few hours. They're treating me like I'm an old man," Sam complained. "The nurses are even calling me 'cutie.'"

He'd been in the hospital for two days after Steven had knocked him unconscious. Despite the concussion, the doctors were confident there wouldn't be any lasting brain damage. Even so, the nurses took extra time to care for him.

Sam propped himself up on his elbows and silently observed Alex. An ugly red and purple bruise marred her neck where Steven had wrapped the scarf. She self-consciously touched the bruise with her fingertips, wishing she'd worn a turtleneck.

It still seemed surreal, but she was thankful everything turned out the way it did. She was okay, Sam was okay, and the dogs were okay. Steven had fed them a mild tranquilizer so they wouldn't interfere with his plan to kill her. Both dogs had recovered beautifully.

Now Steven was behind bars where he belonged, Sam was being released from the hospital, and Alex was on the mend.

Theoretically, everything was fine.

"Will you be okay?" Sam asked.

Alex nodded. "I will. My physical recovery will be much quicker than my mental one, though." She paused, then added, "It might be a while before I can wear a scarf again."

Sam nodded in understanding.

"Obviously this trip didn't turn out the way I'd hoped, but I managed to make some good friends along the way." She smiled at the older man she'd come to care so much about.

"What now?" Sam asked, settling back on his pillow.

"I'm heading back to Charleston this afternoon. I'm going to say goodbye to Simon, then pick up Jackson and my suitcase from your house and be on my way."

"I see," Sam said quietly.

"Gram has been worried sick about me, and I owe her an apology. When she said she was concerned about my safety, I thought she was just trying to keep me from searching for my birth parents. It's time to go home and mend some bridges."

"Well, we'll certainly miss you when you leave. It's been an unexpected and wonderful surprise to make a new friend at this stage in my life. Please promise you'll visit." Sam patted Alex's hand.

"Try and stop me," she teased, then leaned forward to drop a kiss on Sam's forehead.

In just one short week, she'd grown to love this man. Tears stung the backs of her eyes. In an odd way, she felt like she was home.

She walked to the door and turned for a final glance at the man who'd nearly lost his life to protect her and forced herself to stay the tears threatening to fall down her cheeks. With a quick flick of her wrist, she waved goodbye and hurried to her car where she allowed the tears to flow freely.

Alone in her car, she grieved. Grieved for the parents she'd lost, the parents she'd never know, and the new friends she was leaving behind. The emotional roller coaster was nearing an end, but she'd never be the same.

Walking into Simon's office building, Alex braced herself to say goodbye. She paused at his office door, watching him a moment before speaking. "It sure is quiet around here."

Simon looked up, his eyes resting on the bruises circling Alex's neck. "John's funeral was this morning. Everyone's still in shock."

"Suicide by cop is more common than people think. Does anybody know why he did it?" A cold lump lodged in Alex's throat. Any life lost always affected her.

Simon exhaled. "A buddy of mine down at the police station called a little while ago. They found evidence in John's home office that he'd been running an underground gambling operation for the past thirty-five years. The FBI was arresting him for that, along with a slew of other things. In the process of looking through his personal papers, they found evidence that Benny Johnson worked for him as an enforcer. That's why John manufactured the evidence to make sure Benny would stay in jail. Thomas Stone was an avid gambler, and evidently, he ordered Benny to go to his house to collect on a debt. Benny decided to take a little something for himself on the side."

"How could he be so sure that Benny wouldn't tell

anybody who he worked for?" Alex asked, unconsciously rubbing her throat.

Simon shrugged. "Benny didn't know. He'd always worked for a nameless, faceless employer. All he knew was that he got a cut of the collection, but never had direct contact with the guy paying him. That was John's way of protecting himself in case Benny got greedy and tried to blackmail him." He sighed. "To make matters worse, John also had documentation that he paid a prison guard to kill Benny so he'd never have a chance to talk. Then, he and Benny parted ways and John worried Benny's new lawyer would connect the dots and blow the whistle on him. When the guard failed at that, he tried to frame my brother. Then he tried to kill Tony in a staged suicide attempt and threatened to kill Dad if Tony said anything about it."

Alex suddenly felt dizzy. Someone threatened to kill Sam. She braced herself against the edge of Simon's desk. "How could such a well-respected man be leading a completely separate life?"

"There's more, and you may want to sit down for this."

She sat, sure he couldn't tell her anything worse than he already had.

Coming around his desk to sit in the chair next to Alex, he took her hand and said, "He also paid the guard to kill you. He's the one that pushed you off the curb. You were stirring stuff up about the Stone murders, and John was afraid you'd get people asking questions."

"Which I did," Alex stated.

Simon nodded in agreement. "He's also the one who sent you the threatening note, and one to your grandmother."

"No wonder she was so worried," Alex said. Poor Gram. "So what will happen to Benny?"

"He's singing like a canary now. Won't shut up about how far into debt Thomas was, and how he kept it a secret all these years. Thomas owed John a fortune and wasn't paying up. In all likelihood, Richard Wade will have enough grounds to get the murder conviction overturned. The judge will lessen the charge to breaking and entering. He'll be let out with time served. It looks like Benny Johnson will be walking the streets a free man before we know it." Then Simon muttered, "God help us all."

"What about Tony?"

"He'll finish his sentence but has been cleared of trying to murder Benny. It's funny—those two are actually becoming friends. They seem to have a mutual understanding. I never would have seen that coming…" Simon shook his head in disbelief.

"Then who killed Thomas and Sheila?" Alex asked. There was suddenly a double murder with no suspect.

Simon frowned and shrugged. "I don't know. They'll reopen the case, but it's about as cold as they come. They may never find out who did it."

An awkward silence hung in the air before Alex announced, "I'm going back to Charleston today. I've already said goodbye to your dad."

Simon looked as though somebody had just knocked the wind out of him. "Sorry you didn't find what you were looking for," he said quietly, turning his head to gaze out the window.

Alex followed his line of vision. "It was a long shot, but I'm glad I tried."

I'm so tired of losing people, Alex thought. As she looked at the man who'd done so much to help her, she ached at the thought that Simon and his father were going to be added to that list as soon as she left for home.

Pulling her from her growing sadness, her phone rang. "Hello?"

"This is Officer DiVito. I'm sorry the DNA results took so long to get back. These things can take a while, I'm afraid."

"That's okay. I guess it doesn't matter now, anyway. I met Thomas and Sheila Stone's daughter, so I kind of found out on my own that they weren't my biological parents."

"That's not exactly true," Officer DiVito countered. "We have a partial match."

Alex held her breath as she listened to the officer explain the results.

Repeating what she'd just been told, Alex said, "So, you're telling me that my DNA didn't match Sheila Stone, but it did match Thomas?" She looked at Simon. His surprise mirrored her own. "That would mean Sheila wasn't my mother, but Thomas *was* my father. Thank you, Officer." Alex disconnected the call and waved out the window. "That means my birth mom could still be out there somewhere."

A small gasp from behind her caused Alex to turn around. Susan Bentley was standing in the doorway, wide-eyed with her hand on her chest.

82

SUSAN STEPPED FORWARD and examined Alex's face. A tear slipped down her cheek and landed on the front of her tailored navy pantsuit. "It can't be," she said in a trembling voice.

Alex looked at Susan, the woman who looked like she'd seen a ghost the first time they met. The pieces began falling together.

"You're Thomas's daughter. I knew that the moment I saw you. But your mother... I had no idea," Susan whispered. Another tear joined the first one. "I suspected, but thought it was too much to hope for." She reached forward and stroked Alex's cheek. "It's me. I'm your birth mom."

Alex's head jerked back. Her eyes darted to Simon's shocked face. No wonder she'd looked so spooked.

Following Susan's lead, Alex settled into one of the chairs in Simon's office and listened as the woman opened up about her affair with Thomas and the realization she was pregnant with no one to help her raise the baby. Her father, who'd been the senior partner at the firm, made up the story that Susan was going to help another firm for several months. In reality, she was giving birth and saying goodbye to the baby she'd never get to watch grow up. Instead of sharing the joys of motherhood with her friends and coworkers, she was forced to keep her pain a secret, all the while wondering what had become of the child she'd so desperately wanted to keep.

"Robert and Carla Tucker were a Godsend," Susan said. "They could provide a loving home for you. But they got to see you turn into a beautiful young woman. I resented them for that," she confessed. "Not a day went by that I didn't wonder how you were, what kind of person you were becoming."

Alex asked the question that had been on her mind since she found her birth certificate in Gram's attic. "If you were my birth parents, why wasn't your name or Thomas's name listed?"

Susan took a shuddering breath. "I couldn't afford to have people find out about me and Thomas. He was still alive then, and it would have destroyed his reputation. I couldn't let that happen. Nobody could ever know we had a child. Dad knew all the right people to have my name left off the birth certificate as well. But you needed a name, and you needed to have part of your father, so I listed your last name as Stone." Tears flowed freely down Susan's face. "My dad also knew how to get a fake birth certificate issued for you in South Carolina—one with your new last name. That's probably the only one you'd ever seen."

Alex reached across the desk and grasped Susan's hand. It was slick with sweat. "I can't even imagine how difficult this has been for you. First, giving up your child, then never knowing who killed the man you loved..."

Susan sniffed. "I know." The words were barely above a whisper.

"You know what?"

"I know who killed Thomas and Sheila." Susan didn't make eye contact as she spoke.

"You *know*?"

Looking down at her lap, Susan nodded.

"Is he in jail?" Alex demanded.

Susan shook her head tightly and sniffed again.

"Was it John Carmichael?" It was only a feeling she had, but given Thomas's connection with Carmichael, the theory fit.

Again, Sheila shook her head. "No, it wasn't John." Susan hesitated, then lifted her eyes to meet Alex's. "It was my father."

Alex sucked in a breath and leaned back in her chair, disentangling her hand from Susan's. She'd known who killed the Stones and still let Benny Johnson sit in jail for a crime he didn't commit?

As though reading Alex's thoughts, Susan said. "I didn't always know. Before you go thinking bad things about me, I didn't let an innocent man rot in jail all this time. I've only known a few years, but somehow, I managed to make myself forget."

Still, Alex thought. Benny's the one paying the price for what Susan's father did.

"Dad knew he was dying," Susan continued. "He let everyone else think he was okay, but he knew. The night before he died, he confided in me that he was the one who killed them. He said he did it for me. He went to confront Thomas about the position he'd put me in. Things got out of hand when Dad suggested Thomas leave his wife and marry me. He said Thomas laughed. It would be ridiculous, he said, to give up the status that came with being married to Sheila. Dad just snapped." Susan grabbed a tissue and dabbed at her eyes. "I've hated him ever since." Susan took a deep breath then let it out slowly, visibly relieved to have told someone her secret. A single tear trickled down her face.

Alex wondered which one Susan hated more: her father for taking away the man she loved, or Thomas, for being too much of a coward to take responsibility for the hurt he caused her.

"But why did he kill Sheila, too?"

Susan cleared her throat, a deep sound that was thick with emotion. "Dad had been having an affair with Sheila. Mom had been gone for several years and being with a woman of Sheila's age made him feel young again. When she caught him in the library right after he killed Thomas, he knew she'd have to die, too. Two people with bright futures, gone in one night because of my father." She choked out a sob. "I'm the daughter of a murderer."

And I'm the granddaughter of one, Alex thought. So many mistakes, and Susan has been living with the consequences of them for so long.

Warmth spread through Alex's chest. Looking at Susan, she felt compassion for her birth mother—the woman Alex never knew she missed until she found her.

Alex was reminded of the effect one choice can have on countless souls. Susan's decision to place Alex for adoption rewrote the stories of countless people.

83

SIX MONTHS LATER

Alex stood, looking out the window of her apartment at the spring leaves, just beginning to bud. The sun danced on the diamond band glittering on her left ring finger.

Here's to new beginnings, she thought as a bird settled on the windowsill.

Eighteen months.

In just a year and a half, she went from daughter to orphan and back to daughter. Alex and Susan had been in frequent contact during the last six months after a DNA test confirmed that Susan was indeed her mother. Both were delighted to have found one another, and even Gram had taken Susan under her wing.

Like spring follows winter, Alex mused, joy comes from pain.

"Ma'am?" said a voice from behind her. "Are you ready for me to take this?" the mover asked, motioning toward the end table, the sole piece of furniture left in her apartment.

"Yes, thank you," Alex replied, then added, "Actually, let me get something out of the drawer first."

She opened the drawer and carefully withdrew her mother's worn leather journal and a piece of paper—the birth certificate that had changed her life. Carefully opening the journal, she placed the birth certificate inside and closed it. She tucked it under her arm and said, "Now you can take it."

The mover nodded and carried the end table through the living room and out the front door of her apartment to the waiting truck.

Tears burned Alex's eyes as she glanced around the empty apartment. This was where she'd made her first new beginning, her first steps into the world alone.

"Are you ready to go *Mrs.* Caldwell?" Simon asked as he walked up behind her and slipped his arm around her waist. "Joan is waiting in the car."

"I'm ready," Alex said, taking a deep breath. "Let's go."

Pausing as she walked out the front door for the last time, she turned for one final look at the life she'd left behind.

Alex smiled. She would never have to be alone again.

Taking the journal from under her arm, she stroked the marred cover. The course of her life had been changed forever because of the secret within its pages that had been buried long ago.

Acknowledgements

Once again, many thanks are in order for the creation of this book.

To my editor, Deirdre Stoelzle, who provided a keen eye for detail and encouraging comments while suggesting ways to make the story better.

To the wonderful folks at Damonza, for creating another beautiful book, inside and out.

To my husband, Billy, and daughters, Zoe and Nora, as well as many friends and family who have encouraged me through this process. You have no idea how much your support means to me!

Finally, to you, the reader. Without you, there would be no reason to write! Thank you for taking a chance on this book. I hope it has provided you with many hours of good entertainment and that you have enjoyed reading this story as much as I enjoyed writing it.

Until next time!
Erin